Nobody Bodine is a nobody who came from a ..... will always be a nobody.

He disappears into the shadows—no one sees him if he doesn't want them to. He exists in neither the white man's world nor the tribe's, dispensing vigilante justice when he sees fit. There's no other place for a man like him in this world.

Until Melinda Mitchell shows up on the rez. From the first moment he lays eyes on her, he can tell there's something different about her. For starters, she's not afraid of him. She asks where his scars came from, and why he has so many. But more than that, she sees him. For the first time in his life, Nobody feels like a somebody in her eyes.

Melinda has come west to run the new day care on the White Sandy Reservation. She's intrigued by this strange man and his tattered skin, and when she discovers that he's a self-appointed guardian angel for the boy in her care, she realizes that there's more to Nobody than meets the eyes. But how far will he go to keep the boy safe? And will she be able to draw him into the light?

"Oh, no you don't."

The next thing Nobody knew, Melanie had looped her arms around his neck and was holding him in place. "Don't you *dare* kiss me like that and then disappear."

"I don't want to hurt you." There. He'd said what he should have said earlier.

"Then don't hurt me." Her lips brushed over his, a whisper of a touch. Jesus, she was going to kill him. "Just kiss me slow and hard."

He couldn't help the way his arms shook as he tightened his grip on her, her breasts pressed against his chest. It'd been a long time. God, he hoped he wouldn't screw this up. "Yes, Ma'am."

MEN OF THE
WHITE SANDY

NOBODY

Enjoy the Shadows!

Sarah M Anderson

RAGT #4

SARAH M.
ANDERSON

ISBN-13: 978-1-941097-01-4

Nobody (Men of the White Sandy #3)

Copyright © 2014 by Sarah M. Anderson

Edited by Mary Dieterich
Cover design and layout by Leah Hanlin of BlueSky Design
Formatting by www.formatting4U.com

This is a work of fiction. Names, characters, places, and incidents are either the product of the author's imagination or are used fictitiously, and any resemblance to actual persons, living or dead, business establishments, events, or locales is entirely coincidental.

Printed in the U.S.A.

DEDICATION

To all the readers who kept asking me, "Where's Nobody?"

Thank you for seeing him. With your help, we made him real!

ACKNOWLEDGMENTS

I could not have written this book without the generous help of the following people, all of whom I owe drinks and/or chocolate: Jules Bennett, Elizabeth Otto, Maisey Yates, Heidi Moore, and Jill Marsal. Deepest thanks go to Mary Dieterich for editing and Leah Hanlin for designing the book.

CHAPTER ONE

"You didn't tell me we were going to have a campfire tonight!"

Nobody Bodine stepped to the edge of the shadows, his gaze focused on the woman who'd spoken. He knew she wouldn't see him. No one ever did. The thin stand of pines was more than enough cover for him. He stayed back in the darkness, watching from a safe distance. He always kept his distance.

"We have a campfire every night." Rebel came into view, carrying more logs for the fire. He dropped them and then turned to scan the trees. Damn it, Nobody was going to need a better spot to hide. "Everybody is welcome to sit with us."

Nobody's skin prickled. Had he thought this was a safe distance? Safe would be anywhere *but* here. Safe would be heading to a bar to make sure Lou didn't go home and beat the hell out of his wife. Safe would be going to make sure Jamie was gonna be okay for the night. Safe was anything—everything—but watching the woman.

But that's what he was doing. He'd never seen her before but he sure as hell wanted a better look. Proof positive that Nobody was an idiot.

She was crouched down in front of the fire, feeding small sticks into the flame with a wild grin on her face. She wore a long skirt and a tank top. Nobody leaned forward. He could see her bra straps.

He snapped his eyes away from that. He didn't know who she was but she obviously wasn't the kind of woman who would give someone like Nobody a second look.

"Melinda!" There was Dr. Mitchell, marching toward the fire with purpose. "What are you doing?"

1

Melinda. That was a pretty name. Matched her pretty face.

"We haven't had a campfire since—well, since we were kids! Can we make S'mores?"

What the hell was a somore? Nobody took a step forward so he could hear better. If he had to guess, he'd say the two women were related—sisters, maybe? But this new woman didn't look much like Dr. Mitchell, who was tall and willowy with that wild mass of yellow curls.

Nobody watched as Dr. Mitchell came to stand next to this Melinda. Melinda put her arm around Dr. Mitchell's shoulders and leaned against her. They *were* sisters. They had a lot of the same face, the same pale blue eyes—although Melinda's were brighter, like the wide-open sky. Melinda was a few inches shorter than her sister, but considerably more... shaped. It was hard to miss the curves of her body in that thin tank top she wore over a skirt. Her bra straps were hot pink, although he was trying not to think about that. He wasn't doing a great job.

Another way she wasn't like her sister was that Dr. Mitchell didn't wear anything she didn't have to—no jewelry, no decoration. Just her doctor's coat and something to pin her hair back. Melinda was wearing necklaces. He wasn't close enough that he could tell how many she had, but the firelight was catching on the metal around her neck. And in her ears. And on her fingers. She seemed to single-handedly be making up for the lack of accessories for her sister.

She laughed at something Rebel said as he walked back around the side of the house. Nobody had hardly seen Dr. Mitchell smile, much less laugh, but Melinda threw her head back and laughed with a wild kind of abandon. She didn't care what other people thought, Nobody could tell. She would wear what she wanted and do what she wanted. The light of the fire caught her hair, making the colors even wilder. He'd never seen hair with red and white streaks painted in it before, but it made her look like she was born in the fire.

Hell, he was starting to feel a little hot himself.

Rebel looked toward the trees again, but he didn't push the issue. Instead, he settled into his normal spot, telling Melinda Mitchell about life on the rez.

Nobody shouldn't be here. He didn't have a place in his life for pretty, fearless women. He should be keeping an eye on Jamie, or, at the very least, checking on his herd of horses. Those two things had been more than enough to keep him busy.

His feet wouldn't move. Melinda Mitchell was poking at the fire with a stick. Every so often, she'd look at Rebel, but instead of her sister's devotion, Nobody swore she was rolling her eyes at him. Would she roll her eyes at Nobody? Or would she just cower in fear?

She sat back on her heels, that wild joy all over her face. Damn. He leaned forward to get a better look. Her eyes snapped up, right to where he was. She stood up and moved away from the fire. Toward him.

"What?" Rebel asked, following her gaze.

"Is someone out there?" She pointed—right at him. Not even Rebel could find him in the dark—and this strange white woman was staring *at him*.

"No," he heard Rebel say. "Nobody's there."

Nobody moved, pulling back into the shadows until he couldn't see her wild hair or her pretty face. The hair on his arms stood up straight and the hair on his head tried to do the same, despite the tail he wore it in. The darkness wrapped around him until he was nothing but a shadow himself, backing away from the light of the campfire one silent step at a time. When he was far enough away that he could run without worrying about making noise, he turned and raced to where he'd left his horse.

He didn't know how he did it. Hell, he didn't even know what 'it' was. It wasn't anything that anyone had ever taught him. All he knew was that if he didn't want to be seen, he wasn't seen.

Most of the time, anyway.

He wasn't a *sica*, a ghost. For one thing, he was pretty sure he'd never died. Come close a few times, but never actually went over. For another, when he ran, he always had feet. That was the big proof—feet hitting the ground, the earth pushing back against him. Same thing when he got into a brawl. *Sicas* didn't break other people's faces with their bare hands.

The only time Nobody had ever had the same weird sensation had been one time when a storm had blown in over the Badlands.

One moment, the sky had been relatively clear as he'd brushed his horses. The next, lightning had struck nearby at the same moment a fierce wind had almost knocked him over. Every single hair on his head had stood straight out. That had almost felt like when he moved into the shadows.

Almost.

Nobody found his horse, Red. Red was a good horse—quiet and careful. She could move through the uncut prairie grass without blowing snot or shying in fear from every little noise. She wasn't the fastest horse Nobody took care of, but speed wasn't everything. Plus, she had a tendency to stay put, so Nobody didn't have to hobble her.

Nobody wasn't much for fancy names. Most of his horses had names like Spot or Star. Red was red. None of this Whispering Wind of the Plains crap or whatever the people who eventually bought his horses named the animals.

Red came to him with a low whistle, half a mouthful of grass hanging out of her mouth. Nobody patted her neck and then swung himself up on to her bare back. He didn't own a saddle. Or a bridle for that matter. He didn't need them.

Something pulled at the edge of his consciousness. That was the other thing he did without knowing how or why—he felt things. Things he shouldn't feel.

For a moment, his mind turned back to the wild sister of the not-wild doctor. He'd felt something then, too—a pull. Hadn't that been the whole reason he'd stayed so long?

Not something. Someone. Someone named Melinda.

But the pull he felt right now—he shook Melinda Mitchell from his head. No, it wasn't her. He tasted fear.

Shit.

Jamie.

Nobody urged Red into a flat-out gallop toward the center of the rez, silently cursing the whole time. What the hell was wrong with him? He shouldn't have gone to Rebel's tonight.

Nobody may be a nobody who came from nobody and would always be a nobody, but he'd finally found a purpose in this world. Most people—excepting Rebel and his wife—didn't look at him. They were either afraid of him—with good reason—or they refused to acknowledge he even existed.

Kids were different. Oh, they were afraid of him, especially the ones who'd been hurt too many times, but it was a lot easier to change a kid's way of thinking than it was a grown-up who only saw what they wanted to see.

He shouldn't have let himself get distracted by a woman. He should have been watching over Jamie. That was his job.

The taste of fear got stronger. Panic.

Nobody rode harder.

By the time the lights of the small cluster of houses came into view, Red was foaming with sweat, her sides heaving. Nobody slid off her, mentally promising to give her a good rub-down when they made it back home, away from the porch lights and people.

He slipped into the shadows, edging his way around the houses. A dog lifted its head as he passed, but didn't bark. They never did.

Jamie's house didn't have a porch light, but light spilled out of the windows on the side of the house. From thirty feet away, Nobody heard the shouts of Lou Kills Deer, the screams of Myra Kill Dear, the shattering of glass.

Damn it, he should have been here. Lou was a mean snake when he was sober; Myra wasn't much better. Together they were one hell of a pair of vicious drunks. Sooner or later, they'd beat each other to death or drive into oncoming traffic or pick the wrong fight in a bar and that would be the end of them. Which would have been fine with Nobody.

Except for their son, Jamie.

Jamie's light wasn't on. Nobody prayed that the boy had gone to bed before the drunken arguments had started, that he'd gotten his door locked and the dresser moved over before Lou started punching things.

But that pull told him that hadn't happened.

He tapped on the window—once, then paused for ten seconds, then quickly two more times. If Jamie was in there, he'd recognize the signal.

A minute later, the window opened. At first, Nobody was relieved to see the kid—but then he saw the blooming bruise over Jamie's left eye.

5

Damn it all to hell. He'd let himself be distracted by a woman and Jamie had paid the price.

"It doesn't hurt," Jamie said, but his voice wavered and he scrubbed the back of his hand across his nose. "I didn't cry."

Nobody nodded, glad that the kid hadn't given Lou what he wanted.

From the front of the house, Myra screamed.

Nobody slammed his hands on the windowsill and started to heft himself up. He didn't like Myra Kills Deer. She was a shitty mother who used her son as a shield while taunting her husband. In that, she was a lot like Nobody's mother. The only real difference was that Myra didn't hurt her son. Much.

Still, Nobody couldn't listen as Lou killed her.

Then a crash shook the crappy little house, followed by Lou howling. Looking terrified, Jamie put his hands on Nobody's shoulders and pushed. "No—he'll kill you too. Can we just go? I want to go."

Not likely. Lou was a savage drunk, but Nobody had ten years and thirty pounds of muscle on him, not to mention stone-cold sober reflexes. He could go inside and put an end to Lou Kills Deer and be gone before anyone was the wiser. No one else besides Jamie would know he'd been here. No one would be able to find any proof that he'd been involved, even if they suspected him. And they would only suspect him because of his record.

Nobody stood there, half off the ground, listening as the fight escalated. He wanted nothing more than to show Lou exactly what fear felt like. But Jamie's eyes pleaded with him.

He hated this, hated knowing that Jamie lived in the same hell Nobody had grown up in. But most of all, he hated that he didn't do more.

"Please," Jamie begged. "I want to go home."

Finally, Nobody relented. He wasn't here to kill Lou. He was here to protect Jamie, just like he'd always dreamed of someone protecting him.

He dropped back to the ground and turned around. Jamie scrambled out the open window and hung onto him, piggy-back. Jamie buried his head into Nobody's neck as he ran for Red.

Assuming no one died in that awful house, Lou and Myra

would probably spend the next few days drunk and sleeping it off. They wouldn't even notice that their son was gone. And if they did, Nobody didn't think they'd care.

He wanted to ride hard for home to put as much space between Jamie and his parents as possible. But Nobody had already pushed Red as far as he dared. So he lifted the kid off his back and onto Red's.

Then he began the long walk home.

"How bad was it?"

Melinda Mitchell rolled her eyes. She would *so* rather not discuss it. "Pretty bad."

"I gathered." Her sister Madeline, stopped peeling the potatoes and glared at her. "I wouldn't have gotten an irate phone call from the Mitchell Foundation chair if it weren't 'pretty bad.'"

Jim Laird had never liked Melinda anyway. He'd just been looking for a reason to squeeze her off the Board of Directors. "I caught Tyrone getting a blow job in the men's room at the benefit."

"That's bad." Maddie kept peeling, but she was waiting. Older sisters. They thought they knew everything—or had the right to know everything.

But Melinda had been here for two days now and Madeline hadn't pressed the issue here yet. It was a bit of grace—but one that wouldn't last forever.

Might as well get it over with. Melinda took a cleansing breath and tried to find the center—a center that had nothing to do with her abnormally bad taste in men. Really. "From one of the busboys."

Maddie froze for a long second before she said, "Ah." Melinda thought she might be off the hook, but then Maddie added, "And the police had to be called over *that*?"

"I was a little upset, okay?" More like a lot upset. More like she'd been hoping Tyrone would be 'the one.' So much so that she'd already given up her apartment so she and Tyrone could move back into the Mitchell Mansion and set up house. She thought she'd been close to happily-ever-after with a man who understood art and understood her. Instead, in that awful space of time between when the whisper had reached her and when she'd burst into the men's room, the only thing she'd understood was that she'd been wrong. Again. Why couldn't she ever see a man for what he really was?

Shooting her a look that said *a little*, Maddie handed her the broccoli and a knife. "At least the charges were dropped."

"Thanks for putting up with me while the dust settles." Laird would never let her back on the Board, that much was certain. Some dust would never settle.

"Putting up with you? Hardly." Maddie shot her a big-sis smile. "Everyone around here works. You'll make a good Child Care Director."

"I've never worked in a day care before," Melinda grumbled as she took a swipe at the carrots. Secretly, though, she was thrilled she had a justifiable reason for getting the hell out of Ohio. So much better to say she was leaving town to run the White Sandy Child Care Center, funded by the Mitchell Foundation, than to admit she was running away from another relationship doomed by her faulty gay-dar.

Plus, the center was brand new. Maddie had promised Melinda that she could do whatever she wanted with it. She could make it her own.

Maddie fixed her with one of those know-better looks. "You did a great job fostering. This won't be that different."

"That was only the one kid. And aren't you the one who told me how hard it was to come out to the rez—how no one looked at you for weeks, and everyone spoke Lakota so you wouldn't know they were talking about you?"

"Not everyone. Mostly just me." Maddie's face broke into a wide grin as her husband, Rebel Runs Fast, came into the kitchen to get the venison steaks he was grilling for dinner.

A pang of naked jealousy spiked through Melinda as Rebel snaked an arm around Maddie's waist. Her sister had had, what— two boyfriends, tops?—before she came out here and landed the hunk of the century. Melinda had gone through more men than she could count and had now been reduced to living in her big sister's spare bedroom as she started over.

One of these days, she thought as she started chopping the broccoli with more force than she really needed, *the right man will come along.* She could only hope she'd recognize him when she saw him.

Maddie cut her a break and let the rest of the Tyrone disaster lie as they sat down to dinner, which was fine with Melinda. She tested out the venison. *Don't think of Bambi, don't think of Bambi.* Which, of course, made her think of Bambi.

She was in the middle of her taste buds hashing it out with her brain when the knock on the door came, sharp and short. The suddenness of the reverberations sent Melinda right out of her chair. Maddie looked equally alarmed.

"Who is it?" they said at the same time.

Rebel smiled, looking surprised and pleased and just a little bit wicked. Was it wrong to be jealous of her sister, Melinda wondered? Because Maddie had landed one hell of a hunk. "It's Nobody."

The knock was, if possible, louder this time. "Doesn't sound like nobody to me," Melinda said, looking around the trailer for a defensive weapon. Maddie had hinted that Rebel was a psychic or something. Which left the distinct possibility that there was a ghost banging on her door. Which meant a defensive weapon would probably be useless, but she picked up her butter knife anyway, just to be safe.

"Don't be a smartass," Maddie said as she threw a napkin at her husband. She no longer looked alarmed. Hell, she actually looked happy. "For Pete's sake, let him in!"

"Who?" Melinda repeated. But by the time she got the question out again, Rebel was up and throwing the door open with abandon as Maddie set another spot at the table. Whoever this nobody was, he sure had people hopping to attention.

"Maddie?" she whispered as a strange voice bit off short words.

"Rebel's friend. Don't worry," Maddie added. Of course, any time Maddie said that, Melinda had good cause to worry. "He's not as scary as he looks."

"What?" But the question died on her lips as Rebel led someone who decidedly did not look like a nobody—or even a ghost, for that matter—back to the kitchen.

Scary was not the right word. Rebel's friend looked

terrifying. He was a few inches shorter than Rebel, but he filled the doorway with millimeters to spare as he scanned the room with hard eyes.

"Mellie, I'd like to introduce you to an old friend of mine." The unexpected formality of the moment did nothing to distract her from the cowering fear that had her wanting to get behind the table. "This is Nobody Bodine."

Her mouth didn't move—she was pretty sure it was open, but she was powerless to get it shut. Rebel paused only for a second and then continued without her. "Nobody, this is Melinda Mitchell, of the Columbus, Ohio, Mitchells—Madeline's sister. She'll be staying with us for a while."

Maybe a while shorter, was all Melinda could think. Because all she could think was that she needed to put a state line between her person and the likes of Rebel's 'old friend.' The man looked like he'd come straight from the UFC cage fight, and she honestly couldn't tell if he'd won or lost. He had a long scar down his left cheek that didn't look old and burn marks on his right arm that spoke of nothing good.

And then he took his cowboy hat—black, of course—off.

The gasp was out of her mouth before she could stop it. If his face didn't say brawler, his hair did. It was pulled back into a high, tight braid, but shaved on the sides. That wasn't the worst of it, though. Not by a long shot.

Without the hat, his eyes were in the full light. Black as pitch around the edge, with flecks of a lighter brown near the center, the man named Nobody was glaring. At her. Like he was looking for a cage. Then he looked down at her hand.

She shuddered. As if a butter knife would make a dent in that kind of chest, because that was the kind of chest that had been around the cage match on more than a few occasions. *Broad* didn't begin to describe the muscles that were barely contained by a thin gray t-shirt, tucked into a ragged pair of jeans that looked like they'd been through a few fashion cycles. The belt was, hands down, the most fashionable thing about the whole outfit, scars notwithstanding. A huge silver disk, it didn't seem to fit the man who was wearing it.

Maybe he won it, she thought as she tried to stop staring in the general direction of his crotch.

Rebel cleared his throat at the same time Maddie stepped on her toe. "Nobody," Maddie said, sounding nothing like the terrified Melinda felt. Instead, she sounded more like her normal bossy self. She even had her hands on her hips, like she was going to scold this fearsome man. "Been taking care of..." she glanced at Melinda. "Yourself?"

Was the woman insane? Would she even think of trying to boss someone as clearly dangerous as this Nobody was?

"Ma'am," Something weird was happening, Melinda noticed. The cage-fighter look had bled into something more... embarrassed? Was it possible that this strange man was embarrassed? "It healed real nice. Much obliged."

Maddie broke out in a grin that Melinda hadn't seen since, well, it had to be years. "Glad to hear it. Won't you join us for dinner?"

Melinda squeaked. Not that she heard it, but all three eyes turned to look at her. Damn, damn, damn. She needed to get it together and fast, before she managed to embarrass Nobody Bodine right back into fighter. "It's, uh..." her brain froze. *Come on*, she scolded herself. *Pull it together*. "Nice. To meet you."

Wonderful.

The hard lines around Nobody's eyes flexed. "Ma'am," he said again, with a short nod of his head in her direction.

And that was all he said for the rest of the night. Maddie and Rebel didn't seem to mind—hell, they didn't seem to mind that Melinda said next to nothing. They carried on as if this whole situation was the most normal occurrence in the world as they argued about whether a sick someone needed a sweat lodge or just bed rest. At one point, Melinda began to wonder if they'd forgotten they even had dinner guests.

Melinda hadn't forgotten. She was sitting on Nobody's right side, and she could *not* stop staring at the marks up and down his arm. It was a nice arm, if a girl didn't look at the burns. Matched his chest—broad and ripped. Nothing like the pasty twigs that passed as limbs on all those pretentious asses she normally dated. No, this was a solid man. And now that she'd gotten over her initial shock at his appearance, she was getting a different vibe off him. As she watched him stare at the broccoli like it was an alien substance, she wasn't getting cage fighter anymore. Which wasn't to say that he didn't still look like he'd hold his own. She decided he was a man who fought not by choice, but only when there was no other choice. And he had the scars to prove it. Lord, he had a *lot* of scars.

She wasn't a doctor—never had the inclination, the desire, the focus, and most especially not the grades. Hell, she'd practically passed out when she'd gotten her first period because she couldn't handle the blood. Maddie had been pasting on the bandages and pulling out the splinters for as long as Melinda could remember. Dad had been disappointed, sure, but Mom had encouraged her to follow her heart into art, and art was where Melinda had stayed.

She could *not* stop staring at the marks. It was art, all right. A horrible collage on a skin canvas.

They were burns—old ones, she guessed. The newer skin had grown around the semi-circular marks, distorting the topography of his arm. They looked like cigarettes—she'd seen some kids, some of the kids who needed the art the most, that had cigarette burns. She'd called the Ohio Department of Job and Family Services on more that several occasions. She'd fostered Shawna Gell for a month just to keep the girl safe from her father until the Mitchell Foundation provided her grandmother with a bigger apartment. Someone had to look out for the kids. And she was someone.

He caught her looking, and an angry fire raced out across his cheeks. But he looked away. He didn't meet her gaze. He didn't even manage to glare. Nothing.

Suddenly, she knew with absolute certainty that no one had ever looked out for this strange man. Her heart just about broke.

"Mellie," Maddie said with that pay-attention-right-now-or-else tone of voice.

"Sorry?"

"I asked you how you liked the venison." A benign enough question, but Maddie was shooting huge daggers at her. *Stop staring,* her eyes demanded. *Be normal.*

Poor Maddie. Always asking for the impossible.

"What happened to your arm?"

The only sound in the room was the clank of silverware hitting ceramic.

Nobody didn't move, but somehow, he shrank into himself, as if a man that big could just disappear into thin air in the middle of dinner. Then something happened, something... weird. Like he shimmered on the edges. Was that even freaking possible?

The hairs on her arms stood, like she'd been shocked. "Mellie," Maddie hissed under her breath. In the quiet room, it sounded like nails screaming down a chalkboard.

"They're older than the one on your face," she added, sliding her legs out of the way of Maddie's incoming kick. Melinda knew all of her sister's moves. And, after all this time, a girl would think that Maddie would know all hers, too. "How did you get that one?"

Head down, Nobody stood. Moving with all the deliberation of a man who was ready and willing to bulldoze his way out of a tight spot, he settled his hat on his head. Melinda couldn't take her eyes off him. She felt no fear this time, none. Instead, she was fascinated. What would he do? He'd said all of what, seven words? Would he tell her to go to hell? Break a dish? Cuss her out in Lakota?

Underneath the brim of his hat, he met her eyes. They were deep in the shadow, but she could see him looking at her. Surprisingly, he wasn't angry or even a little pissed. She could see a hint of worry shadow his face, but what she really saw was curiosity. Like she wasn't acting like he thought she'd act. Like he didn't know what to make of her.

No, she decided. She didn't need to be afraid. Not of him.

Then the corner of his mouth moved—just as slowly as the rest of him, but still. She detected movement. It was a smile, she realized. A blink-and-you-miss-it smile, but all the same, a smile. For her.

Time seemed to slow down at the same moment the ground opened up. Nothing moved—not Nobody, not her, not Maddie or Rebel or the sun or the moon or the stars above. Everything stopped.

In that instant, she didn't feel like the flaky little sister, the artsy-fartsy weirdo, not even the girl who always, *always* picked the wrong man. In that instant, she felt like a woman in possession of the kind of power she only dreamed about, and maybe that made her a little dangerous, a little to be feared. In that instant, she felt alive—not the treading water she'd been doing for years now, but top-down, damn-the-torpedoes, full-speed ahead *alive*.

Because that's what she looked like in his eyes.

And then he was gone, so fast and so quiet that all she heard was the sound of the door opening and hoof beats fading into the silence.

"That went well." Rebel was already laughing.

"Mellie," Maddie groaned. "I can't believe you *did* that!"

"Who *was* that?"

"That," Rebel said with a grin, "was Nobody."

CHAPTER TWO

Morning came way too freaking early. Melinda ignored it as long as she could—she turned her phone off when it chirped at her and pulled the pillow over her head when Madeline knocked.

However, when her sister stood over her and said, "If you don't get up right now I'll dump this water on you," Melinda was forced to open her eyes.

Of course, Madeline wasn't actually holding any water. Instead, she stood there with a perma-scowl on her face and her lab coat on.

"What?"

"Get up."

Melinda rubbed her eyes. "What time is it?"

"I'm leaving in ten minutes," Madeline said by way of answer as she turned on her heel. "It's seven miles to the clinic—a hell of a long walk *especially* if you don't know the way."

Melinda shot a dirty look at her sister's back. Madeline could be so irritatingly punctual sometimes. Most of the time. It was something that Melinda had never mastered.

She rolled out of bed, threw on the first tank top and skirt she grabbed and headed to the bathroom. This was technically her first day at her new job. The least she could do was brush her teeth.

When she got to the kitchen, she found Rebel sitting there. Shirtless. Damn it. Why did her sister have to marry a man who was just so... well, just *so*? "Morning," she mumbled, trying to figure out where to look.

Melinda had no freaking idea how Madeline and Rebel's relationship worked. The Madeline she'd grown up with was the textbook definition of the uptight, type-A, overachieving control freak.

Everything that Melinda wasn't.

If Melinda's significant other had been parading around half dressed, Madeline would have thrown a fit. Instead, she walked back into the kitchen, gave Rebel the kind of look that made Melinda all kinds of lonesome, and then reached out and stroked his arm. And his chest.

Rebel pulled her into his arms. There was giggling. It was *terrible*.

Melinda's cheeks shot red as she tried to find somewhere to look. This wasn't how it was supposed to go. Madeline had no luck with men, attracting only the most boring males on the planet. Melinda was the one who'd always had boys panting after her. She was the one who'd had six different guys ask her to prom. She was the one who liked sex—early and often. She was the one who loved everything about men, who never felt weird or awkward around a guy.

She was the one hiding out at her sister's house after another horrible break-up, watching her sister canoodle with the sexiest man she'd ever seen.

Unexpectedly, Nobody Bodine popped into her mind. He was not sexy, not like Rebel was. He was hard and dangerous and scarred. By all rights, she should be terrified of him.

But there was something about him that was, in fact, kind of sexy. Not like Rebel was—not sensual and easy-going—but still. Maybe it was the hard and dangerous part. Okay, he was hellaciously sexy when he wasn't scaring the bejeezus out of her. All those muscles—*damn*. She'd never seen another man quite like Nobody.

Funny, she'd sort of thought someone had been near the campfire the other night, watching them—her—from behind a tree. *Nobody*. She didn't know why she thought it could have been him. Rebel hadn't seen anyone, and he would know. He was the mystical Indian. Melinda was just the newest crazy white lady. She had to defer to him.

She'd almost asked Rebel about the strange man, but for once had managed to put the breaks on her mouth. She wasn't out here to rebound with anyone. In theory, she wasn't even out here to lick her wounds. Or to be licked. Or do the licking.

She shook her head. Coffee. Yes. That's what she should be doing while Madeline and Rebel got all... smoochy. She kept her eyes focused on her feet as she worked her way around the table. She'd stayed up way too late playing with fire. As irritating as it was, Madeline was right. Melinda had a job to do. Caffeine would help.

"Ready?"

Madeline's know-it-all voice snapped her eyes up. Rebel was leaning against the counter, gazing adoringly at his wife. But Madeline looked less like a woman who'd just gotten frisky and more like the one who'd threatened to dump water on her only sister this morning.

Melinda held up the mug. "Ready."

"See you this afternoon," Rebel called out behind them.

Once they were in the car, Melinda felt better. Less jealous. She didn't do well with jealousy. This was just her and Maddie. It felt more normal.

The clock in the dash said 7:53. Once Melinda got her bearings, she was going to drive her little Civic in all by herself at a more reasonable hour, that was for damn sure.

They drove in silence. At least it was pretty. Even though it was early, the sun was already bright. The afternoon would be warm—but not sweltering. Not yet—it was only June. In another few months, the heat would be killer.

They crested a low hill. In the distance was a building that would have been a hovel, if hovels were made of cinder blocks. Madeline slowed. "This isn't it—is it?"

Madeline shut off her Jeep's engine in a flat, dusty lot in front of the ugliest box Melinda had ever seen. "Are you kidding? This is a significant improvement over when I showed up last year. You get the new half," she added, pointing to the cleaner side.

Melinda swallowed. "I know you said it was bad, but seriously?"

Maddie had the nerve to smile. "Seriously. Come on in. I'll show you what you've been working for."

First, Madeline took her through the Clinic. She pointed out all the newer equipment that the Mitchell Foundation had helped purchase. Melinda supposed it was all great—and yes, there were a lot of warm fuzzies when Madeline told her about the new x-ray machine and how the art auction Melinda had organized had paid for it.

But even with that, Melinda couldn't help notice how crappy everything was. Yeah, everything was clean, but the waiting room chairs were mostly duct-tape, a stack of what might have been phone books once upon a time propped up one leg of the receptionist's desk. The linoleum looked like it had been scraped clean by angry bears—*hungry* angry bears—and everything that wasn't something the Mitchell foundation had paid for looked like it was being held together with twine.

"You look worried," Madeline said as she brewed a pot of coffee.

"This is *it*?" Melinda knew she shouldn't sound so shocked, but she couldn't help it. She'd spent time in some pretty run-down community centers in Columbus—places where 'urban blight' wasn't a phrase that sounded like a bad case of the flu but a real thing where people died in the street and kids were left to fend for themselves—or worse.

But the White Sandy Clinic took the cake. Maybe it was that it was a building out of context—it didn't blend in with other run-down buildings. It stood alone with nothing to distract from the grubbiness of the building.

"Hey." Whoops. Madeline's voice carried a strict warning in it—criticizing the Clinic wouldn't go over real well. "This is the rez. We do the best we can with what we've got, and we've got a lot more than we had when I first showed up."

"Sorry." It came out as a mumble, which made Madeline give her a hard look.

Melinda hated that look. Always had, always would. It was the exact same look that their father had been giving her since the very first time Melinda had drawn all over her arms, legs and bedroom walls with permanent marker. It was a look that said Melinda would never live up to the fine example that was Madeline Mitchell.

Then everything about Madeline softened and she went from looking like their dad to looking more like their mom. "The first week is the hardest," she said, pulling Melinda into an awkward hug. "It's not so bad, once you get used to it."

Melinda wasn't so sure as she looked around the dilapidated office. "Just seems like a lot to get used to."

Madeline had the nerve to laugh as she gave Melinda another squeeze. "It is. Come see the good side!"

Madeline led her outside and around to the new looking steel door. There were no windows in the front of the building, but at least all the cinder blocks were stacked neatly. However, the gray made the place look more like a prison than anything else.

Maybe the inside would be better? Dear God, please let the inside be better. *Please*.

Madeline unlocked the door and pushed it open. "This," she said with obvious pride as she flipped on a light, "is the White Sandy Child Care Center."

Oh, hell. Melinda managed not to say it, but she sure thought it. The inside wasn't any better than the outside. In fact, it was worse—there wasn't a single window in the place. The only light came from the bare florescent bulbs overhead and the front door.

The place was empty. It had walls, a ceiling, a floor of poured concrete, and the lights. There was a door in the far wall, but she couldn't tell if that led outside or to a back room. That was it. The place was a giant gray box.

"This isn't a Child Care Center—this is a bomb shelter!"

Madeline heaved an impressive sigh. "Yes, I know that— actually, it's a tornado shelter."

"You can't have kids in here—it's too damn depressing!" Hell, she was becoming suicidal and she'd only been in here for two minutes.

Madeline clearly did not appreciate the drama. "Mellie— don't see what it is right now. See what you can do with it, okay? That's why you're here. *You* can make it a Child Care Center better than anyone I know."

Melinda had several choice things she'd love to say but Madeline was giving her that look again. So instead she swallowed down her shock and said, "Um, well, at least it's all clean." It was the only nice thing she could come up with.

"Nobody does a great job."

Melinda froze. Was that small-'n' nobody, or capital-'N' Nobody who barged in on dinners and tried to glare her to death?

"The guy from last night?"

Madeline nodded as she walked through the rectangular space. "He's very thorough."

"Is he..." Hell, she didn't know what to ask. "Dangerous?" That had to be the most relevant question.

Madeline turned and faced her. Even from halfway across the gray space, Melinda could see that her normally decisive sister was at a loss for words. "He's... Rebel says he's trustworthy. He's never done anything to threaten me and he does a good job keeping this place from falling apart. But some of those scars are new. A lot of them, actually."

Melinda thought back to the patchwork of skin she'd seen on his arms. What had been under the shirt?

Jesus. This was insane. "Are you telling me the guy who looks like a cage fighter is your *janitor*?"

"Yes," Madeline replied, her tone crisp. "I am."

Just then, a male voice shouted, "Doc? Sorry I'm late," from out in the parking lot.

"Time to meet everyone." Madeline led Melinda up to the front, where a huge man in hospital scrubs and a bandana was propping the door of the Clinic open with a box fan. "Clarence, this is my sister Melinda Mitchell. Mellie, this is Clarence Thunder, the best damn nurse I've ever worked with."

Clarence had to be six-five, but he still blushed. "I do my best," he said with a nervous smile as he held out a mammoth hand to Melinda.

Melinda practically had to crane her neck up to meet Clarence's gaze. "It's nice to meet you."

"Same to you." Clarence tilted his head toward the barren box next to the Clinic. "It's a good thing you're doing."

Now it was Melinda's turn to blush. "I haven't done anything yet."

"Are you kidding? A day care is huge."

Behind Clarence, a pair of young women who had to be sisters—or at least very close cousins—were getting out of a car, along with some small children. "Oh, that's Tara and Tammy," said Madeline, pulling Melinda past Clarence. "I got the coffee started," she called back to Clarence.

"We're here!" the taller of the two women said. She had big permed hair and her clothes were a tad too tight for her Rubenesque figure, but her smile was warm. She ushered a young girl in with her "Hi, I'm Tara Tall Trees." Before Melinda knew what was happening, Tara had her by the hand and was shaking vigorously. "I'm the receptionist. This is my daughter, Nellie."

Okay, so Melinda didn't always know what to say around adults. Kids were another matter entirely. She crouched down to Nellie's level. The little girl was probably in kindergarten. "So you're Nellie! I've heard so much about you. Do you like to color and paint?"

Although the little girl was half hidden behind her mother's legs, Melinda didn't miss the way she nodded her head *yes*.

"Good—then you're going to help me decorate the center!"

Still safely behind her mom, the little girl started clapping. "Can I, Mommy?"

Tara gave her a sweet pat on the head. "Only if you don't make Miss Melinda mad, honey."

"Not possible," Melinda assured her.

"You don't look like Dr. Mitchell," Nellie suddenly announced. "Your hair isn't as bouncy and it's all different colors."

"Nellie!" her mother hissed. "I'm sorry, Miss Melinda—she's only five."

"Five going on six!" Nellie was clearly insulted by this slight.

Melinda could only laugh even as she caught the uncomfortable way Madeline tried to smile. Her sister had never liked her naturally curly hair, no matter how fabulous Melinda tried to tell her all those curls were. Apparently, it had taken one hot Indian on horseback to convince her to wear it curly. "It's true," she told Nellie. "My mom said I looked more like her mom and Madeline looked more like our dad."

"I look like my dad. He's got some white in him," Nellie said, in complete innocence. "But I'm still an Indian. Uncle Rebel's even teaching me to speak Lakota!"

"That's enough, honey," Tara hissed again. "I'm sorry, Miss Melinda."

"Please, just call me Melinda. We're practically family." She

21

turned her attention to the other woman, who was holding a toddler. "Hello."

"This is my sister, Tammy," Tara said as she shooed Nellie to a chair and headed for the now-ringing phone.

"Oh—the Tammy who'll be helping me?" Tammy was clearly the shyer of the two women. She kept her head ducked down, as if she were afraid to actually look at Melinda. She was a little shorter than her sister, maybe a little more generously proportioned, but she had the same big hair and the same nose.

"Yes. I got my associate's degree in child care." She looked embarrassed by this, but Melinda couldn't guess as to why.

"That's great," she said, trying to sound encouraging.

Tammy still didn't look at her, but Melinda thought she saw a faint smile. "This is my son, Mikey." The little boy, probably about two years old, showed none of his mother's shyness.

He took one look at Melinda and stretched out his arms. "Pwetty!" He said, reaching for her hair.

Tammy looked mortified, but Melinda took the little boy in her arms. "No pulling, okay?" she said as he petted her hair as if she were a new puppy.

"Red!" Mikey announced, clearly pleased with this observation.

"I'm sorry," Tammy started to say, but Melinda waved her off.

"Melinda has a way with kids," Madeline said in such a way that Melinda had to look at her. Was that a note of jealousy in her big sister's voice?

Not possible. Aside from Madeline's total helplessness when it came to style—which had, by and large, remained unchanged since she'd decamped to South Dakota a year ago—she'd never been jealous of Melinda. Why would she be? She was smarter and obviously did better in school. Their parents had always been more proud of Madeline, the straight-A student who brought home awards and honors. Melinda had just brought home strange boyfriends and weird art. Well, maybe Madeline had been jealous of the boyfriend part, but she certainly had never shown it.

She shouldn't try to read too much into what Madeline said. At face value, her bossy big sister was being incredibly complimentary this morning. That was actually really nice—and somewhat rare. Of course, Melinda knew that Madeline was just trying to psych her up for the big, empty box that was her new job. But still.

She untangled one of Mikey's hands from her hair. "Do you like to finger paint, big guy?"

"Yes!" Mikey screeched at top volume. "Paint paint paint *paint!*"

"He paints with mud," Tammy added, looking ashamed. "On the wall."

The way Tammy said it verged on heartbreaking. It wasn't that the boy messed up the walls—heavens, Melinda had done the same thing. It was that, unless she guessed wrong, mud was the only paint Tammy had.

Although she was a flake compared to her sister, Melinda had still gone to college and gotten a degree—two, in fact. One in art and one in psychology. The psychology degree had made her father happy, but instead of following it up with a doctorate, Melinda had focused on art. She'd found the perfect way to combine them—art therapy. She'd trucked boxes of art supplies into inner-city schools—places where the ceilings leaked and the textbooks were twenty years old—and sat down with kids who normally wouldn't hesitate to shoot her—or worse. Kids who'd spent their whole lives struggling against poverty and crime, against abuse and molestation—against a pervasive sense of failure.

Those kids—kids who joined gangs and brawled over everything—those kids had needed art the most. She'd refused to give up on them and instead, helped them channel their hopeless rage at the life they were stuck in into drawings and paintings and even sculpture. Some of those kids had never played with clay or dough. The supplies had never cost that much—paper and pencils weren't expensive—but it had been more than some of them had ever had.

She hadn't been able to save them all. No matter how hard she tried, not all of them could be saved. She'd gone to funerals and cried with mothers over lost children.

But she'd also written twenty-three letters of recommendation for college applications. Those kids were her victories—they'd latched onto art and used it to make something better of themselves.

That was why she'd come out to this strange place so far from Ohio. Madeline had said the kids didn't have anything. Melinda hadn't realized that meant babies were using mud for paint. That was less than nothing.

She had a box without windows. Time to make the most of it.

"We're going to put handprints all over the wall," she told the little boy. "And you won't get in trouble at all!"

"Yah! Paint!" He wriggled out of her arms and bolted back to his mom, jumping up and down. "Paint, Mommy! Paint!"

At that point, a beautiful young woman walked in. She was thin and had long black hair that was woven back into a simple braid. If it weren't for the medical scrubs, she could have been a model. "Sorry I'm late, Dr. Mitchell."

"We're just getting started," Madeline said. "Melinda, this is Jenna Inila."

"Oh—the scholarship winner!" Melinda rushed forward and shook her hand. "Congratulations—your essay was outstanding." Jenna Inila had won the Mitchell Foundation scholarship that Madeline had set up for Native American students who were interested in pursuing a career in medicine.

"Oh. Yes." The young woman looked torn, like she couldn't decide if she was going to shake Melinda's hand back or stare at the ground. "Thank you for the opportunity."

Huh. On Tammy, it had just seemed like shyness, but on Jenna, this no-looking thing felt a lot closer to what Madeline had warned her about—that some people wouldn't look at her, wouldn't talk to her. She was an outsider and it might be a little while before she existed to them.

She let go of the girl's hand. "Keep up the good work." If Jenna wasn't going to look at her, she wasn't going to force the issue.

Then the parking lot filled up and a bunch of really sick people walked in. Sure, medicine was Melinda's birthright, but she'd never done well with blood or barf. Or worse.

No one looked at her, actually—not head-on, anyway. She

caught a lot of people giving her the side-eye, but for the first time she could remember, Melinda was essentially invisible while everyone greeted Madeline with warm smiles and a mix of Lakota and English.

She hadn't thought being ignored would bother her, but she was surprised to realize it did.

Then Nellie slid over to her side. "Miss Melinda, what are we going to paint?"

Oh, right. She didn't have time to stand around and be melodramatic—she had work to do. "Why don't we go talk about it?"

The four of them—Melinda, Tammy, Nellie and Mikey—walked next door. Nellie began skipping around the room in big circles, Mikey chasing her as fast as his chunky little legs could carry him.

Tammy showed her that the door in back actually lead to boys' and girls' bathrooms and a small kitchen, with an additional storage area behind that. Everything was utilitarian. And ugly. But very clean. Not a spot of construction dust to be seen.

Madeline was right. Nobody did a damn fine job.

"Okay," Melinda said after she tested the faucets. At least the water was running. "This place is depressing. How are we going to make it fun?"

"Cars!" Mikey shouted. He began making *vroom* noises and squealing his tires as he kept chasing Nellie around.

The sound of just two kids bouncing off the concrete got louder with every echo. Man, what would this place sound like if they had twenty kids in here?

She'd been in a day care once in Columbus that had foam padding on the walls and ceiling. They needed some of that. A lot of it, actually.

Melinda looked down at the floor. The poured concrete was finished smooth. They could paint it... although carpet would absorb the noise better. Maybe she could make something road-like out of carpet squares? There had to be a solution. "What else do we need?"

Tammy started a list. Tables and chairs were at the top of the list, followed by toys. What fun was a Child Care Center without toys? Nellie and Mikey helpfully suggested their favorites—dolls and cars. Books, shelves to keep them on. Food. The center would serve a hot lunch and two snacks a day. Madeline had already told her that they needed to be 'heavy' snacks because a lot of the kids weren't getting three square meals a day at home, and that they'd need to serve as many fruits and vegetables as possible.

And of course, art supplies. Paper, boxes of crayons, finger paints, enough play clay to build another center—she needed all of it.

There was so much to do—and somehow, she was in charge of it all. A whiff of panic curled at the edge of her mind, but she pushed it back. This was nothing but a really, *really* blank canvas. Madeline was right—the space had a lot of potential.

She and Tammy spent the rest of the day making lists. The funny thing was, even though the center hadn't officially opened its doors, there were still somewhere between three and seven kids in there all day, all running around or spinning in circles. Most had come with their parents who had appointments at the Clinic.

The kids didn't have any problem with her. Sure, not all of them said *hi* or introduced themselves, but they all looked at her and smiled big when she asked them if they'd like to have a train set to play with or if they wanted to help paint the walls. The answer was *yes*, over and over.

The list of things they needed grew. Hand soap and toilet paper. Mops and paper towels. Bleach. Cots for kids to take a nap on—or at least blankets or something, Melinda noted after Mikey collapsed in a corner, his little baby butt up in the air. Things like racetracks on the floor would have to wait. They needed snacks and necessities first.

By the time Madeline stuck her head in and announced they were leaving in fifteen minutes, Melinda was beat. Her feet ached from standing on the concrete all day and she had no idea if there was enough money to get half of the things they needed. Hell, she should probably be happy she had that much money at all. God bless being from a rich family—all the more after seeing this place.

"Tomorrow, I'll get supplies," she told Tammy as the younger woman buckled Mikey into his car. "Food first. If you think of anything else we need, just add it to the list."

She waved to Mikey and Nellie as they drove off. Madeline was still in the Clinic. No one else was around.

Melinda went back inside. Nobody Bodine was the Clinic's janitor—would he also be cleaning the center? Was she paying him out of the center's budget? Was she paying him at all?

She didn't know what she thought about the silent man having full access to her center. All she really knew was that she thought about it a lot.

Hell, there was no way to know. It's not like there was much to clean today, just some dusty footprints on the floor.

She looked down at the list of things she had to buy tomorrow. It was four pages long. She had an extra sheet of paper.

Before she could change her mind, she tore half of it off and dashed off a note. She didn't have a desk or table to set the note on, nor did she have any tape to stick it to the door.

So she folded it into a little tent and set it in the middle of the floor.

She wondered if he'd be the one to find it.

That night, she was so tired that she only managed to sit by the fire outside for about twenty minutes. Although she knew it was ridiculous, she found herself staring at the trees. Would a man walk out of the shadows? Would he come sit by the fire? Would he stare at her with those dark eyes again, like he was daring her to ask another wildly inappropriate question?

He didn't. As Rebel had said, nobody was there.

With a small 'n'.

Nobody stood in the shadows watching and listening. He didn't like to be in the Clinic when other people were there. The woman who answered the phone? Yeah, she didn't like him. She'd even called the law on him a couple of times when he'd had to suck it up and go to the Clinic during daylight hours or risk bleeding out.

Clarence didn't actively hate him, but Nobody always got the feeling that the nurse was just waiting for Nobody to lose it so he could have a crack at knocking him down. It would be a victory if he could take Nobody out, the modern-day equivalent of wannabe gunslingers looking to knock off a Sackett in the Louis L'Amour books Nobody read. Whoever could break Nobody would be the toughest bastard on the rez.

What Nobody would give to *not* be the toughest bastard on the rez. He'd rather not have to go through Clarence to lose the title, though.

So he waited until everyone else had gone home and then, just to be sure, he waited a little bit more. He saw Melinda get into the car with Dr. Mitchell and drive off. Did she know he emptied the trash and mopped the floor? Did she think he was little better than a loser because that was his job?

If she did, he wouldn't blame her. Nobody didn't know a hell of a lot about the Mitchell family—they were from Ohio, as Rebel had said, and had to have some money because Dr. Mitchell had pretty much single-handedly kept the Clinic's doors open for a year. More than enough money that Melinda *had* to look down on a guy who cleaned toilets.

He didn't see anything. It'd been fifteen minutes since Dr. Mitchell had locked up. Except for the couple of times Nobody had caught junkies trying to break into the clinic for drugs, no one came around after hours.

He unlocked the clinic and locked the door behind him again. He didn't want anyone wandering in on him. He didn't even turn on the lights. The shadows inside weren't the same as the shadows outside, but he felt better when light wasn't shining down on him.

He worked quickly, wiping down the exam tables, scrubbing the bathroom and mopping the floor. He was good at this. Of course, he'd had a lot of time to get good at it—eight years in prison with nothing to do but clean and fight. It was stupid to take pride in something as lowly as cleaning up other people's messes, but he knew it was important for a doctor's office to be germ-free. In some pathetic little way, he felt important for the Clinic.

He bagged the trash, took it out to the barrel and... didn't light it up. Damn it all, he wasn't done yet. Dr. Mitchell was going to pay him more to clean up the Child Care Center. He hadn't wanted to do it—and that was before he'd seen Melinda Mitchell. It was one thing to keep a clinic clean. That was necessary. But a day care? He didn't know why, but it felt like he'd lowered himself even more. If it'd been anyone else, Nobody would have turned them down, but Dr. Mitchell wasn't the kind of person—man or woman—who took 'no' for an answer. And really, who was he kidding? He was already so low he couldn't get any deeper.

He unlocked the back door of the center and surveyed the scene. The place looked almost the same as it had when he'd swept it up two days ago—some water splashed, most likely from hand-washing, some footprints on the floor. He went back to the Clinic and got his stuff.

He wiped down the bathrooms and opened the door to the main part. Even though the sun was well on its way to setting, enough light streamed in behind him that he could see.

There was something small and white and folded, in the dead center of the floor. Something that didn't look accidentally dropped or even tossed.

Nobody stood there for a moment, looking at the paper, for that's what it was. Part of him didn't want to even touch it—it felt like a trap of some kind, something dangerous.

He set his stuff on the floor and propped the broom up against the door. Then he walked over, picked up the paper and unfolded it.

Mr. Bodine,

Thank you very much for having the center so spotless for me. I'm sorry to say that we're going to be destroying your clean building in the next few days. I'll be bringing in toys and furniture and we're going to paint the walls. Don't think of it as a mess, although it will be—for a while, anyway. Think of it as creative chaos. Out of disaster can come something beautiful.

Yours,

Melinda Mitchell

Nobody stood there in a state of shock. Mr. Bodine? If that wasn't his last name, he'd be sure that she hadn't meant to leave this for him. Hell, it *was* his last name and he still wasn't sure it was really for him. She'd written him a letter. Him, of all people. He'd never gotten a letter before. What was he supposed to do now? What did normal people do? Should he write her back?

What the hell was he supposed to say? *Thanks, happy to scrub your toilets?* No way in hell that was going to happen. He'd rather get shot again.

His eyes returned to the last part, where she'd written *Out of disaster can come something beautiful* and below that, *Yours*. Her handwriting was deeply slanted, so it almost looked like she was writing in italics. It wasn't creative chaos—the words were perfectly formed, written with a steady, careful hand. And she'd written to him.

She wasn't afraid of him. That stunning realization was quickly followed by another—if she'd written him a letter, she had to have been *thinking* about him.

Was that even possible?

No. No way. At least, not in the way he kind of wanted her to think about him. The idea was ridiculous and he knew it. She might have crazy hair and whatever, but she was still a rich-ish white woman who would be afraid of him, once someone saw fit to tell her all about the nothing that was Nobody.

Women like her might go slumming with a janitor, but not with convicted murderers. And *never* with janitors who were convicted murderers.

No, it was more likely that she was just being nice. One of those people who had been raised to be polite to the help, like her sister was always polite to him, in her disapproving way. That's all this was. A small measure of kindness.

Still... *Yours.*

He folded the note and put it in his back pocket.

Then he cleaned the floor.

For her.

CHAPTER THREE

The note was gone the next morning.

Otherwise, Melinda couldn't see much difference in the place. It was as clean as it had been yesterday, but then, there wasn't much to mess up. But no note meant that Nobody had been there. She didn't have a trashcan yet, so there was no way of telling if he'd thrown it away, burned it in the barrel out back or...

Or if he'd kept it.

The only thing she knew for sure was that he hadn't left a reply. She had no idea if he thought she was insane or ridiculous or what for leaving him a message in the middle of the floor. That wasn't an entirely foreign thing—many of the board members on the Mitchell Foundation thought she was a total flake. Yet another reason she was out in South Dakota instead of in Columbus.

Of course, in Columbus, she wouldn't have had to leave a note on the floor. Even in the grittier areas of town, everyone had a cell phone. Everyone texted. Here? She couldn't even get a signal except at about nine in the evening. On a clear night. It was like going back to the Stone Age.

Her little first-world whine was interrupted when Tammy showed up. She didn't want to text anyone, anyway. All of her friends back in Columbus had thought she was nuts for following her sister out here to the middle of nowhere. No, she was here for the isolation, to throw herself into her work.

Starting now. After Rebel kissed his wife goodbye—Melinda *so* wasn't used to that—she and Rebel headed up to Rapid City in Madeline's Jeep. The Great Stock-Up had officially begun.

And it didn't let up for two weeks—two of the longest weeks of Melinda's life. The fact that she was getting up before seven every morning had something to do with that. Driving the three hour round-trip to Rapid City several times a day also had something to do with that, too.

Almost once a day, she drove to the warehouse store and bought as much food staples as she could get into the Jeep. Then Rebel showed her where the thrift stores and resale shops in town were located. She scored cups, plates, cutlery, books, toys and a couple of couches in decent shape. They had to come back for the couches with a truck—which was how Melinda met Rebel's brother, Jesse.

He had a job on a road construction crew, so Melinda and Rebel had to get up even earlier to make it to his place to get the truck. Melinda wasn't exactly comfortable letting a man she'd barely said hello to borrow her car, but she also wasn't comfortable having kids sit on the concrete floor for story time. So Jesse drove off in her Civic and she and Rebel loaded up couches.

It was a start. At least the kids could all have a snack while she read them stories.

Tammy made admirable progress on organizing what Melinda trucked in while simultaneously keeping the kids from wandering off. She had Nellie in charge of organizing books and Mikey was responsible for stacking the boxes of crackers and cookies. Tammy was good with the kids, in her quiet way. She wiped noses and hugged away booboos like a professional. Melinda may have liked kids—and she did—but she got along better with the older ones who were at least in kindergarten, like Nellie. Babies were beyond her. Thank heavens Tammy was good at changing diapers.

Oh, yeah. She added more diapers to the list. Just another thing to get.

At no point during those two weeks did she see Nobody Bodine. No surprise visits for dinner. No sign of him at the center. No notes left anywhere she would find them. No one else talked about him, not even Rebel and Madeline.

It was like he didn't exist. Except she couldn't get that feeling out of her mind—the feeling she'd gotten the first night that he'd been just out of sight, watching her. Other people showed up to talk to Rebel, but Nobody wasn't among them. This left her vaguely disappointed. How crazy was that?

Finally, the center had enough supplies to function. Melinda was still going to have to make regular trips into town—the kids went through an insane amount of milk on a daily basis—but she was ready to start spending time with all the short people.

She was also ready to stop getting up at the butt-crack of dawn. Tammy was going to handle the morning shift. The plan was that Melinda would roll in around ten, they'd handle lunch together, and then Tammy would head out at naptime. Sure, that meant Melinda would be in the center until the last kid left—no later than six every night, but she didn't mind. In theory, she'd get back to Madeline and Rebel's trailer just as dinner was being served.

Plus, if she was actually in the center, she could start painting the damn thing. Even with the addition of furniture and toys, the whole place was still as depressing as a morgue. In a perfect world, she would have painted the whole place before the kids showed up. However, the kids had come first. Ah, well. Life wasn't perfect.

On Sunday, she made what she hoped was her final run into Rapid City for at least a few days. On Monday, she showed up at the center a little after ten, the car full of paint cans and rollers. Tammy had twelve kids already there, running from toddler to maybe eight. The older kids were outside playing kickball while the smaller ones played in the dirt. The day was bright and clear. Perfect.

The kids all stopped as she got out of the car. Some of the older ones were a little wary around her, but Melinda had already cemented her position as 'crazy white woman who brings cool stuff.' No kid was immune to that kind of fun. "What did you bring today, Miss Melinda?" they all asked as they crowded around.

"Paint!" she announced. "Who wants to paint today?"

The chorus of 'me! me!' was so loud she was thankful she wasn't inside. One of the older kids said, "what color?"

"Oh, I like you. What's your name again?"

"Mark," the kid said, looking at his feet.

"Excellent question, Mark. Today we'll be painting one wall

primer white." The kids all drooped in disappointment. "But tomorrow," Melinda hurried to add, "we're going to start a rainbow! Won't that be cool?"

The kids all whooped and hollered. Melinda made the older kids carry in a gallon of paint while the younger ones got the rollers. Then she set them to work, clearing all the new-to-them stuff away from the western wall of the center. Sometimes that meant the younger kids were literally just throwing toys over their shoulders, but it was progress.

Soon enough, she had the drop cloths down, the kids into the t-shirts she'd snagged from a thrift store to act as smocks and they were rolling primer onto the walls. The kids squealed with joy as primer dripped everywhere. Far too late, Melinda wondered if some of the parents might not be so thrilled if their kids came home with white paint in their hair. Oh, well. It'd wash out. Eventually.

She worked on getting the names down. Kala and Andy were twins. Along with Mikey, those were the toddlers. Jeremy, Paris, Luis and Colby were all three and four. Sasha, the twins' older sister, and Nellie were five, Courtney and Alex were six, and Courtney's older brother Mark was eight.

They were a quarter of the way through the wall when a shadow passed in front of the door, blocking the light. Melinda turned and saw a boy, probably no more than ten, standing on the threshold. Something about the way he held himself was familiar. Head down, arms loose at his side—it was almost as if he was looking for a fight.

Then she noticed the bruises. The left side of his face was a mottled mess of greens and yellows—older bruises that had probably just started to fade.

Something in her cramped up, a pain that more than one person had referred to as Melinda's 'bleeding liberal heart.' *Whatever*, she'd always said. Her heart bled because people hurt kids. Someone had hurt *this* kid. If that made her a soft touch, so be it. Someone should be soft. The world would be too hard a place otherwise.

She shot a look at Tammy, who was doing her level best to keep the paint on the walls and off the floors. "You know him?"

Tammy glanced over her shoulder. "No. Oh, Jeremy!" She rushed toward the boy, who'd started painting a stuffed animal.

Melinda set her roller down and approached the boy slowly. It had been her experience that abused kids didn't like sudden movements. Slow and steady won the race. "Hi," she started out.

The boy didn't respond, except to drop his eyes.

Melinda considered her options. The smart thing to do would be to trade places with Tammy and see if the kid did better talking to another Lakota.

Melinda never did seem to do the smart thing. Another step forward. "You want to paint?"

Ah, a reaction. The kid shrugged. Excellent. Now they were getting somewhere.

"I could sure use the help," she said, pausing long enough to snag another roller. "This wall is monster huge." Another step forward.

Christ. She was close enough now that she could see how big the bruise was, how half of his face was still swollen enough that he looked lopsided. No wonder the kid couldn't decide if he was coming or going. She was probably lucky he'd even made it this far. A bruise that big? How had he not gotten a concussion—or worse? She'd seen kids who'd been hit so hard, so often that it did permanent damage to their brains. It was a hard thing to see, to know it could have been stopped, the kid could have been saved.

She fought the overwhelming urge to pull the boy into a fierce bear hug and tell him no one would ever hurt him again. First off, grabbing the kid would probably scare the hell out of him. And second off, she couldn't make promises like that. She knew damn well at the end of the day that this kid would go home, where he'd be vulnerable again. All she could do was offer him a safe place *here*. Damn it all.

She hated that feeling, the one of frustration that kept her from protecting kids.

"What's your name? I'm Melinda. I'm Dr. Mitchell's sister." Nothing. She took another step closer and held the roller out halfway between them. If he wanted to paint, he'd have to come in the rest of the way. When she got no response, she added, "Do your parents know you're here?" in a quieter voice.

Another shrug, but this one was followed by the boy snaking his hand out and trying to grab the roller out of her hand.

Victory. A really small one, but she took it. He was here, he wanted to paint. Except Melinda didn't let go. "You have to tell me your name first. Everyone here has a name."

He almost let go of the roller, *almost* turned and ran back out the door. Melinda could see the boy was terrified, but she wasn't sure why. Was he scared of her, of what the other kids would say about his face—or of what his parents would do when they found him here?

She didn't want to think about that third option. Yes, she'd had her fair share of confrontations with adults who were violent and/or strung out on something. She'd usually been in a place that had back-up, though—other teachers at community centers, guards at a school, that sort of thing.

Here, she had Tammy and, next door, Clarence and Tara. A person would have to be an idiot to take on Clarence—the man was a tank—but Clarence left at five every day. Melinda was here until the last kid went home.

She wasn't going to let a little fear rule her and she sure as hell wasn't going to let it rule the children—not if she could help it. "Well?" she said, holding tight to the roller.

"Jamie," he finally said, his voice so soft that she wasn't sure she'd heard him correctly.

No last name. Well, it was a start. She let go of the roller. "It's nice to meet you, Jamie." He nodded his head, just a little. She leaned in. "You're safe here. No one will hurt you, okay?"

At that, anything that had started to loosen up about the boy went all unreadable again. For a moment, she thought he was going to drop the roller and bolt on her. But after a tense moment, he started spinning the roller in his hands.

Yeah, this was a kid who needed to paint. "Come on," she told him, leading him to a section of the wall that hadn't been splattered on yet. "You can start here. We'll have lunch in about an hour, okay?"

She kept an eye on the kids—and Jamie—as the afternoon progressed. He kept himself apart from the other kids, painting in careful, measured strokes. Every time she passed him, she made sure to tell him how even his section looked or how neat a job he was doing—any compliment she could come up with, she threw out there.

Not that the boy responded. Half the time, she wasn't sure he'd even heard her over the joyful noise the rest of the kids were making. *With time*, she told herself. Rome wasn't built in a day. The important thing was that the boy had come at all.

By the time Tammy headed out with Mikey, the wall was almost done. Nap time was shot to hell and back, though—the whole room reeked of paint and there was no way the smaller kids would lay down while the bigger kids kept painting. Luckily, on her trips to the warehouse store, she'd bought several fans. Once the wall was painted, she had two of the older kids—but not Jamie—set the fans up while the rest of the kids helped her carry the supplies outside. Thankfully, there was a hose bib at the back of the building so she could get the rollers cleaned up while the kids picked up their game of kickball.

Jamie didn't join in. Instead, he hung back, standing in the meager shade of the building, watching the others. She didn't like that he held himself back, as if he wasn't allowed to have fun. He needed to interact with someone, even if that someone was her. "Here," Melinda said to him, handing him the trash bag with all the used rollers in it. If she really wanted to, she could clean them out, but in her experience, re-using rollers led to shoddy walls. "Hold this."

They worked in silence, with only the occasional break for Melinda to scold or hug, as the case may be. The shadows of the afternoon lengthened and parents arrived to pick up their kids.

Melinda could tell the paint-in-the-hair thing wasn't winning her any friends, but everyone was at least polite. It helped that the kids were obviously having way too much fun. A few parents promised to send the kids in their grubby clothes for tomorrow.

It wasn't until the twins had gone home that Melinda realized Jamie was gone, too. He'd slipped off into the evening as silently as he'd arrived.

Damn. That boy was going to be a tough nut to crack.

She thought about him while she straightened up the center—as straight as it could get with everything on one side of the building. Then she got the rollers all ready for tomorrow. She really wished this place had a window so she could leave it open to air out overnight. Tomorrow, they'd have to open up all the doors and hope for a good cross breeze.

At six fifteen, she wrote a note to Nobody. He was cleaning the clinic, she was pretty sure. The trashcans were always emptied and the bathrooms were always clean in the morning, so someone was doing it. Even if it wasn't Nobody, she owed whoever it was an apology for the state of the center.

Then she walked outside and locked the door. The sky was still a brilliant blue. She stood for a moment and let the sun warm her face.

Then she thought she heard something. Well, maybe not heard, but felt—like when someone was staring at her from across the road? Even as she thought it, she knew it sounded crazy—how exactly did one *feel* someone watching them?

But she did. "Jamie? Is that you?" She got no response as she scanned her surroundings. There weren't a lot of places to hide out here. The immediate surroundings of the clinic were limited to a low hill, a barrel that was used to burn trash, some sad little shrubs and even sadder pine trees that looked like they'd given up. And grass. Plenty of knee-high grass.

She couldn't see anything out of the ordinary—not even a critter slinking around in the grass. But she could feel something. *Someone*. Someone was out there. In the trees? There weren't enough trees to hide behind, were there? "Hello?"

Nothing. And she didn't hear anything else, either. *Long day*, she thought. She was hearing things. "Jamie, if that's you, Tammy will be here around eight tomorrow. I'll be here until six, okay? We'll be here tomorrow. You can come back."

A gentle breeze ruffled the sad trees, but there was no other response. She'd have to ask Rebel about Jamie with no last name. He was the medicine man, after all. If anyone knew about a young boy with a beaten face, Rebel would.

Nobody watched Melinda Mitchell drive away. She'd been wearing another long, hippie-style skirt and bright white tank top—he could still see the hot-pink bra straps. Was the rest of the bra hot pink, too?

Hell. He slammed the door on that train of thought and *fast*. So what if she was sparkling? So what if she'd left him one note?

So what if she'd almost seen him that one time? Or this time? That didn't mean he should be thinking of her like that. He'd had women, sure, back when he'd been a stupid teenager trying to prove himself—to someone. Anyone. It'd been a woman that had led to the fight in the first place.

Yeah, he was done with women. For their part, women were done with him, too. No one wanted a man as messed up as he was. Hell, he couldn't blame them. His own mother had never wanted him. Why should now be different?

Except... except Melinda was different. *Seemed* different, anyway.

Had he done something to attract her attention? Stepped on a twig or something? He was usually silent, but she'd heard him. Jamie hadn't been around by the time Nobody had gotten here. He knew. He'd checked.

This was the first night she'd stayed so late. He'd almost gone into the clinic before he'd realized she was still there.

So Jamie had come after all. He hadn't wanted to. If it were up to Jamie, he'd stay out at Nobody's place, brushing the horses, fishing and reading all day long.

It was one thing for Nobody to stay hidden from the rest of the world. No one cared about him, with the exceptions of Jamie and maybe Rebel. But Jamie was another matter entirely. People would notice the boy had gone missing. Eventually, anyway. Sooner or later, one of his parents would sober up and realize that their son had been gone for days, weeks even. The odds were good they wouldn't care, but there was always a chance that one of them—Myra, more than likely—would report the boy gone.

Nobody knew what happened when kids disappeared. The cops got involved, Amber Alerts were issued, and people looked. People combed the land.

Nobody wanted to keep Jamie out with him, safe from the Lou Kills Deers of the world, but he couldn't risk people finding him. And he especially couldn't risk people finding Jamie with him. The law would take one look at Nobody's record and assume that he'd taken the boy—that he'd meant harm to the boy.

If they locked Nobody up again, Jamie wouldn't have anyone. And Nobody couldn't let that happen.

School was out for the summer. The boy needed somewhere he could go, something to do. Working with horses and fishing were all well and good, but the boy needed more than that. He needed... something. Nobody didn't know what and that was the problem. He knew how to protect the boy, not raise him. Not make him a part of the tribe. He couldn't be the boy's family. That would be condemning him to a life on the outside with no hope of ever being a part of the rest of the world.

So Nobody had told Jamie to go to the new center, that the white woman would keep him safe during the daylight hours. He could be around other kids. He could make friends. He could be a part of the tribe.

All those things Nobody couldn't have, couldn't be.

He forced himself to do the clinic first, but he knew he was rushing. He still had her note in his back pocket. He'd gotten into the habit of reading it again right before he went to sleep. Would she have left him another note? Did he even want her to? He didn't know what to say to her in either case.

Soon, he unlocked the center's door. The place looked like it had been looted by vandals—everything was pushed to one side, and one wall had been painted.

What a mess. How was he supposed to clean that? He wasn't. He couldn't even see the floor—tarps were scattered everywhere. Shaking his head, he turned back through the door to clean the toilets—and then he saw it.

A folded piece of paper was taped to the door at what had to be her eye level, just below Nobody's chin. He snatched it off the door, as if someone else might beat him to it.

Mr. Bodine,

As you can tell, we began painting today. You have my permission not to bother cleaning up this particular mess—I'm only going to make it worse tomorrow. I'm sorry that we've trashed your building so badly, but I promise it'll be very pretty when we're done! Remember—creative chaos!

Yours,
Melinda Mitchell

Nobody smiled—an actual smile, which was rare enough. His building? She had to be teasing him, but it didn't feel like she was making fun of him—not like other women did. And she'd signed it *Yours* again.

Maybe he'd stop by Rebel's again tonight. Maybe she'd be outside at that fire again, burning as bright as the flames themselves. He'd only passed by the place a few times after he was confident Jamie was safe for the night. Those had been late-night visits—long after all the lights had gone out. He hadn't actually seen her again until today.

He promised himself he wouldn't stay long—he had to check on Jamie.

Nothing good could come from it.

But he wanted to see her anyway.

"Jamie," Rebel said, more to himself than to Melinda. "Yes. Jamie Kills Deer."

"Kills Deer? Really?"

"That's not the weirdest of them," Madeline said, grinning over her glass of wine. "Wait until you meet Plenty Holes."

Dude, it got weirder. "He showed up today, a huge fading bruise on his face. Should we call social services?"

Rebel and Madeline shared a worried look. "What?" Melinda asked. "That's what I'd do in Ohio. Call social services. Or the police. Or both."

"It's... complicated," Madeline said.

"What's complicated? Someone's beating the hell out of a kid." When Madeline didn't have an answer for that, she turned to Rebel. "Why is that complicated?"

"Social services will take the boy."

"And that's a bad thing because... why?"

Rebel looked as uncomfortable as Melinda had ever seen him. "They'll take him away. They'll put him in a foster home in Rapid City or Pierre—a white foster home."

"Still not seeing why that's bad—kind of far away, but not bad."

"It's complicated," Madeline said again. "Because Indian kids are Indians, they're marked as special needs, so foster families get paid more to take care of them."

"And?" Because there had to be a catch here, one that would keep people from reporting child abuse.

"Some of the foster homes are in it for the money. Social services takes a child out of the only home and land they've ever known and puts them in a situation where they're treated exactly the same. Not all," he hurried to add as Melinda looked at him in shock. "But once social services takes a child, it's almost impossible to get that kid back to the rez, even if there are relatives willing and able to take care of them."

"What are you saying—that calling social services on a child abuser is asking for a kid to be kidnapped or something?"

"It's happened," Madeline said. "Who was it—last year? A girl didn't get off the bus. Grandmother was waiting for her. Called the police, did the Amber Alert—and it turned out that social services had taken the girl out of school because they'd received a tip that her mother was on drugs. Just a tip. Nothing investigated, nothing proven. Just... gone."

"Sheila is still in a foster home," Rebel said quietly. "They cut her hair and made her take a white last name. Her grandmother cannot get her back."

"He's kidding, right?" Melinda asked her sister. Then, turning to Rebel, she added, "You're kidding, right? Tell me you're kidding."

"It's like the old days," Rebel went on, not meeting her gaze. "They took our children, some in handcuffs, and shipped them to the east. They cut their hair and took away their names. They took away the language. They took away what it meant to be a Lakota. They thought they could break us," he added in an angry tone that Melinda had never heard before. "Kill the Indian to save the child."

An uncomfortable silence settled over dinner. "This is insane," she finally said into the quiet. "You're telling me my options are to either let an Indian beat him or let someone beat the Indian out of him?"

"Lou Kills Deer will not let his son go with anyone else." The sorrow in Rebel's voice told her that he'd already had this argument before. "No one else on the rez will risk pissing him off."

"Not even you?"

That was one of those things she probably shouldn't have said—or, at least, shouldn't have said in such an accusatory tone. But she was furious. How was this even possible? Where was the freaking justice for Jamie and all the kids like him? Because she wasn't so naïve to think that Jamie was the only kid getting smacked around on this rez.

But apparently she was naïve enough to think that she could help him out.

"We have to pick our battles, Mellie." Ever the rational one, Madeline was speaking in her calm-down voice. Which usually only made Melinda that much madder. "We pay for the clinic and now the center. We do the most good that way."

They'd had this conversation, on and off, for years. Melinda always wanted to do more. It hadn't been enough that the family had spent Thanksgiving serving meals to the homeless. Melinda had wanted to spend every weekend at the shelter, trying to make the world a better place, one meal at a time. No, her parents had said. Mom worked on her pro bono divorce cases on the weekend; Dad had seen poor patients on Saturday. That was how they could help the most. Dishing out spaghetti wasn't the proper use of their resources.

Melinda supposed it was true enough. Mom helped women get away from abusive marriages and get child support. Dad saved people's lives and didn't make them pay the crushing bills that went with it.

But it wasn't enough. Not for her.

"This is ridiculous," she said as she shoved away from the table. "Utterly ridiculous."

"Mellie," Madeline called out behind her, but she wasn't in the mood to listen. She stomped outside so hard she was surprised she wasn't leaving craters in the dirt behind her.

What kind of crazy world had she wandered into, where the only two options were both letting a kid's spirit die a little more every day? Yeah, bad things happened to kids all the time in Columbus, too—but she'd always been able to do something—call the cops, help a woman get her family to a safe house, foster a kid... When Shawna Gell's father had killed her mother but was freed on a stinking technicality, Melinda hadn't hesitated to take the little girl into her apartment. It had been inconvenient, sure, but she'd known Shawna was safe. Wasn't that the most important thing? To keep the kids safe?

Not here, apparently. Stupid world.

Melinda's anger burned hot. If she could have, she'd have punched something. Instead, she stomped frustrated circles around the unlit campfire.

What was she supposed to do tomorrow? Check Jamie for new bruises? Send him home with a prayer that nothing bad happened that night? Coast on warm, fuzzy thoughts of how, one day, the meek would inherit something and hope you didn't get beat to death in the meantime?

Shit. She was going to cry.

Melinda hung her head, willing the tears not to get started because once they got started, she'd wind up crying her eyes out and she absolutely hated crying in front of Madeline. Her older sister was always so calm and rational and never, every lost her head over every little tragedy in this world. Oh, Madeline would come out and give her a sisterly hug and a pat on the back to try and calm her down, but she'd never understand how deeply Melinda felt the pain of others. Madeline was too clinical. She didn't see people, she saw symptoms—problems to be solved.

Melinda had always been different. A bleeding heart, a soft touch, an idealist in a realist world. She knew she couldn't save everyone. It was not just naïve to think that if she could just solve inner-city poverty or educational opportunities or child abuse that the world would be perfect—it was downright delusional. But that didn't mean she wasn't going to try, by God.

Something snapped her head up. Had she heard a noise? Maybe not heard—more like what she'd sensed outside the center this evening. She looked over her shoulder. No one had snuck out of the house to try and reason with her. The sun hadn't set all the way, but long shadows cast the trees in darkness. As far as she could see, she was alone out here. Just the crazy woman and the feeling that someone was watching her.

There—in the trees on the other side of the clearing. There was someone there. Was it one of the people who came for Rebel?

No, it couldn't be. They always came up on the gravel road.

What was she supposed to do here? If this were Little Red Riding Hood, a wolf would be stalking her from the shadows and she should go back inside right *now*.

She took a step toward the tree line. "Hello?"

Nothing.

Then something... shifted. Like one part of the shadow got *darker*, somehow, as if the light was condensing into a black hole. Which didn't make any sense. Shadows didn't do that. Not like *that*.

"Is someone there?" There was always a chance it was Jamie. That's who she thought might have been hanging around the center earlier.

Behind her, she heard the trailer door open and shut. She glanced back over her shoulder to see Rebel walking down the steps. He gave her an odd look before he went to get the firewood for the night.

When she turned her attention back to the trees, the strange shadow was gone. Just plain old boring shadows as far as the eye could see.

What the hell was going on in this place?

Before long, another campfire was roaring. Melinda was still plenty pissed at Rebel, though. How many Jamies were there on this rez? On all the rezs? How many kids did they lose in the name of Indian-ness, when even one was too many?

And how could someone like Rebel, who was supposed to be this medicine man who cared for his people, let it happen?

She wanted to tell him he could go to hell so bad, but she was sort of living in his house at the moment. Back home, she would have had any number of couches she could have crashed on until the drama passed. Here? Well, she could go sleep on the couch in the center. For a night, maybe. And then?

She'd already burned nearly every bridge she had in Ohio. She didn't have anywhere else to go.

Rebel sat cross-legged by the fire, staring into the flames. He had his beading things within easy reach, but he wasn't doing anything. Just staring.

He was starting to freak her out—normally, he was kind of chatty. Definitely not the silent, stoic Indian that Hollywood seemed convinced existed in great numbers.

Definitely not like Nobody, her brain reminded her. Had he gotten her note? Would he leave her a response?

"It's good you came," Rebel finally said.

"I had to come, remember? I got myself run right out of Columbus."

He cocked his head to one side, as if he were listening—to what, she didn't know. "You could have gone many places. But you came here."

"If you're trying to make me feel better, it's not working."

He smiled into the firelight. "This isn't me trying to make you feel better. This is me trying to tell you why you're here."

She froze. "What?"

"It's good for him you're here," Rebel went on. "You see him. That makes him real."

"Who, Jamie? How does me seeing him make him real? Are you trying to be all mystical? Because it's not working." She thought about mentioning the weird shadow, but didn't. He already thought she was nuts. No need to dig that hole deeper.

Rebel heaved a mighty—and mighty patronizing—sigh. "You got yourself run right out of Columbus, you say?"

"Go to hell." There. She did actually feel better. Not much, but some.

He laughed, which would have been sexy if it hadn't been so damn irritating. "She did warn me about you."

No question who that 'she' was. "Yeah, yeah—I'm the flakey drama queen. Whatever."

"I understand why you're not happy about Jamie," he went on. "There are no good solutions at this point. But he's not alone. There are those who look out for him, imperfect as it is. To remove him from that would be to cut him off from the only people who actually care about him." Finally, the man turned and looked at her. "You are one of those people, Melinda. Do not underestimate the power of that caring."

She opened her mouth, but nothing came out—no snarky comebacks, no damnations.

"How many people looked at you on your first day at the center?"

"Not all of them," she admitted. "Madeline said they might not."

"Did she tell you why?"

Melinda shook her head. "Just that I wasn't there."

Rebel sighed—less one of frustration this time. Just weariness. "It's a pure form of denial."

"Not the river in Egypt?"

He chuckled. "Not just a river in Egypt. When the white man first came across our territory looking for gold, some of the elders thought that they could just ignore the problem and it would go away. The white men would die when winter came and that would be that."

"It didn't work that way."

"No," Rebel agreed. "You kept coming."

She bristled. "I personally did not destroy your culture, thank you very much."

Rebel shot her a look that walked the fine line between amused and irritated, which was becoming a common occurrence. "The point," he said in a tone of voice that was definitely irritated, "is that we have a long history of ignoring those who do not belong. Because you are an outsider, you see things differently. You see *people* differently. That is how you make them real."

She thought of how the other kids kept themselves separate from Jamie, how he didn't interact with them, either. Did it start that early?

"What if *seeing* them isn't enough?" Just looking at someone couldn't stop them from being beaten. It didn't keep them safe.

He gave her the kind of smile a teacher always gave a student when they were just about to figure it out—the quadratic equation, mitosis—whatever. He was leading her to something. Damned if she knew what it was.

"But what if it is?"

Before she could answer *that* bon mot, he turned to look down the drive. An older man was riding up on a horse at a slow walk.

Rebel barely made sense—seeing made it real? She had no idea.

They'd been talking about Jamie, a boy she'd barely met. But

47

the funny thing was, her thoughts turned back to Nobody, to the way he'd reacted when she'd asked about his scars. Because she'd noticed them. Because she hadn't been able to look away.

What if seeing didn't make something real?

But what if it did?

CHAPTER FOUR

Nobody stood in the shadows, watching her.

She wasn't leaving. Melinda Mitchell normally closed up shop and drove off by this point in the evening, but not tonight. It had to be close to eight—two hours after she normally left. Was that because it was Friday?

What was she doing? Light streamed out of both the front and back doors of the center as she did something inside. He was tempted to edge closer and steal a look in.

She couldn't be painting. In the two weeks since she'd left him the last note, the inside of the center had gone from concrete gray to plain white to rainbows. Maybe that's what she'd meant by creative chaos? Because it was still chaos. He wasn't sure if it was beautiful, but it was definitely wild.

The rainbow colors went vertically up over the walls—even over the foam she'd managed to hang from the ceilings. The foam covered the top four feet of the walls. Not that Nobody made a lot of noise, but even he could tell that the center was more hushed now. Less echo-y.

At the height he'd come to think of as her eye-level, she'd hung bulletin board strips. Papers, splashed with finger paint and crayon scribbles, were tacked up along the wall now, some with kids' names neatly printed at the bottom, others with names that were barely readable.

Then, at kid level, the wall had been covered with tiny handprints. Each set of prints had a name and an age painted onto the wall underneath it. Jamie's hands were up there—no last name, though.

He'd been right. Melinda had taken the boy in. Good.

But that didn't explain what she was doing here *now*. Didn't she know this wasn't the safest place on the rez? True, he hadn't caught any junkies trying to break in recently, but that didn't mean they wouldn't try again.

She appeared in the front door. Light streamed from behind her, giving her an otherworldly glow.

He felt himself breathe at seeing her again. The two weeks since she'd almost walked right into him at Rebel's place had felt long. Time, as marked by days and weeks, didn't have much meaning for him. His world was divided into light and dark, warm and cold. He cleaned the clinic every day. There were no Mondays, no weekends.

But the last two weeks had moved by at such a slow pace that he'd begun to feel... uneasy about it. Not his usual sense of when someone was in trouble. This had been different. He'd wanted to see her just because. Not because he had to keep her safe or anything. Just... because.

But he'd forced himself to stay away from Rebel's. She'd looked right at him, walked right toward him as if he were standing in broad daylight. If she hadn't gotten distracted... no. He didn't believe she could actually tell he was there. Something else had attracted her attention. That was all.

Backlit, she stretched, her body reaching for the dusk sky. Something else began to make Nobody feel uneasy and that something was obvious—Melinda Mitchell had a hell of a body. Part of what had been bothering him had been those curves—those generous breasts, those hips.

How would her body feel? Would she be terrified if he filled his hands with those breasts? Would she be afraid of him if he grabbed her hips and pulled her into him?

Onto him?

Or would she like it? Would she think it exciting to do it with someone dangerous? Would she moan or cry out?

He got hard just thinking of it. Of her.

Then she did something that snapped him out of his thoughts.

She looked at him.

There was no mistaking this—she looked right at him. And smiled.

What the hell?

He started to shrink back, but she turned away from him, gathering up something off the floor. Did she know he was here or not?

He should go.

He didn't.

She was putting on a jacket of some sort—a big thing that came down to her knees. And a... helmet? Yeah, a helmet. A welder's helmet, he remembered.

Then she grabbed a sheet of metal from just inside the door and carried it out to where the burn barrel was. She leaned it up against the barrel and lit a blowtorch.

Nobody stood in absolute shock as Melinda began cutting into the metal. She sure as hell looked like she knew what she was doing—the helmet, the big gloves, the coat? Those weren't things people had just lying around.

Sparks flew as she worked. Nobody wanted to move so he could get a better view of what she was making, but he didn't want to. If she saw him... well, then she'd see him.

He knew he was being stupid. It'd been almost a month since he'd sat down next to her for dinner. A month since she'd talked to him. He wanted...

Hell. He didn't know what he wanted. But he wanted something with *her*.

Chunks of hot metal hit the dirt around her feet, but she didn't jump out of the way, didn't squeal in terror. She just kept cutting.

Finally, she stepped back. She turned the blowtorch off, set it down and then turned what was left of the metal sheet onto its side. She re-lit the blowtorch again, made a final cut, and shut it off a final time.

The metal fell apart, but she didn't cuss or cry. Instead, she stripped off her helmet and coat.

His body clenched as she removed the top layer of clothing. She wasn't any less clothed than she'd been before she started, but she made something as routine as taking off a coat sexy.

"Well?" she called over her shoulder. "What do you think?"

All sexy thoughts fled Nobody's mind. He froze—didn't even breathe. Was she talking to him? Was that even possible?

"I know you're there, you know." She was still admiring her

pile of metal. Not looking at him. "You're stealthy, but you're not invisible. Come tell me what you think."

Shit. She *was* talking to him.

He had two choices here. He could turn tail and run—be the coward people thought he was. Or...

Or he could do as she asked.

"I don't bite," she added, sounding cheerful about it. Like this whole thing was no big deal. "If you want, I won't ask about the scars. Deal?"

She really did know it was him. If he bolted, she probably wouldn't leave him any more extra-polite notes.

He took a deep breath and, heart racing, stepped out into the circle of light.

He saw tension ripple down her bare shoulders but otherwise, she gave no sign that she'd heard him.

He wanted to trail a finger down those shoulders, watch her skin jump at his touch.

But he didn't. Instead, he made damn sure to keep a good distance between them. Say, about six feet.

"There, that wasn't so hard, was it?" Moving slowly, she turned to him.

His lungs quit working. She had the most beautiful smile on her face, all warm and inviting. Especially the inviting part.

God, he wanted to close the space between them and kiss her. It'd been so long... just one kiss. Was it wrong to want that? With a woman as beautiful as Melinda—a woman who smiled at him, for crying out loud?

"Hello, Mr. Bodine. How nice of you to join me on this lovely evening."

The last time she'd asked him a direct question, he'd run back to the safety of the shadows. He wasn't going to do that this time. Not as long as she was smiling.

Still, that meant he had to talk to her and talking was not something he did in great quantities. He cleared his throat, trying to find his voice. "Ma'am."

He wouldn't have thought it was possible, but her smile grew. "How do you do that?"

"Do what, Ma'am?"

She wrinkled her brow at him, but she didn't lose that smile. It lit up her whole face. "That stealthy thing. You're almost invisible."

No 'almost' about it. He *was* invisible to everyone—everyone except her. "Don't know."

"Really? You have no idea how you blend into the shadows like that?"

"No, Ma'am." She kept looking at him like she expected him to say something more, but what else could he say?

"Do you call everyone Ma'am? Or just me?"

This could be worse, he decided. She could be asking about the scars.

But it was still pretty bad. He didn't know how to answer her. He didn't talk to women, really. Just her sister, and only then when he needed stitches. But to say that out loud? 'I don't talk to women all that much and they don't talk to me'?

Hell, no.

So he didn't answer. She waited a moment longer before saying, "It was just a question, Mr. Bodine. It's called a conversation—two people talking."

She was making fun of him. It stung for a moment, but then she made a face at him—like she was waiting for him to laugh with her or something?

"Okay, one person talking." She tilted her head to one side, sizing him up. Studying him. "Anyway, it's nice to see you again." Then, thank God, she looked back at the metal remains on the ground in front of her. "What do you think?"

"About what, Ma'am?"

"Here, you can put all those muscles to good use. Help me, please." She grabbed one of the sheets of metal and poked at the other with her toe. "Thank you."

All his muscles? He knew he was a brute—that's how involuntary manslaughter happened—but the way she said it, it didn't come out as a criticism. It almost sounded like a compliment.

Nobody did as requested, picking up what was left of the metal. What had started out as a solid sheet was now in about forty pieces.

But the piece in his hand had a—well, maybe not a pattern to it, but it didn't look like she'd just randomly attacked it with a blowtorch. Circles and swirls were cut into it. Same with the piece she was holding.

"Now," she said, heading toward the door, "do you think that part should go on the outside or the inside? Here, hold that one up to the top of the door."

Nobody stood there, unable to move as she bent over and jammed her section against the bottom of the door. Even in her non-skin-tight skirt, the outline of her ass was enough to give any man pause.

She straightened up but didn't move away from the door. "Well? Go on." She shooed him forward.

Nobody hefted the metal up against the door, but he was having trouble focusing. Melinda was closer now—barely two feet away from him now. He could smell the tang of hot metal, but underneath that was a bright scent of... oranges? She smelled good enough to eat.

"What do you think?" she asked again.

He couldn't really tell, not while he was holding the metal up. But she'd asked him that several times now, so he felt like he had to come up with some sort of answer. "Looks good."

For some reason, that made her laugh. It was a pretty sound. It fit her well. "Here, take your piece down." Then, thank God, she stepped away from him.

Nobody did as she asked. By the time he set his metal down, she was already behind him, grabbing the parts she'd cut out off the ground. "See, it's going to be a reverse image. On this side, we'll have the bottom piece here and these that I cut out of the top. Then, on the other side, we'll have your part on top and the pieces I cut out of the bottom in roughly the same place." She held a few of the smaller bits up, which had the effect of stretching her body right in front of his eyes. The skirt may not be skin tight, but the tank top sure as hell was. "See?"

The only thing he could see was the black bra strap that couldn't be contained by the tank top. Black would look so good against her creamy skin. God, so good.

He forced himself to take a step back. Then another one.

"Yeah," he offered when she snapped her head around. "Looks good."

"You're not leaving, are you?"

He needed to. She was messing with his head in a way that he wasn't used to and didn't know how to handle. Women didn't make conversation with him. They didn't flaunt their bodies around him. They didn't ask his opinions on—on—hell, he didn't even know what to call whatever she'd done with a blowtorch. Art. No one asked his opinion on art. Ever.

"Don't go yet." That was even worse, the way she said that with a soft voice and a softer look in her eye—like she'd be sad if he disappeared back into the dark.

Oh, yeah—she was messing with his head. Badly.

"Are you... are you afraid of me?"

Yes. Oh, hell yes. She scared the shit out of him, out of what he wanted to do with her. He'd rather get shot again that admit that out loud. "No."

Everything about her changed. He couldn't say how, though. She was still giving him those big doe eyes, still had an easy smile on her face. "But you're scared of my sister." It wasn't a question.

Yeah, Dr. Mitchell scared the hell out of him, too—but not like this. He always got the feeling that Dr. Mitchell was disappointed in him every time she sewed him back up. But she trusted him, too, with the keys to the clinic and all the drugs in it. He didn't want her to think she'd misjudged him.

He didn't answer. What was he supposed to say? Yes? What if she went back and told her sister what he'd said?

"She has that effect on a lot of people," Melinda went on as if he'd spoken out loud. "I'm the nice one."

He had no idea what she expected him to say. Hell, he had no idea what was even proper to say at this point. She'd spun his head around way too much. So he nodded his head.

"You don't talk much, do you, Mr. Bodine?"

"Why do you call me that?" There. He'd said something.

"It's your name, isn't it?"

He stared at her for a moment—the kind of stare that backed everyone else up.

She didn't flinch, though. If anything, she looked... pleased?

Damn it, she did. And damn it all, it looked so good on her.

Then he heard it—a rumble carried up to him on the breeze. Crunching. An engine revving.

Damn.

"Get inside." He moved as he spoke, so that he'd barely said the words before he had her by the arm, pulling her back into the building.

She squeaked—a sound he'd heard before, when he'd first seen her. He'd scared her. Well, that was too damn bad. "The lights."

He ran back to the rear of the building, locking the back door and shutting the lights down. He knew that sound. Someone was coming—fast. That kind of noise at this point on a Friday night? Nothing but trouble.

He raced back up to the front as Melinda shut the lights off. He grabbed the door, but didn't shut it. He left it open a crack. Why didn't this place have windows?

"What's wrong?" Melinda sounded scared—but she wasn't exactly whispering.

"Quiet."

"I don't—" Then she grabbed his arm as the car crested the hill, did a donut in the grass and squealed toward the clinic.

"Who is it?" At least she was quiet about it. But she'd leaned into him, putting her sweet mouth closer to his ear.

Nobody shifted—to block her from the door, not because she was making him nervous or anything. If this were junkies coming to rob the clinic again, things could get ugly, fast. He didn't mind fighting—hell, it was one of the few things he was good at. But Melinda? She'd probably never been hit in her life. She might panic, and a panicked woman combined with meth heads tweaked out of their skulls was a bad combination.

She leaned into him again, the weight of her breasts pressing against his arm. Jesus. "Do you have a gun or something?"

He shook his head before he realized she probably couldn't see it. The center was pitch-black and he was blocking the only light with his body. "No."

"Why the hell not?"

Why the hell not? Because the difference between an assault

charge and an assault with a deadly weapon charge was measured in years, that's why. But he figured that, if he tried to explain that right now, she'd probably want to know how he knew something like that and it was difficult to defend her and argue with her at the same time. "Because. Quiet."

The car cut one final donut in the grass before coming to a stop. Bodies piled out—male. Short. Giggling? Young, he realized. Kids—out joyriding. Probably drunk. Looking to stir up shit, but hopefully not to break into the clinic.

More giggling. Someone was passing around a joint. Then one of the taller guys stepped in front of the headlights. Great. Just *great*. Dwayne LaRoche was here.

What Nobody didn't need right now was some piss-ant, low-level criminal who was trying to fashion himself as an Indian Godfather using this particular building for his initiation 'rites'. Nobody tried to remember what Dwayne was calling his little gang now—Indian Killerz? Something stupid like that. At least the name fit. He was a dealer—pot and meth. He was doing a damn fine job killing people all by himself.

He snapped a beer off a six-pack and tossed it to a kid who didn't look more than fifteen. "Well, Georgey-boy? What's it gonna be? You run with the Killerz?"

Georgey-boy? He didn't recognize that name. Not someone Jamie had told him about. Which was good. Wasn't much point in keeping the boy safe from his father if he was going to join a damned gang.

"What's going on?" Melinda whispered in his ear.

He didn't answer her. The boy chugged the beer, burped, and caught another, longer can Dwayne threw at him. Spray paint? Hell, no. Nobody worked too damn hard keeping this building clean to let a bunch of wannabe gangsters mess it up.

He turned his body—not enough that the idiots outside would notice the movement through the crack in the door, but enough that he could talk to Melinda without them hearing him.

He almost hit her in the face with his elbow. Without thinking about what he was doing, he lifted his arm up, dropped it behind her, and pulled her in tight. He was just going to tell her something. He only needed to pull her in closer so she could hear him. It had nothing to do with the way her body fit against his or how she came willingly into his arm.

Right.

He lowered his head to hers. The scent of oranges got stronger as her hair brushed over his nose. God. She was going to kill him. "Lock the door behind me, then hide. Whatever you do, don't let them see you."

"Where are you going?"

He couldn't help it. He gave her waist a little squeeze. He felt the way she sucked in air, made a little noise that wasn't the same terrified squeak she'd made earlier. Closer to a gasp. They were almost alone in the dark. No one knew they were here. He could close the door and pull her in so close that she wouldn't be able to do anything but gasp.

"Do it!" a chorus of voices started chanting outside, egging Georgey-boy on.

"Be safe," he whispered, his mouth against her ear. He forced himself to let go of her, to push her back further into the darkness.

Then he went outside.

CHAPTER FIVE

What the hell was he *doing*?

Melinda stood there in a state of shock as Nobody slipped out the open door. As he did, he almost... disappeared before her eyes. Like he'd walked out into a shadow, sorta. How the hell did he *do* that? It was like he bent light or something out of a Harry Potter movie. Did he own a Cloak of Invisibility or what?

She should do what he told her—shut and lock the door, go hide somewhere. But she couldn't. She was watching Nobody.

He wasn't invisible, though. She watched him edge along the side of the building, then out into the darkness behind the car, where he really did disappear. But then, she couldn't see anything behind the car. Not even the outline of the trees.

None of the others acted like they had seen him. The guy who everyone else was egging on shook his can and turned toward the building. Vandalism? Really? Hell, she'd let him come paint the outside whenever he wanted! Why did he feel like he had to sneak around in the dark?

Then, suddenly, everything changed. One guy screamed in pain, a second one yelled, "Holy shit!" and a third one went down. It happened so fast that she couldn't see what was happening. Just a blur of black.

The kid with the spray paint spun around, took one look at the fight scene and dropped the can. In seconds, he'd also disappeared into the darkness at a full run, but Melinda didn't figure he'd done anything so brave as to circle back on Nobody.

Jesus—that man was taking on all ... she did a quick count. Three on the ground, one running away, two standing. Nobody had disappeared back into the darkness, three guys down. They were moving, so he hadn't killed anyone yet.

Then Melinda almost giggled, in that hysterical kind of way. Had she really just thought *yet*?

Oh, yes, she had.

The remaining two guys—one of whom appeared to be the ringleader—scrambled off the car hood where they'd been sitting and stood back to back. "Who's there?" the ringleader shouted.

To her ever-lasting surprise, Nobody walked out of the shadow. He'd lost his hat, but that didn't make him look any less menacing. If anything, he looked like he really *could* kill someone.

Nobody moved forward with a coiled ease that reminded her of a wolf stalking its prey. Not that she'd ever watched a wolf stalk its prey—not that many wolves in Columbus—but Nobody walked into the light in the way wolves were depicted in movies. Dangerous power seemed to roll off him.

"Dwayne, man," the second man was saying. "We should go."

"Fuck, no—I'm not going to let this nobody get in my way." Then the ringleader—Dwayne—reached into his back pocket and pulled out a switch-blade knife.

Melinda shoved her fist into her mouth to keep from screaming, mostly because Nobody had already seen the knife and didn't seem to be the least bit worried about it.

"You know what, freak? I'm tired of you."

Even as Dwayne said it, Nobody took a step to the side and kicked one of the downed guys who'd managed to make it back up to his knees in the ribs. With an agonizing groan, the guy went back down and stayed there. Nobody didn't hesitate—for God's sake, kicking that guy didn't even break his concentration. It was as effortless as Melinda picking a stray hair off her skirt—something that was easy. Second nature.

She'd been right, when she'd first seen him a month ago. He was a fighter, one who was exceptionally good at it. He was the most dangerous man she'd ever seen—maybe *the* most dangerous, because he'd taken down three men without a weapon. Just his fists.

"Fuck, Dwayne—he's not real! I ain't messing with a *sica*!"

A what? What was a *sica*? Whatever it was, it appeared to be scary.

NOBODY

"He's real. Watch. I'll make him bleed," Dwayne shot to his sidekick as he slashed through the air with his knife. Then he turned his attention back to Nobody. "What do you say, freak? Wanna dance?"

She had a good view of Nobody at this angle. His face showed no emotion—he wasn't scared, not like she was, but he wasn't having fun. She thought. Hell, he might be enjoying this, for all she knew.

Dwayne's back was to her, so she kept the door open, as horrifying as it was. She did *not* want to see Nobody get killed. Actually, she wasn't that keen on seeing anyone else get killed, either. But she couldn't bring herself to shut the door. If something happened to Nobody, she wanted to be able to help him. Although she knew damn good and well she was no match for a bad guy with a blade.

Nobody turned his head to the side and spat, which was apparently an agreement to 'dance.' The sidekick shrank back as Dwayne and Nobody began circling each other.

Melinda wanted to shout, *No, don't turn your back on the other guy!* But she shouldn't have worried. When Nobody got close to the sidekick, he spun with a speed she hadn't imagined he possessed, grabbed the guy's arm, and threw him—*threw him*—the ten feet or so to the car. The guy cleared air before he hit the side of the door with a sickening thud.

"You don't scare me. You ain't no ghost. You're nothing but a nobody and nobody can hurt me." Dwayne shouted.

To Melinda's ears, he did sound a little bit afraid. *He should be*, she thought. He may be holding the knife, but Nobody had just taken down four men all by himself.

Nobody hadn't said anything yet. Big surprise there. At least it wasn't just her. He really didn't talk.

The circling continued for another painful few seconds. The tension was killing her—would they fight or would the Dwayne guy bolt? Because she couldn't see Nobody turning tail, not when he knew she was still in here.

Nobody made a movement like he was going to charge at Dwayne, but then pulled back. It must have done what he wanted it to, though, because Dwayne started and then lunged forward in a less-than-organized way. Nobody had pulled him off balance, she saw. Dwayne rushed forward, knife out. Nobody easily sidestepped the blade and, turning as Dwayne went past, brought down a huge fist on the back of Dwayne's neck.

Dwayne went to the dirt and for a second, Melinda hoped that was where he would stay. But he scrambled back to his feet and lunged again.

Nobody spun again, but not fast enough this time. Dwayne caught him on the arm. Suddenly, there was a red hole where black t-shirt had been. But if Nobody felt it, he sure as hell didn't show it. Instead, he backed into Dwayne. Melinda couldn't quite see what was happening, but she would guess that Nobody was driving his elbow into Dwayne's midsection, over and over.

The sounds coming from the fight turned her stomach. Dwayne was grunting in pain and the sound of Nobody hitting him was like a meat tenderizer hitting a T-bone steak.

Even as he was being pummeled, Dwayne kept fighting. Melinda couldn't see what happened, but suddenly Nobody shoved him off.

Oh, he was hurt. He didn't cry or shout, but he leaned down, one hand on his knee, trying to catch his breath. Dwayne looked like he'd been hit with a cement truck, but he swung around and caught Nobody with the blade again.

Sweet Jesus, the knife hadn't just scratched him this time— she could see the handle sticking out of his side. Melinda cried out in horror. *No, don't*, she wanted to shout, but she couldn't do anything else.

Apparently, though, that was enough. Dwayne's head shot up in confusion at the noise, which was all the opening that Nobody needed. The next thing Melinda knew, he was screaming in pain. Nobody had gotten hold of his knife hand and had bent it back until his knuckles were touching his arm. The sound of bone's snapping was sickening.

Dwayne collapsed onto the ground as Nobody twisted his broken wrist. Then, knife handle still jutting out of his midsection, he punched the downed man. Hard.

Dwayne fell sideways, unconscious.

Melinda flew out of the center. "OhmyGod—he stabbed you!"

Somehow, Nobody managed to stand up straight. Looking her in the eye, he pulled the blade from his gut. He didn't even wince in pain when he did it. He could have been zipping up his pants for all the emotion he showed. But then he blinked, and she saw the pain register on his face.

She ran to his side, sliding her arm under the part that hadn't been slashed in the fight. "OhGodohGod," she heard herself say.

Finally, he spoke. Even as he let her take some of his weight, he said, "Woman, I told you to lock the door."

Then he stumbled, going down to one knee and pulling her with him. "Nobody!" she shouted, trying to pull him back up. It was like trying to lift a refrigerator.

"Rebel," he grunted as he managed to get both feet back under him. "Sister."

Oh, right! Duh! What the hell was the point of standing around panicking when she knew exactly where the local doctor lived?

"My car—it's this way," she said, trying to push him in the right direction.

"Red," he wheezed.

"What? No, my car. It's this way."

"Red," he said again. It sounded like it really hurt.

"Damn it, Nobody, whatever red is it can wait. I've got to get you to Madeline *now*." She made the mistake of looking down.

Dark stickiness covered the front of Nobody's shirt, with more blood coursing down his arm. Her stomach turned again. They had to get to Madeline before she passed out.

"*Now*," she repeated, more to have something else to focus on than what was dripping off him.

"Lock the door." For a wounded man, he was awfully argumentative.

"Nobody—"

"Door." He pushed her toward the center door.

Fine. She had no idea what was red or why it was important but she could see the logic of locking the door. Those guys would wake up sooner or later and they'd probably want revenge.

So she fumbled with the keys until she got the door locked, then they stumbled toward her car together. She got the door open and him in the passenger seat, and then they were driving for Madeline as fast as she could.

She laid on the horn when she hit the drive to Madeline's trailer. By the time she pulled up in front, Madeline and Rebel were waiting. "Where have you been?" Madeline demanded, but then Rebel pulled the passenger door open and Nobody fell out. "What the hell? Nobody!"

"I was cutting metal—for the door—and Nobody was there—and then these guys pulled up!" She raced around the other side, trying to get Nobody back on his feet. "Six guys—they were going to do graffiti—and Nobody! He went out there and knocked four of them out—and the one ran away and the one—the last one had a knife." She drew in a ragged breath and Nobody groaned as the three of them basically dragged him up the five steps into the trailer.

"Damn it, Nobody—you got yourself cut up over graffiti?" Madeline sounded like she'd gotten over her initial shock and was already in doctor mode. She even had on gloves.

Which was great. Exactly what Melinda wanted, because she couldn't even begin to go into any other mode besides panic. Still, it was irritating as hell that her sister could keep it together and Melinda was on the verge of hysterics.

"Rebel," Nobody grunted as Madeline cleared off the dining room table. "Red. They'll wake up. Don't let them hurt my horse."

"Red is your *horse*? You've been arguing with me about a horse? Jesus, Nobody—you're, like, bleeding out and you're worried about a horse?"

"He's not bleeding out and you need to calm the hell down right now or I will kick you out of this house myself," Madeline said as they leaned Nobody against the table and swung his legs off the floor. She sighed. "I hate it when you bleed on my table, you know."

"My apologies, Ma'am."

"You guys talk like you've done this before."

"I know, I know." Her voice bordered on gentle. Was Madeline being... nice to Nobody? She paused long enough to shoot her bossy look at Melinda. "Are you going to help or not?"

Nobody reached out and took hold of her hand. The same

hand that had beaten five men to a bloody pulp tenderly gripped her fingers. "It doesn't hurt," he said through gritted teeth as Madeline began to cut off his shirt. Then, to Rebel, he got out, "Dwayne."

"LaRoche?" Rebel whistled. If it was humanly possible, he seemed even less bothered by the bleeding man on his dining room table than his wife did. "What did you do?"

Nobody didn't say anything, so Melinda answered. "That was the guy with the knife, I think? After he stabbed Nobody, he broke his wrist and then knocked him out. It was..." *Horrifying*. But she couldn't say the word.

Nobody gave her hand a gentle squeeze. But he didn't say anything else. He just lay there with his eyes closed as Madeline tried to get the shirt off him.

She was in her nightgown, Melinda realized with a giggle. Did she normally do outpatient surgery in her nightie?

"Keep it together, Mellie," Madeline said under her breath.

"Rebel," Nobody said through gritted teeth.

"I'm on it." He grabbed a phone and made several calls, but Melinda couldn't tell who he was talking to, mostly because he was speaking Lakota. When he was done, he came back over with a handful of towels that looked like they'd been washed in mud. "Tim's on his way to get Clarence. They'll clean up the mess."

"Red," Nobody said.

"I'm going." Rebel leaned over and kissed his wife on the cheek. "Need me to bring you back anything from the clinic?"

"If I give you antibiotics," Madeline said to Nobody, "will you take them?"

And the damn fool shook his head no.

Madeline sighed. "Another bag of blood? I think I've got an extra pint of saline here."

And she'd thought the fight had been insane? That had nothing on Madeline keeping pints of blood in the house. "Why is everyone so calm?" Melinda demanded. But at that moment, Madeline cut the rest of his shirt off and suddenly Melinda was faced with a bare, muscular, and *very* scarred chest.

"Because," Madeline said in an everyday voice, "we've done this before."

Melinda had no snappy comeback for that, mostly because she was trying to process the magnitude of Nobody's skin.

Jesus Christ—the scars. So many scars. How was this man still alive? How was he *not* dead? He looked like he'd been used for target practice—repeatedly. For *years*. She'd never seen anything like it.

Of course, if he fought like he had tonight on a regular basis, with absolutely no thought to his own personal safety—well, yeah, maybe she shouldn't be shocked by what she saw. A gunshot wound on his shoulder. Cigarette burns—other burns that were bigger. Long, jagged scars, small neat ones.

"Oh, my God," she whispered.

"Doesn't hurt." Was he trying to reassure her? Really?

"Be still, Nobody. I've got to run this IV." Madeline was serious, too—she had an IV pole.

She pulled his uninjured arm back and ran the line. The man actually flinched as the needle went in. "Seriously?" Melinda asked him. "You got stabbed and you act like that hurt?"

"Don't like needles," he got out, breathing heavily.

"I'm sorry, Nobody," Madeline said, "but you lost too much blood this time and I'm not about to lose you. Do you know how hard it is to find someone who cleans the Clinic the way I like it?"

Nobody grunted.

Then, to Melinda, Madeline added, "Hold this flashlight steady. Can you do that or do you need to leave?" Melinda might have expected Madeline to sound disappointed in her inability to handle the gore, but instead her big sister sounded more understanding about it.

"I can hold the flashlight," she said, hoping it was true.

Madeline began to rinse out the wound in his chest. Water and blood poured onto the towels—not mud-stained towels, Melinda realized. *Blood* stained. They really had done this before. Oh, God.

Finally, the rinsing stopped, which was good. However, Madeline then started poking around. "I don't know how you manage it," she said more to herself than to anyone else.

"Manage what? Manage being cut to ribbons?"

"Yup. Missed all the major vessels. Didn't even perforate

your intestines—by millimeters." She sighed. "Anyone else would be in big trouble, but not you." Madeline was still ignoring her.

Melinda did not appreciate being ignored. "What? What are you talking about?"

"Another flesh wound. They're always flesh wounds," she added, finally talking to her sister.

"Always?" She looked down at the map of Nobody's skin. Even if they were all 'just' flesh wounds, there were a hell of a lot of them.

"Always," Madeline agreed. At least this time, she sounded a little impressed by the fact. "Hold the light steady, Mellie. I've got to sew him back up."

"You aren't even going to give him something for the pain?"

"No drugs," Nobody growled.

"You see what I'm working with here?" Madeline was back to muttering to herself. "He won't let me give him anything and she's about to pass out. Where is Clarence when I need him? Good lord. Next time, Mellie, *call* me and I'll come down to the clinic, okay? I hate getting blood on the table."

Next time? The way Madeline said it made it perfectly clear there would be a next time. And she ate dinner on this table! God, she was going to be sick.

Suddenly, she wished that Rebel were still here. Rebel would be able to hold a flashlight still. He'd be calm and cool and collected—not on the verge of sobbing and throwing up or passing out. "Uh..."

"Chair," Madeline said, pointing with her chin. "Sit down. But hold the damn light."

"Okay." Melinda pulled the chair over with her foot and sat heavily. Yeah, that helped. She propped her arm up on the table, which helped steady the light.

She closed her eyes and leaned her forehead against her other hand, the one that was still clasped in Nobody's hand. He was breathing, but other than that, he wasn't making a sound. "Doesn't it hurt?" she whispered, unable to block out the sounds of Madeline sewing Nobody shut.

He didn't respond. At first she thought he might have blacked out—she sure would have under the circumstances—but then he gave her hand another squeeze, like he was trying to make her feel better.

She squeezed back. "It was just some graffiti. I would have let the kid paint the walls, Maddie. I really would have. That boy didn't have to sneak around. No one needed to get hurt over graffiti."

"It's not the graffiti," Madeline said. "Dwayne LaRoche is a gang leader. That was probably an initiation rite for some stupid kid. Marking their territory."

"Oh." Of course. Why hadn't she realized that? Because she had assumed gangs were a city problem and they were in the middle of nowhere. "He still didn't have to get himself all cut up over that." She realized she was talking about Nobody as if he wasn't in the room. "*You* didn't have to get yourself cut up over that, you know."

No response. Of course.

Her brain, apparently operating on autopilot, replayed the fight again. "What's a *sica?*"

Nobody tensed, which made Madeline hiss at him. "It's a spirit," Madeline said after Nobody had relaxed again. "A ghost of someone who died but didn't go on."

Melinda opened her eyes and stared at the hand in hers. It sure as hell felt real. And there was all the blood.

But... but there was that way he sort of blended in with the dark—so much so that no one else could see him when he didn't want to be seen.

He'd been outside the campfire her first night here, she realized. Even Rebel hadn't seen him. But she'd sensed him. And tonight? Before the fight, that was—she hadn't exactly seen him standing in the trees, but she'd seen an outline, a shadow darker than the rest. A *large* shadow. And she'd figured that it was him, that he was waiting to do his job.

That he was watching her.

"What are you?" she whispered, although with Madeline standing less than a foot away, keeping her voice pitched low was sort of pointless.

Nobody tried to let go of her hand, but she wouldn't let him and Madeline hissed at him. "If you don't stay still, I *will* drug you, Nobody. Don't think I won't!" Then she said to Melinda, "It is my professional opinion that this man is just that—a flesh-and-blood man. Not a ghost, not a spirit, and definitely not someone who died. Although he's probably on his twenty-second life by this time."

"I'm sorry," Melinda said to Nobody again. "I didn't mean it. Be still." He responded by relaxing his hand against hers.

Silence settled over them. Nobody was as still as a statue, Madeline was focused on her sewing, and Melinda was determined not to throw up or pass out. Every so often, Madeline would tell her to move the light and she'd have to look. Then she'd go back to not throwing up again.

Dad had *so* wanted both of his daughters to follow in his footsteps into medicine, but Melinda could *not* stomach this. She tried to think of something—anything—else so that she wouldn't replay the knife plunging into Nobody's chest, wouldn't have to think about the hole Madeline was closing from the inside out.

Her thoughts turned back to the last time she'd sensed him outside the campfire—the day Jamie had shown up at the center for the first time. The boy had healed up and almost smiled at times since that first day, but he still held himself apart from the other kids. From her, too.

That night, Rebel had told her that she saw people—*him* was what he'd said—and that made *him* real. She'd thought he was talking about Jamie... but what if he hadn't been? What if he'd been talking about Nobody?

What if no one else *could* see him? Was that even possible?

"Okay," Madeline said, taping gauze to his chest. "Where else?"

"Arm," Nobody told her. Melinda could hear the strain in his voice.

Madeline shooed Melinda out of the way so she could get to the cut on his arm. After looking it over, she said, "You wouldn't have come in for this by itself, would you?"

"No," Nobody agreed, although he still sounded like he was holding on to consciousness by the skin of his teeth.

"You are the most stubborn man I know," Madeline said in that absent-minded way of hers as she began to clean the wound.

"And I'm married to Rebel—so that's saying something."

"Yes, Ma'am."

In short order, she had his arm stitched back together. Seventeen neat stitches crossed over his bicep. Melinda only looked when Madeline said, "Anywhere else?"

Nobody shook his head, but only once and that seemed to take a lot of effort.

"Then you're done."

"Thank you kindly." As he said it, Nobody did something that Melinda sure as hell hadn't expected. He let go of her hand, sat up and swung his legs off the table with a pained grunt. "Much obliged."

"Oh no—you're not going anywhere." Madeline grabbed his arm just before he pulled the IV out. "*No*, Nobody."

"Problem?" The front door banged open and Rebel jogged in, a bag of what had to be blood in his hand.

"He thinks he's leaving," Madeline said.

"Nobody, sit down," Melinda hissed as she tried to grab his hand again.

"You got Red?" he asked Rebel.

"Yeah, she's outside. Sit down, man."

"I gotta go home."

"No, you've got to get some more fluids in you. Mellie—hold him down."

"Uh..." She'd seen this man in action—there was no way in hell she could just hold him down, for crying out loud. But she did as she was told. She put her hands on his shoulders—his bare shoulders—and held on tight.

She felt the tension ripple through his back, but she had no idea if that had to do with her or if it was because all this movement was pulling on his brand-spanking-new stitches. But he stopped trying to get up, so she held onto him.

"Babe," Madeline said, clearly exasperated.

Rebel stepped in front of Nobody. "You're gonna crash here tonight, man."

"No. I gotta go home." It was, hands down, the rudest thing Melinda had heard him say yet.

"Yeah, you are. You can't ride Red like this anyway.

Madeline's going to hook you up to some more fluids and you're going to sleep here. We have a perfectly good couch. You'll like it."

Under her hands, Nobody flinched. "No."

"I swear to God, Nobody, I will inject you with enough sedatives to knock a rhino to its knees. Not even you will be able to walk away." Madeline was now peeling her gloves off. "I don't want to, but I will. I'm not going to have you ride off and die alone."

His shoulders sagged and, ever so slightly, he leaned back into Melinda's touch. "I want to sleep outside."

"What? Why?" she asked.

Rebel shot her a look she couldn't read over the top of Nobody's head. "Not gonna happen. You're in no condition to ride and you know she'll want to keep an eye on you. It's one night on the couch."

Nobody must have been wearing down—more than he already was—because he stopped arguing. It was weird, hearing him talking that much—weirder still to hear him expressing an opinion on something. Melinda had no idea why it was so important that he get home this very minute—and what the hell was that about, sleeping outside?

"Okay, onto the couch. I've got to hook this bag up." Madeline was back to her bossy voice. "Melinda, you get on his good side. Rebel—"

"I'm on it." He waited for Melinda to get under Nobody's arm and then hefted the bigger man to his feet.

Nobody swayed, coming dangerously close to falling on top of Melinda, but Rebel got under his wounded side and together, they stumbled to the couch.

This time, when Nobody went down, he did take her with him. They landed on the couch with an audible *whump*, followed by a low, involuntary moan of pain.

"Are you okay?" It was quite possibly the most pointless thing she'd ever said—the answer was obviously *no*. She was trapped under his arm—against his bare chest.

Madeline rolled the IV pole over to the couch. "Mellie, you need to move."

Nobody's arm clamped down on her. He wasn't going to let her go. "I need to get up," she said in a quiet voice. She needed to decide if she was going to throw up or not and she definitely needed to wash his blood off.

His grip tightened.

"Nobody, please—let me up and I'll come back, okay? I'll come sit with you tonight. You won't be alone."

His chin was tucked to his chest, but he rolled his head toward her. "Promise?"

"Promise."

His arm lifted off her and she was able to slide out. She caught Madeline giving her an approving look before she ran to the bathroom and turned the hot water on full blast.

She scrubbed down, trying to wash away everything that had happened after the moment Nobody had slipped out of the center door. As she showered, she forced herself to think about the other time Nobody's arm had been around her—in the dark, in the center.

She'd been scared then, too—but he'd pulled her into his chest and put his mouth against her ear, whispering so quietly she had only heard the way his breath moved over her skin.

Yeah, better to think of the way she'd broken out in goose bumps at the way his body had pressed against hers than to think of the blood.

She wrapped herself in a towel and hurried to her room. She normally didn't sleep in a lot, but she had a pair of capri yoga pants around here somewhere. She wore a lot of tank tops in the summer—she had nice arms, so why not? But now...

She dug out a t-shirt she'd gotten for finishing a 5K Fun Run for Juvenile Diabetes and slipped it on. She didn't know why. As she did so, she heard the bathroom door click shut.

She padded back out to the living room on bare feet. Rebel was sitting cross-legged on the floor, watching Nobody. For his part, the man on the couch didn't look like he'd moved since she'd left his side. His head was still down, his chest was still naked, his eyes closed.

"Madeline is cleaning up," Rebel said in a low voice. "She told me to remind you that he would be fine."

"Oh. Okay." As carefully as she could, she sat on the edge of the couch next to Nobody. "I'm here."

He didn't move much, but she saw his chest fall as he exhaled. "Cold," he finally said.

"I'll get a blanket," Rebel offered, hopping up. "We don't have any shirts big enough to fit him," he added as he headed toward the linen closet.

"Do you, uh, need some pillows braced against your side?"

"Yeah," he whispered after a moment. She couldn't tell if he was hurting that much or if he was ashamed to be admitting any form of weakness.

She grabbed a couple of throw pillows from the edge of the couch and, lifting his wounded arm up as slowly as possible, stacked them against his side. The bandage Madeline had layered on over his chest wound wasn't showing any blood, so Melinda just had to hope he wouldn't bleed through to the pillows any time soon.

He settled his arm back down, but she saw the way he shivered. Rebel came back with a blanket and together they wrapped it over his shoulders, careful to avoid the IV.

"Better?" she asked. In reply, he shivered again.

Only one thing left to do. She didn't know why she was nervous—Nobody had never done a single thing to threaten her in any way, shape, or form. But there'd been the way he'd taken on six men without batting an eye. Not even being stabbed—twice— had stopped him.

Another chill ran over him. Rebel had settled back onto the floor, as if he meditated over wounded men all the time. Maybe he did. Hell, she didn't know anything anymore.

She sat back down and—again, careful to avoid the IV line— leaned under his arm and rested her head on his shoulder.

"Better?" she whispered.

His arm settled around her. "Yeah."

She tried not to think about the blood that was dripping into him—better in than out—and instead focused on the warm, hard muscles underneath her hands. Because she had to put her hands somewhere, and wrapping her arm around his waist seemed like a good way to keep him warm—as long as she kept her hand away from the stab wound.

"Sleep now. I'll be here when you wake up, okay?"

"Yeah," he repeated. He shifted briefly, settling her against him, and then his chest rose and fell in even breaths.

Madeline emerged from the bath. "How is he?" she asked, wearing a fresh nightgown.

"Sleeping. He said he was cold, but he feels pretty warm to me."

Madeline stood next to Rebel, who started rubbing her leg. "I wonder if I could give him a shot of antibiotics while he sleeps? Or would he wake up and kill me?"

"Let him lie, babe."

"I can't believe he's still here," she said in a more quiet tone. "I figured he would have disappeared by the time I got done showering. He always does." She looked down at her husband. "You going to sit?"

"Just in case he doesn't remember where he is when he wakes up," Rebel said.

It sounded like a perfectly innocent thing, but Melinda caught his meaning—in case he woke up violent. Rebel was going to sit here all night to make sure that she was safe. But they were talking about the same man who'd fought to protect her.

She had no idea if she was supposed to be terrified of Nobody or what.

Madeline yawned. "Are you going to be okay?"

"I think so," Melinda said, hoping it was the truth.

"Call me if you need anything."

"We will," Rebel said. "Get some rest."

After Madeline went to bed, silence settled over the trailer. Despite his claims of being cold, Nobody's body was warm. The deeper he slipped into sleep, the more his body relaxed. Soon enough, Melinda felt herself being hypnotized by his breathing. It pushed back the horror of the fight, the blood that had been spilled—everything faded until there was only Nobody's chest, rising and falling.

Finally, she slept.

CHAPTER SIX

The pain pulled Nobody back from the blackness and into the gray at a relentless pace. He didn't want to feel the pain, but it wasn't paying a damn bit of attention to him.

He wanted to wake up and do something—what, he didn't know—but he let the gray fade gradually. As it got lighter, the pain began to define itself. His side hurt. He could feel the stitches pulling with each breath. His arm wasn't great either, but at least it wasn't throbbing.

And... his other arm. Shit. He had a needle in him.

That realization jolted him the rest of the way awake. He was already moving to pull the needle out—damn, but he hated needles—when he realized he wasn't outside. Hell, he wasn't even alone.

There was a head in his lap. A head with wildfire hair that was spread out over his jeans—over his groin. *Melinda.*

He went hard in an instant, the overwhelming desire pushing the pain back so far he didn't feel anything but where she was touching him.

Because she was touching him. Her head laid on his thigh, her hand next to her chin. She was facing away from him, which meant that if she woke up, she wouldn't see the huge hard-on that was taking control of his body.

He blinked a few times, just in case he was having a dream. He didn't dream, not that he remembered anyway. Sleep was just darkness. But there was a first for everything, because if he were going to have a dream, waking up with Melinda Mitchell's head in his lap would have to be near the top of the list. He even gave his head a shake, but nothing changed.

She was really asleep on him.

In addition to his throbbing dick, his heart began to pound. Why was she asleep on him? And why was he on a couch? Where was his fire? Where were his horses? Where was he?

He looked down at his arm, the one with the needle it in. Yeah, he was hooked up to an IV—a clear bag of what looked like water was hanging on a pole. Only one person would do that to him—Dr. Mitchell.

But that realization was blown away when he saw where the arm in question was resting. His hand was on Melinda's bare skin, just above where the waistband of her black pants should have met the bottom of her t-shirt.

She was laying on him. He was touching her.

God, how long had it been? Hell, how long had it been since he'd even touched someone? Dr. Mitchell touched him, but he was usually bleeding at the time. Jamie—he carried Jamie on his back some times. And he beat the hell out of whoever deserved it.

But none of those situations were like this. There was no pain—not that he felt at the moment, anyway—no suffering.

Just a beautiful woman under his hand.

His mind spun and spun wildly. He'd had women, back when he was young and stupid and clawing for survival every single damned day. He'd taken the comfort girls had offered him, both of them looking to escape the hell of their reality for an hour at a time. He liked sex—well, he had back then, anyway. But he'd been a kid. A big, mean kid who wasn't good at anything but fighting.

He hadn't had a woman since...

Well, hell. Thirteen years was a long time by anyone's standards.

What would it be like, if she rolled over and undid his jeans? What would it feel like if she took him in her mouth, her lips moving up and down, her tongue licking him? What would it look like, her wild hair wrapped around his fist as she moved faster and faster?

And when she was done? It'd be his turn. He'd lay her back and taste her like she'd tasted him, licking and sucking and exploring her sweet body until she cried out his name—his and no one else's. Would she grab his hair, pulling his face down into her soft body until he was surrounded by her? Would she demand he finish her off with his mouth or his dick? Would she want it slow and sweet or hard and rough?

Jesus, he was going to come in his jeans just thinking about it.

Despite the crazy bent of his thoughts, he was actually afraid to move, afraid to wake her up. Because as much as his dick was trying to think for him, the odds of her doing anything of the sort were slim-to-none. What was more likely was that she would wake up, take one good look at him in the light of day and freak the hell out.

And he wouldn't be able to blame her a bit if she did. He'd told her to close the door last night and hide. He'd known what was about to happen—not the stabbing part, exactly, but he knew the fight would be ugly. He'd been trying to protect her—there was always a chance he could lose a fight or worse—but the truth of the matter was that he hadn't wanted her to see it, to see him like that. He hadn't wanted her to know what he really was—a violent man. Because that's what he was. That's what he'd always been.

Before last night, she hadn't been afraid of him—not much, anyway. And now that had probably all changed. As soon as she realized where she was—and who she was sleeping on—she'd look at him and see what everyone else saw—a man to be feared.

Then her voice floated up, and he remembered hearing her say, "*What* are you?"

If she still saw him as a man at all.

So he didn't want to move and ruin this moment with her body on his. She was warm and heavy against his leg, curled into a ball on her side. He breathed deeply, letting her scent of oranges fill him.

A little of her hair was covering her cheek. Even though he didn't want to move, he found his needle-free arm lifting toward her, his hand brushing the hair back from her face. So soft. Her hair felt like silken threads as it slid under his touch.

Then his fingertips were brushing against her skin. Up this close, he could see the pale freckles that kissed her face. Even without the wild reds and white that were painted into her hair, she was so beautiful that it crushed the air out of his chest.

At his touch, she stirred, which froze him immediately. What was his freaking problem? He didn't want her to wake up and break this contact between them—and yet, he was waking her up? Damn it all, he didn't know how to be around a woman. This was exactly why.

Then she moved, rolling onto her back—and toward him. Toward his aching dick.

His arm—the one that still had the Goddamned needle in it—stung as she turned, so he was forced to lift his hand and let it skim over the skin on her belly.

God, for a moment, this felt like he'd always imagined normal would be. Waking up with a pretty woman in his arms, watching her blink the sleep from her eyes, her mouth parted just a little.

Was this why Rebel had given up the outdoors? Why he slept in a house, on a bed now? Because this was how he woke up every day?

Nobody hated being inside almost as much as he hated the needle in his arm, but the moment her beautiful eyes—a deep blue that veered into green—locked onto his, he thought, *It's worth it*. No matter what happened in the next thirty seconds, he'd take this time with her to his grave.

Then it got better. Instead of recoiling in horror or throwing herself off his lap—instead of doing anything he expected her to do—she smiled. That perfect strawberry-red mouth of hers curved up into a lazy grin that set his body to throbbing again, in the best way possible.

"Hi," she whispered.

God, to be normal. To know what he was supposed to say when he woke up with a woman in his arms. Even back when he'd had women, he hadn't spent the night with them. Never.

She saved him from having to come up with something. "You didn't die on me last night?"

"Nope." But before he could get another thought formed, she did something else unexpected. She rested her hand on top of his—the one on her belly. And she didn't even lift his hand up and cast it aside.

Instead she—sweet Jesus, she pushed her fingers in between his. She held his hand to her bare skin. She made him *keep* touching her.

"How do you feel?"

"Fine." Better than fine. He felt amazing.

She wrinkled her brow. "You scared the hell out of me last night."

"Didn't mean to." Then, just because he couldn't help himself, he brushed his free hand over her hair again. He wanted to say things to her—for no other reason than to prove that he could talk, could *think*—that he wasn't some dumb killing machine. But he didn't know how.

Then the moment was over. Rebel walked into the living room. "You need to go home."

"What? Why?" Melinda sat up, which pulled at the needle in his arm. Damn, he hated needles. "He's still wounded!"

Rebel gave him a serious look. "Tim's coming. He can't decide if he's going to arrest you or not."

Nobody's stomach fell in, killing his hard-on in a wash of fear.

"Tim? Tim who? What's going on?"

"Get this out of me," Nobody growled, starting to pull on the IV.

Melinda grabbed at his hand. "No, wait—let Madeline. Why do you need to leave right now? Who's Tim? What's wrong?"

"Tim's the sheriff. He's coming to talk to me about the fight last night. He's not too happy about it." Rebel walked into the kitchen and started making coffee. "He's no fan of Dwayne's, but he knows you were there. And if he arrests you..."

Nobody nodded. He needed to get gone—the faster the better.

"No—wait for Madeline," Melinda said, pulling his hand away from the needle. "Don't be so stubborn, Nobody."

"I'm not going back to jail," he said. He wanted to pull his arm away from her—he could do it—but he didn't want to hurt her.

Thankfully, Dr. Mitchell walked in. She gave him a surprised look. "You're still here? Really? Never thought I'd see the day, Nobody."

"He's going to rip the IV out," Melinda said, still clutching his arm.

"Oh, for heaven's sake," Dr. Mitchell clucked. "I haven't even had my coffee yet."

"He's got to get gone, babe," Rebel explained, handing her a cup. "Tim'll be by in a bit."

The doctor took a long drink and then pulled the IV. Damn it, that stung. He hated feeling something inside of him like that. Drove him crazy. "Who's going to take him home? You?" Then she stuck a bandage on him. He felt ridiculous.

"You know if Tim shows up and I'm not here, he's going to get suspicious. It's obvious you patched him up. Tim was mad enough last night that if he thinks I'm hiding Nobody, he might just throw the cuffs on me until he cools down."

"I don't understand what's going on," Melinda said in an unsteady voice.

Nobody flexed his freed arm. Now that the irritation of the needle was gone, he could think a little better. "I'll ride home."

The fact was, no one—besides Jamie—knew where he lived. Not even Rebel. It was better that way. Rebel didn't have to lie when he told people he had no idea where Nobody had disappeared to, and Nobody didn't have to worry about endangering the only man he counted as friend. Because Rebel would not fare well in a jail cell. That was one of the things they had in common. Both of them needed to feel the ground underneath their feet.

He stood—and wobbled. The pain spiked up from his side. His arm was fine, but his side... Melinda scrambled to her feet and slipped under his arm again. He didn't want to admit how good she felt there, so he didn't.

"I don't like this," Dr. Mitchell said. "You're in no condition to ride."

"Me, neither," Melinda said. "What if you fall off your horse or something? You'll bleed out in a ditch and then what?"

Rebel looked at him. "I'll ride you home if you want..." He let his words trail off, clearly thinking the same thing that Nobody was. Then Rebel would know how to find him. That wasn't how it worked—it was better for everyone if Nobody stayed un-findable.

"I'll go with him."

Nobody had to look around for the person who had spoken—and was stunned to find Melinda looking up at him, a determined glint in her eyes. "No."

"Yes. I can ride—not as good as Madeline does, but I took

lessons for years. I'll make sure you don't fall off."

"Are you sure?" Dr. Mitchell was worried about sending her sister off with him. He understood that.

He didn't understand Melinda. Shouldn't she have turned tail and run for cover by now? Shouldn't she want him gone so she could go back to her real life in some big city somewhere?

"No one else knows I was there, so this sheriff won't be looking for me. I'll get him home."

Except that would mean she'd see his home.

"No," he repeated, but was horrified to see that he hadn't let go of her slim shoulders yet. How was he supposed to leave her behind if he couldn't even stop touching her?

"Or you could stay here and talk to the lawman." Oh, hell—a woman should not look that pleased with herself, but she did. She had him cornered and they both knew it.

And the fact of the matter was, he wasn't sure he could stay up on Red at this point. He didn't own a saddle, which meant he had to physically hold himself on. And he was starting to sweat just standing here.

"I'm going to go put on a pair of jeans and a bra. Then I'm taking you home."

Nobody's mouth flopped open at this. If he'd had any power to make her stay, she'd just blown it out of the water. Instead, his eyes dropped down to her front—to where two little points topped the most amazing breasts he'd ever seen through a t-shirt.

"I don't like this," Dr. Mitchell said again.

"I'll get him on the horse," Rebel told Melinda. They changed places and Melinda ran back to her room.

But before Rebel could get him out of the house, Dr. Mitchell was up in his face, wagging a finger inches from his nose. "Listen, Nobody. You've always done right by me and I don't want anything to happen to you but if something happens to my baby sister, next time I'll stand by and watch you bleed out. Do I make myself clear?"

Like he'd do anything to Melinda. "I'll keep her safe. That's a promise."

Dr. Mitchell's face softened. "You better." Then she walked down the hall.

"Are you sure about this?" Rebel asked as they watched his wife disappear.

Was he sure about bringing Melinda Mitchell out to his home? About showing her where he lived? About riding the five or so miles with her?

No. He'd never been less sure about anything in his entire life.

But he was in no position to say no.

Not to her.

CHAPTER SEVEN

"Here." Madeline burst into Melinda's room with a backpack. "Take this."

Normally, Melinda would have given her big sister crap for barging in while she was in the middle of changing. But now was not the time. Honestly, she was surprised Maddie wasn't making a bigger deal of this. "What's in it?"

"Bandages—you'll probably have to change his when you get there. Can you handle that?"

"Um..." She'd seen quite enough blood the last twenty-four hours to hold her for a lifetime, thank you very much. But Maddie gave her *the look*, so Melinda hurried to add, "Sure. No problem. What else?"

"Water, granola bars, a round of antibiotics—maybe you can get him to take them, I sure as hell can't—a walkie-talkie, the GPS, and..." She opened the bag and pulled out a knife. "Just in case."

Melinda looked at the five-inch blade in a leather sheath. "Do you think I'll need it?"

"I don't think so, but..." Madeline shrugged. "You're always doing this—going off into dangerous parts of town by yourself, after dark. *I* wouldn't do this, but that's never stopped you before."

Melinda looked at her sister in shock. Sure, she knew Maddie had probably always thought that—but she'd never actually said it out loud. She must be really worried. "Says the woman who came out to the rez all by herself—this is the least safe place I've ever been!"

Madeline tried to sneer at her, but she didn't pull it off. Not this time. "Just... be careful, okay?"

Melinda pulled her shirt back on. "I will. Besides—he's wounded. What's he going to try?"

"I have no idea. No one does. Not even Rebel." Then her bossiness took back over. "The walkie-talkie has a ten mile range, so it won't work if you get too far away. But if you get into trouble, there's a button on the GPS you can push that will send up a distress signal at your coordinates, okay?"

"Okay—but it'll be fine. I'll try to be home for dinner, all right?" She grabbed the pack and slung it on her shoulder.

The next thing she knew, Madeline had her in a fierce hug. "You better be."

"I will." Then she hurried outside.

Rebel had gotten Nobody up on a beautiful red horse—Red, of course. And he had his hat back on—Rebel must have found it when he'd gotten the horse. However, she could see the strain on Nobody's face. "How is this going to work?"

"Here—climb up on this stump." Rebel motioned to a two-foot tall hunk of wood. "Then put your arms around him and hold onto the horse's mane, okay?"

"Sure." Because it sounded just *that* easy.

She got up on the stump and Rebel wheeled the horse around so that she could slide on behind the wounded, shirtless man. Right. No big deal, that whole putting her arms around him thing. Gotcha.

Moving slowly—it seemed like the thing to do—Melinda slipped her arms around Nobody's side, working extra hard not to hit the bandages. Finally, after what felt like a long time, she was able to tangle her fingers in the horse's mane.

Nobody's back against her chest was so warm as to be downright hot. Was he running a fever? Hell, what she wouldn't give for a little bit of Maddie's medical know-how. She'd have to try and get the antibiotics into that man.

Maddie came out, looking pissed. "Do not let him fall asleep up there. No matter what, keep him talking."

Both Rebel and Melinda turned to give Maddie a look. Even Nobody turned his head in her direction. Melinda wondered what was worse for him—talking to her or being stabbed.

"Yeah, that won't be hard at all," she replied.

Rebel chuckled as he patted the horse on the flank. "Get gone, Nobody. Don't be seen."

Nobody grunted. "Never am." Melinda felt him touch his legs to the horse's side. Red began to walk.

She didn't know where they were going. She didn't know how she'd get back, either. Within ten minutes, they'd left anything familiar behind. She'd normally try to memorize the landmarks, but there were none. No house, no road. Just grass and, off in the distance, hills with trees on them.

She wasn't sure if she should be touching Nobody or not, but it wasn't like it was an option at this point. Every part of her front was pressed against every part of his back—thigh to thigh, chest to back, calf to calf. If she hadn't had to hold onto the horse's mane, she could have leaned back at least enough that she'd have some place to put her face. But as it was, it was difficult.

She managed to put enough distance between them that she wasn't resting her chin on him, but that just gave her the full view of his back. Had she thought his arms were scarred? Had she really been surprised by the damage on his chest?

Because his front had nothing on his back. Huge, inch-wide scars were scattered around at intervals that looked almost regular. Some of them were nearly circular, but others looked more like maybe they'd gotten infected. And that didn't even include the jagged scars, what looked like an exit wound on his shoulder and God-only-knew what else.

The scars... they looked a lot like the cigarette burns on his arms. But bigger.

Cigar burns.

She realized that they'd been on the horse for close to fifteen minutes and she had *not* kept him talking. Oops. Maddie would have her head on a platter if Melinda let him fall asleep—and fall off the horse. "Tell me about these," she said.

Nobody grunted—but didn't reply.

"You're supposed to talk, you know. Madeline said so."

She didn't get a response.

Oh, so that's how it was going to be, huh? "I *will* make you talk."

"You don't scare me." But the way he said it, with just a hint of nervousness in his voice, told her otherwise.

"Fine. We'll do this the hard way." He snorted at this

challenge, but Melinda leaned forward and pressed her lips against the round scar closest to her mouth.

He jolted, but didn't make a sound.

She tried again. "Who did this to you?" As she asked it, she circled the scar with the tip of her nose.

"Don't." It was half an order, half a plea for mercy.

This qualified as talking. Sort of. "Oh, I will. I'm going to keep asking until you tell me." Then she kissed the scar again.

This time, she let her lips linger over his marred skin, let her mouth kiss over the edge of the scar onto a small patch that wasn't damaged. It was a very small patch.

"Please," he said, and this time, there was no ordering about it. Just begging.

"Talk. Tell me who did this." When he didn't immediately respond, she leaned forward again, ready to kiss his bare back a third time.

He tensed and tried to lean away from her, but then sucked in air. The movement must have hurt because he leaned back, his shoulders drooping in resignation. "Don't remember his name. They never had names."

"Who?"

"The men my mom brought home. No names. Just fists."

It's not like it wasn't obvious that that was exactly what had happened, but it still hurt to hear it. She tried to imagine what Nobody Bodine had been like as a boy, but she didn't do a very good job. "Why didn't she do something to stop them?"

"Because." The words seemed to take a lot out of him. "She... She thought it was funny."

"*What?*"

"She burned my arms. Liked to try and make me cry."

"Oh, my God." How could a mother do that to her baby? "When did it start?"

"Dunno. Just... was."

"Did you cry?" Because she was pretty sure she'd heard a *try* in there.

"Sometimes. If she snuck up on me. But I got good at not crying."

"You got good at not feeling the pain." That explained why

he didn't want pain killers for surgery, for Christ's sake. He'd trained himself not to feel. She wasn't sure she'd ever heard a sadder thing in her life.

"Yeah."

"So these?" She leaned forward and traced the tip of her nose around the scar again. "When did these happen? How old were you?"

"Thirteen. I tried not to go home, but I had to. No where else to go. They were waiting for me."

"Jesus, Nobody." He sucked in a deep breath. At first she thought he was dealing with the horrific memories—but then he reached over and slid her arm away from his wound. Oh, yeah. She probably shouldn't squeeze him that hard. "Sorry."

"Didn't hurt," he said without a trace of emotion.

She was afraid to keep asking questions—afraid to find out more. But overriding that basic instinct of self-preservation, she felt like she *had* to know more, for his sake. No one person should have to carry this sort of weight alone. Plus, he was actually talking to her. She was performing her duties as ordered. He hadn't fallen asleep and hadn't fallen off the horse.

"What happened?"

"They had a bet. He said he could make me cry. She said he couldn't."

"Did you?"

He didn't say anything for a while. Red took a left in the middle of nowhere. Melinda couldn't tell if the horse knew where she was going or if Nobody was somehow guiding her. How, she didn't know. But she didn't know how he did anything.

He was quiet enough that she was afraid he might be falling asleep. So she leaned forward and kissed his scar again.

He jolted. Yeah, he could be all impassive and unfeeling, but he was fully aware of what happened on the surface of his skin. "Don't do that."

"Why not?"

"Just... don't."

"Then keep talking. So you were thirteen, you came home, they were sadistic bastards who trapped you and he—what, he tried to see how many times he could burn you before you cried?"

"Yeah." Again, no emotion. No feeling.

She leaned back as far as she could and started counting. Eleven scars that were roughly the same shape and size. A few others that might be from the same time, but might have been something else.

"I was this big kid, but I'd never fought back before. I didn't know I could. I didn't know how. Then..."

She leaned forward again, trying not to picture him being held against his will, someone probably sitting on him, using his back as an ashtray. "Then?"

"I didn't cry," he said defensively. "But he started to pull my pants off. He was gonna *make* me cry, he said."

"Oh, God, Nobody. I'm so sorry." She didn't know what kind of person would burn a kid on his back, but to go for private parts? Even if the guy had just been going to burn his butt, that was terrifying. But...

"My mom was *laughing*..." he said, his voice quiet. It sounded as if he were talking from very far away—but he was talking. "When the guy stopped sitting on me and started pulling on my jeans, something just snapped."

"Yeah?"

"I hurt him," he said in a small voice—which was impressive, given his size. "He wasn't ready for it. I kicked him, I punched him. I broke things. His nose, maybe his jaw. Ribs, probably his arm."

She could see it, too. Her mind easily substituted the fight last night for the fight so long ago. "Good for you. You had the right to stand up for yourself, Nobody. No one has the right to treat a kid like that, no matter how big he was for his age." Her thoughts turned to Jamie, the disappearing boy at the center. She couldn't save Nobody from his mother. Was there anything she could do for that boy?

Nobody was silent again. He'd said a lot, she figured—probably more than he normally did in a week. Maybe he needed to recharge a bit. But she couldn't risk letting him fall asleep on her. Plus, she had the sinking feeling that wasn't the end of the story. "So you fought back?"

"Yeah."

She swallowed, knowing she wasn't going to like this answer. "Then what happened?"

He swung his head in a funny manner. At first she thought he was blacking out, but then his braid flopped down over his other shoulder. "My mom... she grabbed me by my hair and dragged me into the house. She locked me in a closet—barricaded it shut with a dresser. Then she left. I was so hurt, I couldn't get out. I... I lay down to die."

Everything about him seemed to shrink in on itself. Melinda was sure that if they were near some of the trees that never seemed to get any closer, he'd find a shadow and melt into it and she might never find out what happened.

"You didn't, right? Madeline says you're not dead." She didn't know if she was asking to make him feel better—or to reassure herself that he wasn't just a very warm ghost.

"Guess not," he admitted.

"How long were you in the closet?" He had to have gotten out. At some point.

"Three days, maybe."

"*Three days*? That's flipping insane! Why didn't she let you out?" Although maybe she'd wanted him to die, too. Nobody Bodine's mother was quickly rising to the top of her Worst Moms Ever list.

"Because." He took a deep breath and looked up at the sky. The morning was still cool, but the sun was rising higher and there were no clouds. If they didn't get to where they were going soon, they were going to fry on the back of this horse.

"Because *why*?"

"Because she and that guy went to a bar and got drunk and rolled her car on the way home. They died. And no one knew where I was."

For one of the very few times in her life, Melinda was completely, utterly speechless. Those horrible people had deserved nothing less, but..."Three days locked in a closet, burned like this, with no food and water? If I weren't looking at the scars..." Then the light bulb went off in her head. "That's why you don't like to be inside."

He nodded his head once, but didn't say anything else.

89

"Well, how did you get out? What happened next?" She was desperately searching for the silver lining and she knew it, but there had to be a bright spot in this story somewhere. He'd lived. He'd grown up and they hadn't.

When he didn't respond immediately, she kissed his scar again, letting her lips linger as if that could siphon some of the pain away from it. "Don't you dare fall asleep, Nobody Bodine."

"Not gonna happen with you around," he said with what sounded like a smile. Was it possible? Was he cracking an actual joke up there?

She leaned forward, but this time, instead of kissing him, she rested her chin on his shoulder. "Then tell me how you got out."

"Albert found me."

"Who's Albert? Why didn't Rebel come get you?"

"Rebel'd gone away. Albert was his grandfather."

"Oh." That didn't explain much but she'd rather not waste his valuable talking on information she could get from Rebel later. Rebel could explain where he'd been and who Albert was. "So Albert found you and nursed you back to health?"

He nodded.

"But that can't be the end of the story. You have so *many* scars. And how do you do that thing where you disappear, almost? Why couldn't they see you before you attacked them last night? And where are we going?"

"You talk a lot. More than your sister," was all he said.

She got the distinct feeling that story time was over and that she wouldn't get much more out of him—at least, not about what happened when he was thirteen. But, hell yeah, she talked a lot. "Where are we going? Where do you live? You don't live in that same house, do you?" She couldn't even imagine that—having to return to the scene of so much pain all the time.

"No. It burned."

The way he said it—had he burned it? She waited, but he didn't elaborate. Actually, she should probably be more surprised that he'd elaborated on anything at this point. A new thought occurred to her. "Who else knows about these? I mean, knows the how and why?"

He didn't answer her, but he didn't really have to. A man

named Albert who was Rebel's grandfather probably knew most of it. But if Rebel hadn't even been here—wherever he'd been—then she wondered if he knew about the attack.

"So why did you tell me?"

He tilted his head to one side, as if he were really thinking. "Don't know." Then, after further reflection, "You asked."

"Well of *course* I asked. I mean, you've got some hellacious scars going on here." But what he said sunk in. "Why hasn't anyone else ever asked? Not even Madeline?"

His back stiffened. "I ain't a good man. You saw what I did last night."

"What a load of crap, Nobody. You had a rough life and you survived. That doesn't make you a bad man. Just a..." she almost said *broken*. Almost. But for once in her life, she got the brakes slammed on. "Just a scarred one."

He shook his head a time or two, as if he thought this statement to be woefully incorrect, but he didn't disagree with her. *At least, not out loud*, she mused as Red took another unmarked turn and finally the trees on the hills got closer.

They'd been riding for about forty minutes now—more than enough that she was going to be a bit bowlegged after this. After a lifetime in a small city like Columbus, she couldn't believe that there was this much untouched space in this country. Out East, there were just so many people and cars and buildings. Who would have thought that there were still places that existed where you could ride for an hour and never see another living being, much less a car or an electricity pole?

As the horse began to climb up a gentle incline, holding on to Nobody got a lot harder. His breathing seemed more labored. To think, this stubborn man had wanted to do this himself—and, given the way Maddie had talked about being surprised he was still in the living room this morning, he usually did.

She had to actively counterbalance her weight to keep from slipping off—or letting him slip. "Are we almost there?"

He grunted, which was probably a normal thing but made her nervous. He'd managed a decent amount of talking, for him anyway, but the ride was clearly taking its toll and he was fading. If they didn't get there soon, she didn't know if she'd be able to keep him awake without doing a hell of a lot more than kissing.

She looked at the body underneath the scars. No, no—none of that. This man was wounded. In more ways than one.

Plus, the ride was taking all her attention now. Each step was a full-body workout. "Talk to me, Nobody. Don't fall asleep."

He grunted again, which was probably as good as it was going to get.

"How much longer?"

"Soon," he said, the strain obvious.

"Why do you fight so much?" She was digging, but she needed him to keep awake. He probably weighed at least two hundred pounds—far beyond what she could heft. No yoga class in the world could get her to dead-lift two hundred pounds.

"Good at it," he got out through what sounded like clenched teeth.

The fight last night replayed in her mind. "Okay, yes, you're extremely good at it. But that doesn't mean you have to. We could have called the cops last night. I didn't want you to get hurt." *Again*, she thought as she looked at his back. *Again*.

He didn't say anything as the hill got steeper. "Talk to me, Nobody. Ask me a question."

The pause was longish, but finally he said, "You can see me?"

"What, you mean like right now? Hard to miss you, given all the holding you on a horse and stuff."

Seeing makes it real, a voice in her head whispered that sounded just like Rebel. Was this what he was talking about? Or..."Do you mean that other people can't see you in the dark?"

"No." He was going past sounding pained and was rapidly moving into agonized.

Melinda found herself counting the steps of the horse. Which was not a productive use of her time, frankly—she had no idea how much longer they had to go. But it was something to do. "Why do you live so far away from everything?"

"Safer."

There was nothing 'safer' about a wounded man in an unreachable location. She wondered if they were still within the ten-mile radius for the walkie-talkie that was still in the bag on her back. Along with that knife.

"Madeline gave me a knife, just in case. But you're not going to hurt me, are you?"

That was one of those things that popped out of her mouth and usually earned her a stern look or a swift kick from Maddie. But she didn't want him to find it and freak out on her. She couldn't have him thinking she meant him harm.

"No." He said this with more conviction. Good, she hadn't lost him yet.

"Will you take the antibiotics?"

"No."

"Why the hell not?"

"Don't take drugs."

Of all the ridiculous positions to take on the matter. "Well, yes, *hurray* for not taking 'drug' drugs but I don't want you to get sick and die on me. I've gone to a lot of trouble to make sure you stay alive. Try to keep it that way, okay?"

He was breathing harder now, slumping forward. It put a huge strain on her forearms. She couldn't hold him up with her arms alone. "Lean back. You're going to break my arms."

"Sorry." But he didn't lean back. He only sat up straighter.

"Oh, for the love of Pete." She put her chin on his shoulder and sort of pulled him backward until his back was resting on her chest. It took some of the strain off her arms, but man, he was heavy. And hot. But at least this way, she could see where they were going instead of where they'd been.

The trees were thicker now and a clear path was visible. Red seemed to know where she was going. If Melinda didn't know any better, she'd say the horse was picking up speed. "Are we there yet?"

"Quit asking," was the short reply she got, but again—was he teasing her?

"Then stop trying to fall off this horse. You're not exactly a feather on the wind, you know."

They rode on, Nobody leaning back on her and her leaning forward to keep him from pushing her right off the back of this horse. *Keep him talking.* "I've never ridden a horse without a bridle. How'd you get Red to do that?"

"I train 'em."

Two options there—was he starting to slur his words or did

he have more than one horse? "How many horses do you have?"

"Twenty-seven."

"Seriously? What the hell are you doing with twenty-seven horses?"

He didn't answer. The trail got very steep for about five feet—actual switchbacks appeared in the hill. It took everything she had to keep the both of them on the horse.

"I can't do this much longer," she told him when the trail suddenly leveled out. Her legs were burning from gripping the horse's sides and her arms were starting to shake from the effort. This was more work than a 5k run.

"S'okay," he said, his voice getting fainter. "Here."

"What?" Then she looked over his shoulder and saw a small clearing filled with stuff. Crazy stuff. Stuff that had her blinking her eyes to make sure she was seeing what she was seeing.

Yes, off to one side was what looked like a cabin being held up by cobwebs alone. On one side was a nearly ceiling-high stack of firewood. That was what she would have expected. But the power cord that ran from the roof of the cabin to one of those old-fashioned trailers—the kind that Mom had always called a pregnant silver-dollar camper? The trailer was set off to one side, the shiny silver top completely covered over with low-hanging branches. A bright blue and white awning hung out over the front. Underneath it was an outdoor café table with two matching chairs. She blinked, but the floral pattern tablecloth covering it didn't change.

Oh, but it got weirder. She shook her head, but there really were twinkling stars hanging from the awning, as well as a chaise lounge with a different floral print cushion situated near a copper fire pit. Of all the possible things she might have expected to find in the middle of this particular nowhere, pregnant silver dollars with twinkle lights and floral patterns weren't high on the list.

"What the hell?"

"Home," he grunted out. "Chair." He managed to lift a hand and point at the chaise lounge.

"Okay." The horse seemed to understand and plodded over to the lounge, stopping a few feet away. "We have to get you off this horse." The moment she said it, she realized there was a problem.

How was she supposed to get him *off* this horse?

CHAPTER EIGHT

"You first," Nobody said. His side was throbbing and his head felt like steel wool that had been left in the rain for a month. But they were home.

"Um, me first?"

If he'd been able to, he would have smiled at her. "Slide off. I won't fall."

"But the horse..."

"She'll be fine. Go. Now." He needed to get in his chair in the worst sort of way before he blacked out.

She pulled away from him, which left him feeling more wobbly than he wanted to admit. What had been harder about the ride out here—her making him talk about his scars or having to feel her full breasts pressed against his back, her thighs pressed against his legs? Or the way she kissed him? Yeah—that. Feeling her mouth pressed against him—not because some drunk friend at a bar had dared her to kiss the *sica* and not because she had something to prove. He was pretty sure about that.

But why? Had she kissed him just to keep him from blacking out? Or...

No. There was no *or* and to think so was stupidity, plain and simple.

Except, now that she was off the horse, she was standing there, looking up at him with her big blue eyes. With a hand on his leg. And another on his arm. The thing was, he saw plenty of concern in her eyes, but very little that looked like pity. And none of the scolding her sister always had in store for him.

He looked away. He needed to quit thinking. He'd never been real good at anyway.

"Easy, now," Melinda said. "Lean forward onto her neck and take it slow. Try not to crush me on your way down, okay?" She said that last bit as if it were funny, but maybe not so funny at the same time.

He did as she said and laid down onto Red's neck. Even though the horse had been carrying a lot of extra weight, she held still as Nobody managed to get his leg over her back.

Normally, he could dismount a horse at a full gallop and land on his feet at a dead run. But today? Yeah, no. The pain ripped up through his side and he more or less flopped to the ground. He did not like having weak knees. Being able to stand up and walk away was how you let your enemies know you were *not* defeated.

But Melinda Mitchell was not an enemy. She'd already seen him at his lowest, unable to even get himself outside or on his own horse.

He didn't like it.

He couldn't do a damn thing about it. He hung onto Red's neck with everything he had, trying to focus on the smell of horse sweat and *not* the way her arms looped around his waist, *not* the way her breasts pressed up against his unwounded side and *not* the way she ducked under his upraised arm to try and take some of his weight.

"Five feet," she said, sounding as if she was talking about the end of a marathon. "Ready?"

He nodded. It was all he could do.

"One," she said, tightening her grip on him—which hurt. But then, so would collapsing in a heap. "Two..."

On "Three," he let go of Red and tried to take a step back. It didn't quite work, but she didn't let him fall. She couldn't hold him up, though, so they half-stumbled, half-fell into the chair.

"Ow. You okay?"

No. But he wasn't about to admit that to her. So he grunted instead.

Then he realized that he was laying down. With her in his arms, tucked against his good side.

Suddenly, he didn't hurt so much.

"What do you need? Water?"

Yeah, a drink would be good right now. But he wanted to

hold onto her just a little bit more. "In a minute," he managed to get out.

"Okay." She moved the arm that was across his chest, probably just to avoid touching his bandage. But she didn't pull away or anything. Instead, she laid her hand down in the middle of his chest. "You still with me? Didn't die or anything, did you?"

"No."

"Yeah, not really sure which question you were answering there." She kind of made this noise that could have been a sigh of frustration or could have been a giggle but was probably a giggle of frustration. "No dying allowed, got that?"

"Yes, Ma'am."

"So, where did you get all this stuff? I mean, I'm pretty sure the cabin was here, right? But what the hell is this trailer doing here? And why are there so many floral prints? I figured you for more of a plaid guy, frankly."

As tired as he was, he felt the corner of his mouth curve up. No one had ever figured him for anything before, really. No one thought about him enough to do any figuring. "Borrowed it."

"*Borrowed*? What—you stole it?" Then she did sit up, pulling her other arm out from under his back. But she didn't get up. Instead, she leaned up on her elbow, her one hand still warm against his chest, and looked at him. "Are you telling me you *stole* everything here?"

He wouldn't have thought it was still possible after all this time, but his face grew hot. Was he blushing? Shit.

Of course he'd stolen all of it. He didn't have a lot of money and what money he did have, he spent on the horses and Jamie. The only things he bought were food, books, and clothes. The books and clothes always came from thrift stores and he hunted a lot for food.

He tried to take things that no one else used. He'd kept his eye on the trailer at a storage lot for two whole years, but no one had come for it. It had just sat there, forgotten. So, after a particularly cold winter night, he borrowed a truck from the rez, drove to the lot, and went through the trailer. He kept the stuff like the sheets, but anything that looked like it might have personal value to the previous owners, he set aside, leaving a small box of belongings in the empty space where the trailer had once been.

He did that with all the stuff here. Some of it, like the chair they were in, had been left beside a dumpster. He'd cut out the busted webbing, restrung it with some rope, and borrowed a cushion from an outdoor store. Good as new. The twinkle lights had been outside an apartment. They cast a soft glow that was better than campfire for reading, but not as spotlight-bright as the lights in the trailer. The hose had been left out overnight in a park.

He didn't take things he didn't need and he never took things that would cause a hardship for someone. He just took what he needed to survive.

But he didn't think he could say that in words she'd understand, so he tried ignoring her. But that was impossible, frankly. She was staring down at him. Then she began tapping her fingers on his chest, each fingertip sending a flash of something he thought might be desire through his body. Each flash pushed back at the pain.

"I'm waiting," she said in an impatient tone of voice.

"Wanna sleep." Then, before he was aware of what he'd done, his good arm had curled tighter around her waist, pulling her back down against his chest.

For a moment, it felt like she was going to go along with that. Her body started sinking against his—sweet and easy and something he knew he'd dream about for many a long winter night. Except for the stabbing part, he'd hold this entire twenty-four hours of contact with her deep in his memory until the day he finally did die and go on to the other side.

Then she pushed back against him. "You need water. And I have to change your bandage." The way she said it—nervous—was so unlike her sister that he felt himself start to smile again.

"Sink in trailer." His mouth was tired from all the talking. As much as he wanted to keep holding her, he really did need the sleep. He usually healed fast, but then, he usually didn't lose this much blood.

As she peeled herself off him, she said, "So, you have electricity and running water? In the middle of nowhere? How the hell did you pull that off?"

"Cabin," he replied. He'd found the cabin four days after he'd slipped off Albert's couch in the middle of the night. He'd stayed long enough that the fever had gone down and most of the scabs had crusted over. Even though the old man had been kind to him, sleeping on his couch had brought on such a feeling of claustrophobia that Nobody had needed to get away.

Once, this had probably been some hunting cabin. It was a piece of junk, but the power was on and the water was clean. Someone, somewhere, was paying the bills, but in all Nobody's years out here, he'd never seen a hunter—or hell, another person. Except for Jamie, of course.

And now Melinda. Man, that was going to take some getting used to. Her knowing where he lived—*how* he lived—gave Nobody a deep feeling that was so unsettling, he'd almost rather get stabbed again instead. At least physical wounds healed.

Finally, she was up. The sudden loss of the heat from her body made him shiver. Another sign of weakness he didn't like.

He couldn't keep his eyes open, but his ears did all the seeing for him. He heard her walk up to his home and open the door. He heard the trailer creak as she stepped inside.

If he could have cringed in anticipation of her response, he would have.

Sure enough, seconds later a very loud gasp came out of the trailer. "Holy crap, Nobody—what are all these *books*?"

He didn't bother to answer. He couldn't have said anything loud enough for her to hear it, anyway.

"Dude, this is like, every Louis L'Amour ever published! And Zane Grey? Wow." There was a longish pause. "I've never even heard of half these guys. Who is Elmer Kelton? Are these seriously alphabetized? Where do you *even* sleep in here?"

Then he heard the cupboard doors opening and shutting. She found the glasses on the third try. Wasn't that hard—only three little cabinets in there. He heard the water turn on, off, and then heard the trailer creak as she came back out.

But instead of her coming over to him, he heard her pause, then the sound of something dragging. He managed to get his head turned to see her pulling one of his table-chairs over to where he lay.

Damn. She wasn't going to lay down with him again. Even though he had no right to be disappointed—no right to want her to—he still was.

"Here." She held a glass up to his lips. "Drink."

God, he'd never felt so helpless, not since those days in the closet and those nights on Albert's couch. He'd been stabbed, shot, burned and cursed, for crying out loud, and in all his years he hadn't been hurt so bad he had to have a woman hold a glass for him.

Unfortunately for him, he was in no shape to take the water away from her, especially not as the cool, clear liquid began to trickle down his throat. And his chest, but he didn't care. Most of it was going in his mouth and it tasted so damn good.

But then she said, "Oops, sorry," as she took her hand—just her hand—and started to brush away the water that had dripped down his chest. His bare chest.

At some point, her touch went from brushing the water away to stroking him—slow, teasing movements that set flames against his skin.

Defensively, he grabbed her hand away from his chest. She couldn't touch him like that. She really *didn't* know what he was capable of, no matter how good an idea she thought she had.

But his brain felt like it was sloshing around in his head and before he knew what he was doing, he'd pulled her hand up to his mouth and kissed the palm. *Her* palm.

And the funny thing was, she didn't jerk her hand back or call him names or slap him. He kept waiting for the blow, but it didn't come.

Then her mouth was against his ear and she whispered, "I *see* you," as she moved her palm away from his mouth and rested it against his cheek.

He couldn't find the strength to say anything, but that was just as well, since he had no idea what to say. All he could do was breathe in and out and feel the pain push back. In its place, the building blackness of sleep was taking over.

She said, "I'll, uh, change your bandage and let you rest, okay? Is there anything else you need?"

You. He wanted to tell her that—wanted to wake up and feel her body against his again. But now that the water was hitting his guts, he couldn't push back at the darkness of sleep.

Until he heard a twig snap and Melinda gasped. "*Jamie?*"
Well, hell.

Melinda blinked, sure she was hallucinating. Had the boy just walked out of the woods like he belonged here? "What are you doing here?"

The boy froze, his mouth open. He glanced around as if he wanted to bolt, but then he saw Nobody laying on the chaise lounge. He didn't say anything, though.

So that's what it was. Jamie Kills Deer was following in Nobody Bodine's footsteps. That explained his silent, distant attitude. For the love of Pete.

Was this what Rebel had been talking about? Was Nobody one of those who'd look out for the boy? Was this why she couldn't call social services?

"Boy." They both turned to look at Nobody, who was trying to prop himself up on his elbows. The effort left his face looking ashen. He apparently couldn't get anything else out, but he looked at Jamie.

"I fed the horses," Jamie said, dropping his eyes to the ground. "Brushed them, too."

"Rub Red down good, feed her." He had to pause after each word as beads of sweat began to roll down his face. "Get Star and Socks. Take her home." Then, spent, he fell back.

Jamie just stood there for a minute, still looking torn between doing what he was told and running. Melinda tried to help him out by smiling, but she was pretty sure that just made the situation worse.

"*Now,*" came the order from the chaise lounge with more force than she would have thought Nobody could put into it.

The boy moved. Without looking at Melinda, he patted Red's neck and then effortlessly slipped up onto her back. Dang. She may have had about a decade's worth of riding lessons, but there was no way in hell she'd ever be able to *just* hop up onto a horse.

She watched Jamie ride the horse out of the clearing. The trees were thick, so she couldn't see where he went. Where on earth was Nobody keeping another twenty-some-odd horses?

She turned her attention back to the man on the chair. He still looked like he'd been run over by a steamroller and blood was starting to show on his bandage.

Okay, make this quick. She dug into the pack and came up with sterile gauze, tape, and antibiotic cream. That would have to do—she didn't think she could get any pills down his throat.

"I'm going to take this one off," she told him, but she got no response. Boy, she really hoped peeling the tape off his side wouldn't wake him up.

Then she remembered an old trick her dad used to do when they had to take bandages off knees. She went back into the trailer. Man, what a weird place. If she had to guess, she'd say the trailer was late seventies, early eighties. Back in the day, it'd probably been a very expensive trailer. Maybe thirty feet long, it had wood paneling that was so clean it shone, an olive-green microwave that looked older than she was, and orange macramé-fringed curtains. The front had a dinette table and a couch that probably folded out, along with a swivel chair that looked as if it'd been recovered by a fourth-grade girl in wrapping paper—a hideously bright fabric in yellow and pink. *Pink*!

But beyond the clashing vintage stylings, what threw her the most were the books. The dinette table was packed three feet high with them—and underneath as well—leaving only a slim six inches or so of usable space. Those were all by one author—Louis L'Amour. The couch was similarly stacked, with books going up past the windows and only a space big enough for one to sit. A big section of those were Zane Grey.

She peeked past the kitchen area to the back. There was a bathroom, done in a hilarious baby-blue color scheme that somehow seemed just as inappropriate as the pink chair did. And two twin beds, one on each side. All stacked high and deep with paperbacks. As far as he could tell, they were all Westerns—and all in alphabetical order by author's last name. She didn't recognized most of the names.

It was like walking into a time warp/library combo, because there were paperback books *everywhere*. Where did he sleep? Or did he not sleep in here at all—just out in the chair?

She wouldn't have guessed the books—but then, she wouldn't have guessed the pregnant silver dollar trailer or the twinkle lights. One thing was for sure—Nobody Bodine was a man of few words and many, *many* mysteries.

She looked in the bathroom and under the kitchen sink, but didn't see any paper towels. Finally, she found a washcloth that she hoped he wouldn't mind getting bloody and soaked it in the sink until it was sopping wet. Dad had always wet down Band-Aids when they were kids or pulled them off after a bath.

When she came back out, Jamie was standing next to Nobody's hopefully-not-lifeless form. He didn't say anything—what a shocker there—but he looked up at her, the question obvious in his eyes.

"Some guys came by the clinic and there was a fight," she told him. A pointless, stupid fight that didn't need to happen and had left at least two men in really bad shape. Again, frustration with him bubbled up. Why had he felt the need to risk getting himself killed?

But the bigger question was, what would he have done if she hadn't been there? "Nobody, I'm going to put a wet cloth over your bandage, okay? Don't freak out, okay? No needles, I promise."

He grunted, a noise so quiet she wasn't entirely sure she'd actually heard it.

"Is he gonna be okay?"

She touched the wet cloth to Nobody's side. He didn't even flinch. "Madeline said he'd be fine," she replied, hoping it was true. "I've got to change his bandage and then he needs to rest."

Water tinged with blood dripped down Nobody's side and plopped on the cushion. God, she hoped the stitches had held. She could change a bandage, but she couldn't sew a man back together.

They sat for a few minutes until Melinda thought it'd soaked enough. Even then, the medical tape pulled at Nobody's skin.

She forced herself to look at the wound, which made her tummy do some highly acrobatic flips. But, as far as she could tell, the stitches were all in one piece. There wasn't even that much bruising. She used a corner of the washcloth to wipe the area clean and breathed a huge sigh of relief when more blood did not well up in the cut.

She looked at Jamie, who had turned an unusual color of green. "Can you go find me a dry towel or something?" she asked, hopeful that a job would distract him. "Please?"

He didn't even hesitate. And since the boy probably knew his way around that trailer better than she did, she only had a few moments alone with Nobody. She leaned down close to his ear. "Nobody, you and I are going to have a little *chat* about that boy just as soon as I'm sure you're not going to die on me. Understand?"

"Don't... scare... him." Each word seemed to be a thousand-pound weight on his chest that he struggled to push through.

"Isn't that the funniest damn thing I've ever heard, coming from *you*," she muttered as Jamie came flying back out of the trailer with a handful of paper towels.

Melinda smiled at him even as she mentally smacked herself upside the head. "Thanks. Can you rinse this one out for me and hang it somewhere to dry?" Jamie nodded and was off again.

She dried the stitches as gently as she could and dug into the backpack for the bandages. Just as she saw the antibiotic cream, she noticed the small square at the bottom. Where there condoms in here? Oh, for heaven's sake. Her sister was insane to think that Melinda would sleep with a wounded man.

She slathered on a healthy layer of the antibiotic cream. "I'm going to leave the antibiotics. I'd consider it a personal favor if you took them."

She wasn't sure, but she thought he made a noise that could have been, "Ha."

"Laugh all you want, but I'm serious. Otherwise, I'll... I'll come back here and make you talk some more."

One eyelid fluttered about half open. Was he trying to give her a look? He needed more practice.

"Oh, I will," she told him, hoping that what passed as his sense of humor was a good sign. "I almost know where I am. You have a hell of a lot to explain—all those books, what that child is doing here, where you're hiding twenty-seven horses? A *hell* of a lot."

One corner of his mouth curved up into what was almost a smile. As she looked down at him, she was struck by the wonder of it all. His face relaxed into sleep, the color coming back to normal. He looked... at peace. It took everything hard about him and made it softer. God, he was a handsome man.

And a wounded one. She placed the gauze over the wound, instantly feeling better now that the stitches were covered by white cloth, and taped the whole thing on with what seemed to her to be three times the amount of tape Madeline had used. But hey—it was a darn *secure* bandage.

Jamie came back out, looking a little better. Yeah, having a concrete task helped her, too. "He's going to rest for a while. Can you get the horses, please?" This time, the boy didn't bolt off to his chore. Instead, he gave Nobody a plaintive look.

"I'll get lost if I try to go home myself," she reminded him, which was God's honest truth. "And you have to bring the horses right back here."

In other words, she wouldn't make him go back to his parent's house and she wouldn't keep him from coming back to Nobody.

Honestly, she didn't want to. If he came back here, then there'd be someone keeping an eye on the man who was currently unconscious in a chaise lounge. That was a reassuring thought. If something went really wrong, Jamie might be able to get to Madeline in time.

The boy thought this over for a bit and then nodded before he headed down the same path he'd taken Red earlier.

Whew. She went back into the trailer and found a light blanket. She threw it over Nobody's shirtless form and then refilled the water glass and put it on the chair next to him. Then she opened the little fridge in the trailer. There wasn't much there but carrots, so she dug out a few, rinsed them off, and found a baggie to put them in. There. It wasn't a gourmet meal, but if he woke up, he'd have something to eat and drink. Then she grabbed the backpack and took out anything she thought he might need— the rest of the bandages, the antibiotics, the granola bar. Just in case.

"I'm leaving," she told his sleeping form as she slung the pack over her shoulders. "Don't you dare die while I'm gone, okay?"

She didn't get a response, but then, she didn't expect one. She could only hope that, somewhere in his dreams, he'd heard her.

She leaned down. "I'll send Jamie back, okay? And I'll see you later," she told him as she heard the clip-clop of hooves. "I promise."

Then, because she couldn't help herself, she kissed his forehead and said, "Thank you for protecting me, Mr. Bodine."

He sighed in his sleep.

Now why did that make her feel so good?

CHAPTER NINE

"Let me guess," Melinda said, looking at the mare who appeared to be considerably older than Red had been. Had that man put her on a geriatric mare? Oh, when he wasn't having a medical emergency, she was going to tear him a new one.

This horse had a big burst of white right between her eyes. "This one's Star, right?"

Jamie gave her a short nod.

Melinda looked around, but she didn't see a convenient stump or stepping stool or anything that she could use, beyond the café chairs. "I need help," she told the boy.

He gave her a look that, in another two or three years, would probably be the full-on teenage eye-roll. But then he slipped back off the other horse's back and came over to her.

Without a word, he laced his fingers and let her step into his cupped hands. Then, with more force than she would have given the kid credit for, he gave her a big boost onto Star's bare back.

Would she even be able to walk tomorrow? It'd be a bow-legged experience, that was for sure.

Jamie slipped back onto his horse, Socks—who had four perfectly matched socks on her legs—and led the way out of the clearing. Melinda looked over her shoulder at Nobody's sleeping form as they rode away.

Be okay, she thought at him. *Don't die because of me*. She couldn't bear the thought.

She and Jamie rode in silence until they broke through the tree line at the bottom of the hill. Then she goosed Star forward so that she was riding parallel with the boy.

"So," she began, watching him cringe at the sound of the voice. It was clear that he'd be perfectly fine not talking the whole way home, but that was too damn bad. She had him completely alone—no one would see them talking or hear what they said. This was her best chance to learn everything she could.

"Your name is Jamie Kills Deer?"

He nodded. *Oy.*

"How long have you been helping Nobody out?"

"I don't help him. He helps me," came the short reply. But hey, it was a reply! Progress!

"How does he do that?"

There was a longish pause. She looked at his face. The bruises were faded, the swelling gone. "Keeps me safe."

"From who?" Nothing. So she added, "from your dad?"

He nodded.

"Your dad hurts you?"

He gave her that look again, the nascent teenage-eye-roll that said *Duh* loud and clear.

So she changed directions. "How long has Nobody been protecting you?"

She didn't get an answer. Oh, this kid thought he could just clam up? Hell, no. They had about forty minutes of riding left. He was going to talk whether he liked it or not. If Nobody was the reason she couldn't have this child removed by social services, she needed to know exactly what he did for the boy.

"I'm not going to tell anyone. Not even Rebel," she said. "And you know Nobody wouldn't have shown me where he lived if he didn't trust me."

At least, she hoped that was true.

"So why don't you tell me how it is that you're grooming his horses and he's protecting you." Then she added a Nobody-esque, "*Now,*" just for good measure.

Jamie's look was a little less smart-ass this time. "My dad— he drinks. Mom, too."

The image of Nobody's scarred back and arms popped into her mind again. "They're mean when they drink?"

He nodded. "I guess I was about seven. My dad hit my mom—knocked her out—and I was..."

She waited. At least he was talking.

"I was screaming," he finally said, as if a seven year old being terrified of watching his mom get beaten was something to be ashamed of. "And my dad was coming toward me. He was gonna hit me, too."

"He do that a lot?"

"Yeah," he admitted, not looking at her. But then his tone changed. "And then... this shadow just kind of pulled off the wall. I mean, I know I was just a little kid, but it was like something in a dream."

"Yeah?"

"Yeah," he said, his voice full of wonder. "I mean, it was scary. One minute, my dad was about to punch me and then this shadow walks into a man and hits him so hard... I thought he was dead, but then this shadow-man kicked him and he groaned and I knew he wasn't dead and that made me so mad. *So mad.*"

"Because he wasn't dead?"

"Yeah." The more the kid talked, the more animated he was becoming.

Melinda almost smiled at him. He may be learning how to be all closed off from Nobody Bodine, but that wasn't his nature.

"Then this shadow-man came at me and I was so scared he was going to hurt me, too. But he didn't." Jamie said this last part as if he still couldn't believe there were men in this world who wouldn't smack a little boy around. "He just crouched down before me and asked me if I was okay. Said if I stopped crying, he'd take me some place for a few days where no one would hurt me and I could ride horses."

She cringed. It sounded like something a pedophile would say to a vulnerable kid to lure them into a trap. Stranger-danger, never take the candy. Never. But to a kid in a crappy situation..."Yeah?"

Jamie nodded. "Put me on the back of a horse and we rode to his place."

"What did you do there?" She kept her voice light and easy. Now that he'd gotten going, the boy seemed more willing to share than his mentor had been.

"He made me some dinner, cleared a spot off one of the beds and let me sleep there and then, the next morning, showed me his horses. Said I could ride one if I could brush it, then he showed me how to do it. Didn't hurt me," he added defensively. "He *doesn't* hurt me. He keeps me safe."

She looked at him. He met her gaze without flinching or looking away. He was telling the truth, thank God for that. "How does he do that?"

Jamie shrugged. "Sometimes, he comes and gets me and I stay out a few days. That's the *best*. He got me a fishing pole—there's a creek down on the other side of the hill—and I can read any book I want as long as I put it back where it came from." He was quiet for a moment. "I hafta eat a lot of carrots, though."

Melinda grinned. That man took his literature seriously. But that just lead to more questions. Like, had he stolen the fishing pole? Where did he get that many books? And, beyond that, *why* did he have so many books? Had he graduated from high school? She could see how it would be hard if he didn't have a home or a family to make sure he got to class every day, but most kids who dropped out didn't have several hundred paperbacks in a trailer somewhere.

"What do your folks say when you're gone that long?"

Dang, that was the wrong question. Jamie shut down on her, barely muttering, "My folks never notice when I'm gone."

She scrambled to come up with a re-direct. "I'm glad you started coming to the center. You've been a big help getting it painted."

"He made me come."

She'd lost him. He was back to not looking at her, sitting rigidly on his horse's back. Crap. She shouldn't have pushed him to talk about his family.

"You know where Rebel and my sister live, right?"

He shrugged.

Okay, that was going to be a problem. She looked out over the sea of grass, trying to get her bearings. The hills that hid Nobody were some distance behind them now, but she couldn't see anything in front of them that looked the least bit familiar. *Great Plains, indeed*, she snorted to herself.

She slung the bag off her back and dug out the walkie-talkie. "What are you doing?" Jamie asked, alarmed.

"If you can't get me to Rebel's house, he has to come get me. I don't have a *clue* where I am." Then she shot him a side look. "And I got the feeling we were done talking, so..."

She clicked the walkie-talkie on. "Hello, Rebel? Maddie? Hello?"

Then she realized that Jamie had stopped and was ten feet behind her. She spun in the saddle. Was he trying to pull a Nobody-style disappearance? "Oh, no you don't," she said, pointing her finger at him. "You have to know where they live so that you can come back and get us if Nobody gets worse."

Jamie's face twisted in confusion. "But..."

She could guess what was going on. Nobody had told the boy not to be seen coming or going from the camp.

"Melinda?" Maddie's voice crackled over the walkie-talkie, making both of them jump. "Where are you? Are you okay?"

She kept her eyes on the boy. "Don't you move," she said under her breath. "I'm here—in the middle of nothing but grass."

"Are you okay?" Maddie insisted.

Something in her tone made Melinda pause. Jamie's eyes pleaded with her. "Fine. Everything's fine." She left it at that. "I got turned around on the way home. Any chance Rebel can find me?"

Maddie chuckled. "Yeah, he's good at that. Give him a few minutes, okay?"

"Okay." She stuffed the walkie-talkie back in the bag. "Listen, kid—here's the deal. I don't tell anyone I know where you go *if* you keep coming to the center. You miss more than three days and I come looking for you. Got it?" Never mind that she'd never find her way back to Nobody's trailer in the woods. He didn't need to know that.

He shot her a look that might have been intimidating on an older kid.

She just grinned at him. "Yeah, you don't scare me. If Nobody wanted you to come to the center, you keep coming to the center. Got it?"

He twisted his mouth in displeasure. She took it as a 'yes.'

"Second, from the center, you follow that road for about a mile until it hits..." Crap. Directions had never been her strong suit. "Until it hits the bigger road. Go right on that for three or four miles." She could see the trip in her head, but she'd never seen a street sign. "Then take a left on the gravel road, follow that for about two miles, then right on the dirt drive. Rebel and Madeline live in the trailer at the top of the hill, okay? I live there, too. If something goes wrong, you come get us, okay?"

Jamie didn't reply, but she could see him thinking through the directions in his head. He nodded this way and that before finally saying, "Okay."

Oh, thank God he wasn't going to fight her on that. "What about the horse?"

Jamie shot her a smary look. "Don't worry about her." Then he spun his horse around in a tight circle and took off.

She sighed as she watched him go.

What else could she do?

She turned her horse back in the direction that might have been toward the house and nudged her on to a slow walk. After about fifteen minutes of what felt like moving in place, she heard, "Melinda? You out here?" from somewhere off to her left.

"Rebel?" she yelled back. "Over here!"

As they got closer, she saw that Rebel wasn't alone. He had another man on horseback with him. Whereas Rebel was wearing jeans and moccasins and a gray t-shirt—proving he did actually own shirts—this other man had on a denim work shirt and a black cowboy hat with an eagle feather tied to it. And a badge on his shirt pocket.

Oh, crap. Suddenly, she was thrilled Jamie had bailed on her. It was going to be hard enough to explain what she was doing out here in the middle of nowhere. But if she'd been with the boy, that would have made everything else more complicated.

As if it weren't complicated enough.

"There you are." Rebel's tone made it sound like she was a little sister that had wandered off and gotten lost.

Which wasn't that far from the truth. "Here I am." She didn't know what else to say. The whole reason that she'd had to get Nobody home was that the sheriff was coming. By the look of things, the sheriff was here. "Hi. Melinda Mitchell."

"Tim Means," he said in a business-like tone, his eyes

searching the horizon. "There was an incident at the clinic last night." His gaze snapped back to her. "Know anything about it?"

Melinda swallowed as she let her face fly into a surprised look. Years of sneaking out past curfew to go out with boys her parents most definitely did not approve of made lying easy. "What happened?" she gasped.

Rebel notched an eyebrow at her, as if her play-acting abilities were something of a shock.

"*Somebody* beat the hell out of some gangbangers," the sheriff said, looking over her horse. "Would you know anything about that?"

Oh, crap—the horse. The horse she was currently sitting on without a saddle or a bridle. That wasn't normal—well, maybe it was normal on the rez, but it was most certainly *not* normal for a white chick.

She needed to stall for time. If this were Columbus, she'd just start flirting. She was good at it. Never underestimate the power of her boobs. But this was the rez and she hadn't gotten all the rules down yet. "Was anyone hurt?"

"Nothing fatal." Tim's voice trailed off, as if he weren't sure about that last one. "I think they were going to trash the child care center. You're in charge of the center, right?"

"Oh my gosh, is everything okay there?" She nudged Star's sides with her heels. If she had to go check on her building, she could get out of this conversation.

"Ms. Mitchell," Tim said in the kind of voice that no smart person *ever* walked away from, "where have you been all morning?"

She looked back at him and this time, she noticed the gun strapped to his leg. Tim Means was a nice-looking guy—solidly built, probably about six feet tall, with a look that could be considered imposing—if one hadn't just spent a day in the company of Nobody Bodine.

Okay, time to play the dippy white woman card. "I was camping," she said in a gushing kind of way. "I can't believe how much *space* there is out here, you know? Without cars or lights? I mean, I didn't even see, like, a plane fly overhead?" Suddenly, every statement ended on an up note, as if the world were a question.

She flashed him a big smile and leaned forward just enough that her breasts shifted. "It's just so beautiful out here, you know? Maddie and Rebel have been great, but I thought we could all use a little... personal time." She raised one eyebrow to emphasize her point.

It worked. The sheriff wasn't so green that he blushed at the suggestion of sex—both the solo and the duo kinds—but he suddenly was staring at the hills again. "Did you see anyone while you were... camping?" The last word kind of stuck in his throat.

"No—isn't that amazing? I mean, a person could get lost out here, you know? Well," she added with a giggle, "I guess I sort of did. Which is why Rebel had to come get me."

Rebel gave her the side eye. *Dial it back a notch*, he seemed to be saying.

Men. "I need to get back and check on the center," she said, trying to strike the balance between flirty and concerned. "But thank you so much for telling me what's happened. I'll make sure I'm not there alone."

The sheriff nodded. "I've assigned a deputy to keep an eye on the place—Jack. Even if you don't see him, he's there. I don't want there to be any reprisals." He tipped his hat to her. "Ma'am," he said as he urged his horse forward—and away from the direction she and Jamie had ridden.

She thought. There was a lot of grass.

"Ready?" Rebel asked, turning around and setting his horse at a walk toward what she hoped was home. She needed a shower and some food. Star fell into step with Rebel's horse.

They rode in silence for a while before Rebel twisted in the saddle and scanned the horizon. "How is he?"

"Stubborn," she replied, unable to stop from rolling her eyes. "But okay, I think. I'm not a medical professional, you know."

"Trust me, I know."

There it was again, that teasing tone that made her feel like his little sister. "Yeah, well, I got him into a chair and got him water and changed his bandage. Then he fell asleep."

She waited for the questions—where did he live, what was it like—as well as questions she didn't have answers for. But Rebel didn't ask them.

"Who's Jack, the deputy?"

Rebel let out a pretty heavy sigh. "He's a tracker. Usually works for a rancher on the other side of the rez. Best hunter I've ever met. Tim only asks for his help when he really needs it."

She didn't like the sound of that. "So is he going to protect the clinic or..."

Or wait for Nobody.

Rebel didn't have an answer for that.

CHAPTER TEN

The sheriff may have said that the deputy named Jack wouldn't always be visible, but it was hard to miss a guy sitting in a rusted out Ford pick-up on the edge of the parking lot late Monday afternoon.

Yes, she felt a little safer with a deputy on-site. According to Rebel, the ringleader of the gang had been taken to Rapid City to get his arm put back together, but he'd already been released. Rebel didn't seem too worried that the guy would come back to the center anytime soon, but then, Rebel hadn't seen the guy drive a knife into Nobody's side.

Where was Nobody? The rest of the weekend had passed with no word from him or from Jamie. Melinda had kept her promise and not mentioned the boy. Madeline had assured her that it was perfectly normal for Nobody to disappear for days or weeks on end—against medical advice, she stressed—and then show up as if nothing had ever happened.

"Who cleans the Clinic when he's gone?" Melinda wanted to know. She was counting on him showing up for his job, at the very least.

"If it's not clean when Clarence gets in the next morning, he wipes everything down," was the non-committal answer.

So here she was, waiting. There were only three kids left—and Jamie hadn't shown up, either. If Nobody wasn't going to put in an appearance—which, given the deputy who was probably authorized to shoot upon sight, seemed unlikely—the least the kid could do was give her an update on his condition. All she could do was pray that Nobody was still alive while she swept up.

Tuesday was much the same. She spent the day in a crap-tacular mood. If that boy didn't show up, she was going to have to track him down. But where? His house? That seemed like a tremendously bad idea, even by her standards. She didn't want someone who beat his wife and kid to know who she was. However, despite her bluff to the boy, she held no illusions that she could retrace the way out to Nobody's place.

So she was stuck, waiting. And waiting, as Wednesday passed. Star was still at Rebel and Madeline's, munching grass without a care in the world, and Jack the Tracker was still spending his evenings watching the center.

Frustrated, she went up to his truck and knocked on the window. Jack was a wiry guy with a sharp hooked nose that matched his sharp chin. He rolled down the window and shot her a grin. "Yes, Ms. Mitchell?"

"Hi, how's it going?"

Chuckling, Jack made a show of looking out the windshield. "Quiet, I'd have to say."

"Can I ask you a question?"

"You mean, another one?"

Smartass. "Yeah. Are you waiting on Nobody?"

A little of the cockiness faded from his grin. "Maybe."

"What are you going to do when you see him?"

Jack the Tracker cranked his head from side to side, thinking. "First off, I won't see him unless he wants to be seen. Second off, I won't arrest him if I don't see him do anything stupid. The sheriff's got it out for him, but I don't have a problem with him as long as he's on one side of the rez and I'm on the other. Besides, it's not like Dwayne's gonna press charges—not when Tim's looking for him, too."

Jack gave her a look that might have been worry. She got the distinct feeling that what he wasn't saying was that Dwayne was going to handle this his own way. This did not make her feel any better. "But if Dwayne comes back, you'll arrest him, right?"

"Yup. He's got outstanding warrants."

Yeah, not exactly comforting. "Thanks, Jack."

Thursday, however, brought Jamie to the clinic. She gave him the meanest look she had—which was still only half as mean as Madeline's—as she hissed, "Where have you *been*? I've been worried sick!"

To which he shrugged. She was so frustrated that she wanted to shake him. She didn't of course, but she wanted to, by God. "Is he okay?"

The look he gave her this time was... different. If she didn't know better, she'd say the boy looked jealous. Instead of answering her, he handed her a little slip of paper that had been folded approximately thirty-seven times. Well, really, about four, but still—who folded paper like that?

The answer was Nobody, of course. She unfolded the paper, trying not to grin like a schoolgirl who'd just gotten her first mash note. "I'm okay," it said in stiff, all-caps letters.

And that was it. So much for the theory that a man who didn't talk much might, you know, actually *write* things down.

Still, he'd sent her a message. And beyond that, he wasn't dead. She looked up at Jamie, who was acting like she'd taken the last piece of cake for dessert. "Thank you."

He nodded just as the twins got into a fight over a toy.

She sighed. Nobody would have to wait. But not for much longer, she hoped.

The ride was hard. That was the difference between getting shot in the shoulder and stabbed in the gut. Shoulders only hurt if you needed to use your arm, but a stomach wound was gonna pull no matter how you moved.

Still, it'd been a week since the fight. Nobody felt bad that he hadn't been able to make it into work. That meant that Dr. Mitchell was going to give him one of those looks of hers and do some scolding.

But he had a feeling that he needed to steer clear of the clinic for a while—the kind of feeling that he'd learned not to ignore. Might be that the sheriff had it staked out. That wouldn't be a bad thing, he decided. There'd be someone around to make sure Melinda wasn't on her own.

But it meant he couldn't do his job and he couldn't watch Melinda. At least, not at the clinic.

But at Rebel's? Yeah, he could tough it out for the ride in and see if she was doing okay.

He took the long way, looping back through the hills and over the White Sandy river before coming up to Rebel's house from the south. Took a lot longer, but if the law was watching Rebel's house and Nobody got caught, he didn't want anyone to guess where his place was.

He left Red about half a mile away and went slow, paying attention to the world around him. Nothing felt off, so that was good. He hoped to find Jamie at the fire, sitting next to Melinda. Maybe she was helping him with his reading. Even as the image assembled itself in his mind, he wondered why the thought had occurred to him.

He'd sent the boy home—a thing he hated doing. Every time he did, he worried that this would be the time he didn't get there to stop Lou Kills Deer. But he couldn't keep the boy, especially now that the law was looking for him. Again.

By the time he got to the house, it was probably past midnight. Rebel would sit up at night if he thought he needed to, but Nobody was surprised to see that it wasn't Rebel sitting next to the fire. Instead, it was a woman with fire hair sitting cross-legged with one hand on her chin, a far-away look in her eyes as she stared at the flames.

Melinda. A weird thing happened in his chest—a tightness he'd thought was a pulled muscle released. Suddenly, he could breathe without pain.

He waited in the shadows to see if anyone else was lurking around, but outside the crackling of the fire, the night was quiet.

He wanted to go to her, but he didn't know how. Rebel had always said he was welcome to sit at the fire, but Rebel wasn't around. Probably inside, sleeping with his wife in his arms.

Like Melinda had been in Nobody's arms back at the camp, her body pressed against his, his arm around her waist. Like lovers.

No, not like lovers. Just because she'd helped him out in a tight spot did not mean he got to think like that.

She hadn't noticed he was there yet. Or she was forcibly ignoring him. That thought made him nervous. Was she? Why would she do that? For a man who didn't want people to see him, suddenly not being seen made him nervous. Maybe there was a lawman staking out the house. He'd been so anxious to get here after the long ride that he hadn't done a very good check. Nobody didn't have friends. The list of people who might be lying in wait for him started with the sheriff and went on for several pages.

See what thinking about a woman got him? Careless. *Stupid.* If he got caught, he deserved it.

He left the glow of the fire behind and did a couple of wide circles around the house and the hill it rested on. Nothing. No sign of tracks in the grass or dirt, nothing in the trees, no one hiding in the barn.

Finally satisfied—and his side throbbing—he worked his way back up to the house again. The light seemed dimmer and a shot of panic caught him off guard. What if she'd gone to bed while he was checking?

No, no—that was fine. He didn't need to see her again. She was fine. That was all he needed.

Except it wasn't. He just didn't realize how much he needed until he could see her form next to the dying embers. He needed something more.

He hadn't even stepped into the clearing when she looked up at him. Anyone else wouldn't have known he was there, but she knew. "Did everything check out?" she asked in a quiet voice.

She'd known he was here. Maybe not when he'd first gotten here, but she'd realized he was around and waited for him.

He stepped out. The light from the fire was negligible and the house was dark. There wasn't much moon, but the stars were bright enough for him to see every detail about her.

What was left of the firelight caught the colors of her hair as she smiled a wide, open smile at him. She was sitting on a blanket, her skirt fanned out around her. "I've been waiting on you, Mr. Bodine."

He whipped his hat off his head. "Sorry to have kept you waiting. I was making sure."

She accepted this. "I was worried about you."

He wasn't sure what he was supposed to say to this. People didn't worry about him. At least, they didn't worry that he was all right. More than likely, they worried that he was around and up to no good.

She looked up at him, her eyes shining in the low light.

"Come," she said, patting the blanket next to her. "Have a seat."

Nobody didn't move. It was one thing to have had her in his arms—on his lap, essentially—when he'd been too wounded to be considered a threat. But he was better now. Not great, but better. Most people would be afraid of him.

Not her. "I don't bite," she said, her tone light and teasing. "And I won't make you talk this time. Just... come sit with me. Please."

He wanted to do just that, maybe slip his arm back around her waist again and feel the weight of her body anchored against his. It was the sort of thing that probably happened all the time. Rebel sat like that with his wife on a regular basis. There was something about it that seemed normal.

He wanted to sit with her. She wanted him to do just that. So why couldn't he make his feet move? Why did he feel like maybe he shouldn't have come?

"Nobody?" Her voice was soft in the night—concerned. "Why won't you come sit?"

He realized he was crushing his hat. He tried to stop but it didn't work, so he ducked his head. He couldn't even come up with a response to a simple question.

He couldn't be normal.

He heard her get up. She was probably going in—had probably given up on him. Just as well. He began to move back into the shadows. He'd go check on Jamie. Yeah, that's what he needed to do.

"Don't." He startled at how close her voice had gotten. His head popped up. She was walking around the fire. Toward him. "Don't go."

He stood, rooted to the spot as she closed the distance between them. One of her pretty little hands reached out and settled on his side, where the bandage was. "How are you?"

Her voice was like the trickle of water in his stream, cool and inviting after a hot summer day. "Good," he managed to get out as her fingers skimmed over his shirt.

She took another small step toward him, her hand settling on his hip. "Do you need Madeline to look at it?"

"No, Ma'am. It's healing." She gave him a soft smile as she

took another step in. His heart began to pound. He didn't like it. He could face down six men and get stabbed in the gut and not be nervous about it at all, but one woman with wildfire hair made him all jumpy.

"Did you take the antibiotics?" Her other hand settled around his waist. The only thing keeping her chest from his was his hat.

Jesus, she was playing with fire. She had no idea what he was capable of. *None*. "No."

He waited for the scolding. At least, that's what her sister would have done. But not her. Her fingertips dug into the waistband of his jeans, pulling him forward. Into her. "Not even as a personal favor to me?" she asked, her lips curving into the most secret of smiles.

Nobody set his jaw. She was playing with him, that was all. She was just dancing with the devil in the pale moonlight because this was all a joke. Maybe she got off on him being dangerous. Maybe she was just trying to prove something to her sister.

She tilted her head to one side, looking up at him through her lashes. He'd read books where the woman would do that and then lead the man over the edge of a cliff. He'd never understood why any man would fall for it—until now.

It was the same look she'd given him when she'd woken up with her head in his lap. God help him, she wasn't afraid of him. He didn't know why she wasn't, but he was pretty sure he didn't care anymore.

"I'm going to kiss you," she said, her voice barely a whisper as she stood up on her tiptoes.

His fingers dug into his hat. It was a good hat, but he didn't mind that it was meeting its death in the line of duty like this. He braced himself for her touch. He would *not* lose control. He would *not* do anything that hurt her. "Okay."

She stopped then and he was just sure that he'd blown it by opening his big, fat mouth and doing the stupid thing—talking. But instead she just stared at him like—like—like he was the only man in the world. Just him. "Are you going to kiss me back?"

He didn't have a clue what he was supposed to say to that. So he didn't say anything. Instead, he let go of his poor hat and pulled her into his arms and crushed her lips against his.

She made a little squeaking noise in the back of her throat. Damn it all to hell, this is what she did to him. He made a promise to himself that he wouldn't hurt her and what did he do? Scare the hell out of her.

He pulled away, fighting the urge to bolt. "Sorry," he mumbled, wondering if it was worth it to get his hat before he ran. He let go of her. "I—sorry."

"Oh, no you don't." The next thing he knew, she had looped her arms around his neck and was holding him in place. "Don't you *dare* kiss me like that and then disappear."

"I don't want to hurt you." There. He'd said what he should have said earlier.

"Then don't hurt me." Her lips brushed over his, a whisper of a touch. Jesus, she was going to kill him. "Just kiss me slow and hard."

He couldn't help the way his arms shook as he tightened his grip on her, her breasts pressed against his chest. It'd been a long time. God, he hoped he wouldn't screw this up. "Yes, Ma'am."

She made a sound that could have been a giggle but could have been a sigh as he pressed his lips against hers. So, so long. Too damn long. Going slow was harder than he'd thought it would be, but he wanted to remember everything—the way she tilted her head to one side and sighed, the way she felt in his arms—the way she made him feel. Strong and real and *alive*.

Then she traced her tongue over his lips. He heard a noise and realized that it was him, groaning. She tasted of sweet oranges and sunsets and something wild and free.

He had to be careful. If he hurt her, he'd never forgive himself. So instead of filling his hands with her ass, he forced his hands to glide down over her clothing. Instead of ripping her shirt off and feasting himself on her breasts, he focused on kissing her.

Which was a good plan until her teeth nipped his lower lip— not hard enough to draw blood, but more than enough to make his dick stand up at attention. The desire hit him so hard that it worried him. What if he lost control?

Better not to. "Don't," he growled, grabbing her arms from around his neck and holding them to her side.

She shook her head in a slightly dazed way. "What? Why

not?" Then she realized that he had her arms pinned. She raised an eyebrow at him as she flexed her wrists, testing his grip. But amazingly, she didn't scream or sob in terror. She just licked her lips. "No biting. Got it."

"I didn't say that."

"Then why shouldn't I?" She leaned forward and he was powerless to stop her as her teeth skimmed along his neck. "If you liked it."

His arms shook. 'Liked it' wasn't the way he'd describe it. It made him rock-hard for her. It made him want to do things that he had no business doing to her.

And the fact that she kept pushing him instead of running away from him—it made him mad. He didn't know why, but it did. "Why aren't you afraid of me?" he demanded. It came out meaner than he meant it to, but he couldn't help it. Why couldn't she see the dangerous man everyone else did?

"Why are you afraid of me?" she replied in her quiet tone.

"I'm not," he snapped back even as he knew he was. He was scared of this fearless woman. He didn't like being scared of anyone, especially beautiful women. "You should be afraid of me. I'm a bad man. I hurt people." These were unavoidable facts. No one would dispute them.

"You protected me. You keep Jamie safe."

"You don't understand."

She stared up at him, all wide eyes and innocence. Could she really not see the truth? "Then make me understand, Nobody. I like you. You're an unusual man with an unusual talent and a code of honor that's all your own. A gunslinger from the Old West— minus the gun—just like the hero in a Louis L'Amour book. How does that make you a bad man?"

He wanted the talking to stop. He wanted to go back to the kissing part and he wanted to let the kissing go on and on until they were tangled up in each other, unable to tell where his skin ended and hers began.

But to do that would be to lie to her. And he wasn't going to do that. Not to her.

Stupid codes of honor. He would have rather her never known what kind of animal he was but she'd forced his hand, all because she wasn't afraid of him.

He couldn't bear to look her in the eyes. So he roughly pulled her into his chest and put his mouth near her ear. At first she was soft against him, like she was ready for the kissing to start back up.

"You should be afraid of me," he began, feeling the goodbye in his throat, "because I killed a man with my bare hands. I did hard time. I am *not* a good man."

Her body went ramrod straight. He let go of her and took a step back. Her eyes were wide-open with shock, her mouth stuck in a silent scream.

Yeah. His work here was done.

He turned and began to run. Not away from her—not because he was afraid of her, damn it all. Because that was the best way to keep her safe. To stay the hell away from her.

"Nobody," she called out after him.

He didn't stop.

CHAPTER ELEVEN

Melinda didn't sleep.

Of course he'd killed someone. Why did that surprise her? He was a rough man living in a rough place. She should probably count her lucky little stars that he hadn't killed anyone right in front of her the other night.

But she'd gotten this romantic notion in her head that he only fought out of necessity. Really? *Really*? God, she was so mad at herself. Of course he didn't fight out of necessity. It hadn't been a matter of life or death at the center, had it? No. Just some kids out looking for a little mayhem. And Nobody had gone in like a bull in a china shop. A *big* bull.

She'd been so distracted by the stabbing part of the fight that she hadn't realized how much he'd been the one starting the fight. They could have closed the door and called the cops—or at least Rebel—and then she could have painted over the graffiti. No one had to get hurt.

She was still sitting at the table when Rebel got up to make the coffee. Shirtless, of course. "Why didn't you tell me?"

He froze, back to her. "Tell you what?"

"Don't pull that innocent attitude with me. Nobody Bodine is a convicted killer."

He filled the carafe. "Who told you that?"

"He did."

"Did he, now," he replied in a casual tone.

She wanted to throw something at him. Something heavy. And pointy. "So let me get this straight, Rebel. I can't get help for that boy because the best possible option is to leave him in an abusive home so that he can continue to spend quality time with a convicted murderer?"

Rebel turned and gave her one of those irritating, all-seeing looks. "You didn't sleep."

"Quit changing the damn subject. Why didn't you tell me about him? Why did you let me think he was just some misunderstood guy with a hard-luck story?"

But instead of explaining himself, Rebel just kept staring at her as if she'd grown a second head overnight. "He didn't tell you how it happened." It wasn't a question. More of an observation.

"He killed someone! Isn't that what happened?"

"Who killed who?" Madeline stumbled into the kitchen wrapped in a thin cotton robe, her hair a wild nest of curls. "What's going on?"

Melinda had forgotten it was Saturday. "Nobody Bodine. He killed someone."

Madeline looked alarmed. "Last night?"

"No. Last night he just—" *Kissed me.* But she couldn't say it out loud.

She couldn't bring herself to admit that, once again, she'd found the least suitable man in a tri-county area and taken a shine to him. It wasn't the same thing as Tyrone getting blowjobs on the side, but was it really that different? Her taste in men was horrid. Abysmal. She should hie herself to a nunnery as fast as she could and stop inflicting the world with her romantic disasters. Because they were all disasters. All of them.

Rebel and Madeline shared a look, which only made Melinda that much madder. "Okay, fine. I kissed him. He kissed me back. And then he told me he was a convicted killer and disappeared off into the night. Another winner, right?" God, she really was going to throw something at the rate she was going. "I sure know how to pick 'em."

"Mellie..."

She cut Madeline off. "No, it's okay. I totally get it. I'm the outsider here and everyone thought it'd be best if I didn't know the sordid history of the man who cleans my child care center. I can see why that wouldn't be an important piece of information to add to the employee profile. I can see why you two have gone to such great lengths to make sure I knew you didn't think he was a dangerous guy. Because obviously, as a murderer, he's not, right?"

"Mellie." This was less a plea and more an order. "Calm down."

"Did you know?" She demanded of her sister. "Or did *he* not tell you, too?"

For once in her life, Madeline looked away. "I knew. Clarence told me. But it happened a long time ago."

She threw up her hands. "Oh, for God's sake. *Really?* That's your defense?"

"Calm down."

Was she hearing things or was the sanctimonious Rebel Runs Fast actually issuing orders? "I'm not listening to you." Then, even though some part of her realized it was childish, she crossed her arms and turned her back on him.

"It is not my story to tell," he said, pulling a chair up to the table. "So I didn't tell you."

"Bullshit. Still not talking to you."

"He was seventeen, from what I understand. I hadn't returned to the rez yet. I didn't know him. When I came back home..." There was a new note in his voice, one that was almost wistful. He cleared his throat. "Albert gave me some newspaper clippings. There was a fight in the bar. He claimed self-defense. He lost."

She fought the urge to stick her fingers into her ear and go LALALALA.

"According to the newspaper, Nobody had punched the guy just right and snapped his neck. He was dead before he hit the ground."

Her mind took the fight from last week and transplanted it to a bar—except instead of a guy's arm, it was a guy's neck. She shuddered. "Oh, and that's supposed to make me feel better?"

"She's like this," Madeline explained. "She promises she's not going to talk to you and then does it anyway. It's really irritating."

"Shut up," Melinda snapped. "You're not helping."

"He was tried as an adult and convicted of involuntary manslaughter. Sentenced to twelve years in prison, paroled after seven with time off for good behavior. Came back to the rez and disappeared into the back country."

It was weird to hear Rebel talk like this—just listing the facts instead of being all mystical and psychic over there. "According to the newspaper? What—are you saying he never told you?"

"Nope." He slurped his coffee, as if this were just another Saturday morning.

Nobody hadn't told Rebel? She felt a little better. But not much. She wondered if he'd ever told anyone about his childhood or if he only trusted her with that. "Why didn't you tell me?"

"It was not my story to tell." She rolled her eyes at him. "Everyone else here already knows what happened, or close to it. They have made their judgment and nothing will change that. I did not want to rob you of your chance to make your own judgment."

She glared at him. Stupid, compassionate medicine man. "Does he know you know?"

"Of course."

"And?"

Rebel gave her a sad look. "I gave him the newspaper articles and built the fire so he could burn them."

Her brain provided the scenery for her—Rebel and Nobody standing around a fire in the dead of night, burning the past away. What a miserable scene. What a miserable life. Or it had been. Was it still miserable? "You're trying to make me feel sorry for him."

He notched an eyebrow at her. "Is it working?"

"No." She wouldn't let her lousy judgment get the better of her and that was final. "Even if it was self-defense, he's still going around and picking fights like a—a vigilante, for God's sake. He shouldn't be around children. He shouldn't be around that boy."

Rebel gave her one of those searching looks that drove her bonkers. "That's your judgment to make, is it?"

And she was mad all over again. "Someone should be the grown up here," she snapped, fully aware that she wasn't the most mature person in the room. She went over to where the backpack was hanging by the door. It still had the knife in it. She grabbed the whole thing, then headed to the fridge for a couple of bottles of water. "If you won't step up, then why shouldn't I?"

"What are you doing?" Madeline asked with true concern in her voice.

"I'm going to go find that man."

Against Madeline's protests, Melinda loaded up some granola bars, water, the knife—just in case—and grabbed a hat. His hat. The one he'd left in a crumpled mess right after dropping the mother of all bombshells in the middle of what had, up to that point, been some really nice kissing. Such nice kissing that she would have been just fine if things had gone to second base. And maybe third.

Melinda seemed to recall her responsible older sister telling a tale about being so mad at Rebel that she wandered off into the plains with no water, no hat and no plan.

Well, Melinda would be different. She had a plan. Find Nobody's hidden little camp and drag the truth out of him. It was his story to tell? Fine. He'd damn well better tell it or she'd call social services first thing Monday morning. She wasn't about to let Jamie live in danger for a moment longer than was absolutely necessary.

Star, the horse she'd ridden home on, was still munching grass in the pasture behind Rebel's barn, which sort of surprised her. Nobody hadn't taken the horse home and Jamie hadn't come back for her.

"Here, girl," Melinda called. When the mare came plodding over, she said, "Do you remember how to get home? You do? Yay! Let's go home, girl!"

Using the pasture gate, Melinda climbed up on Star's back. It'd been one thing to ride a horse with no bridle or saddle with Nobody or Jamie leading the way, but this? She was basically powerless up on the back of this horse.

"Here we go," she said more to herself than to the horse. Star nickered and headed toward the wide-open spaces. "Good girl."

"Mellie, wait!" Madeline came jogging out of the house.

Melinda cringed. Must be time for another lecture about how irresponsible she was being and how she just needed to go to her room until she could calm down, as if she were still eight. "I'm going, Maddie. You can't stop me."

"I'm not stopping you. Here, you forgot the walkie talkie."

Melinda looked down at the proffered device her sister was holding. "What?"

Madeline shot her a look that was part glare, part grin. "First off, when has trying to talk you out of something impulsive ever worked?"

"Really?" She gaped at her sister. "Have aliens taken over your brain?"

"Don't make it worse," Madeline scolded her. "And second, you're trying to do right by a kid. I couldn't stop you from that even if I wanted to. But I don't. I asked you to come out here to take care of the kids and that's what you're doing."

Melinda was aware she was staring at her sister, but she couldn't believe that responsible, careful, *boring* Madeline was just going to send her on her merry way to confront a convicted murderer. Was she off the hook here or what? "Um... yeah. I am."

Madeline gave her a look. Oops, not off the hook yet. "But, that said, I expect you to be careful. I don't believe Nobody is a danger to you or that kid but that's no excuse not to be smart about it, okay?"

"Yeah, yeah, got it. Don't sneak up on him in the dead of night and yell *boo*." She touched her heels to Star's side.

"Check in when you can," Madeline called after her as Star headed down the hill and out toward the big, empty plain of grass. "Please."

"Okay, *Mom*," Melinda called back, knowing it would drive her sister bonkers.

"Mellie!" came the frustrated reply.

Star must have been ready to go home, because she didn't plod along. She walked with purpose, only occasionally stopping to grab a mouthful of grass. Melinda busied herself with trying to memorize the landmarks. She kept looking over her shoulder, hoping to keep Rebel and Madeline's hill in view. But after half an hour, it was just another hill, indistinguishable from the rest.

She looked forward. More hills, none of which had an obvious path running up them. Then it happened. Star stopped walking and began to graze in earnest.

"Come on, girl," Melinda said, kicking her sides a little harder. "There's grass at home, I bet. You can do it!"

Nothing.

Great. Just freaking great. She looked behind her again. Maybe the horse had bent enough grass that she could retrace her steps?

Nope. Nothing but amber waves of grain. Damn it.

She slid off, trying to get her bearings. Oh, crap. That was a bad idea. The grass in this prairie came almost up to her chest and she had no way of getting back on the horse. Looked like it was walking for her from here on out.

She patted the horse's neck. "Good try. Close, but no cigar, right?" Now what? She had no idea if Jamie had taken the same route away from camp as Nobody had taken toward it. She remembered the horse making random turns in the middle of the prairie before finally getting to the trees, but she couldn't replicate those steps if she'd been paying attention, and she'd been focused on making sure Nobody hadn't fallen off the horse first.

As she turned in a circle, feeling hopelessly lost, she... well, she didn't see something. But she *almost* saw something. Like the grass bending against the wind instead of with it.

"Hello? Is there someone out there?" Honestly, she didn't know what answer she was looking for. If it wasn't a *someone*, it might be a *something* and she'd heard the occasional howl of a wolf or a coyote or something that sounded hungry late at night.

She backed up against the horse, who seemed unconcerned. Okay, she would not panic. If the horse wasn't concerned, that probably put the chances of being eaten by a wild animal pretty low.

Wait—the horse wasn't concerned. Like, if there was someone out there, Star knew that person.

Like her owner.

Nobody was following her.

"You can come out now. I know you're there."

At first, nothing happened. She stepped away from Star and did another slow circle, trying to see where the grass was going the wrong direction again. It wasn't until she'd made a complete turn that suddenly, he was there, like he'd just materialized out of thin air about five feet away from her.

"Jesus, Nobody, stop sneaking up on me!"

He looked funny without his hat—something he seemed to realize, as he eyed it resting on her head. "This the first time I've snuck up on you."

"Yeah, okay, maybe." He was right. Usually, she could see

him there, which he didn't always like. "Why didn't I see you this time?"

He had the nerve to smile at her. It was a quick thing, barely a curve of his lips that softened his features from *brutal* to *striking*, but she saw it nonetheless. "Grass isn't see-through."

Now she felt silly. "And your horse? You have one, right? Red?"

"Sent her home."

"Of course." She glared at him. Because stalking her through the tall grass was easier on foot. He'd have been too visible on horseback. "Okay, talk."

The look of panic on his face made it clear that he'd been happier if she'd pulled a gun on him. "Talk?"

"I know it's not your strong suit, but I don't care. You kissed me last night and then dropped this huge bombshell and ran away and I'm not going to stand for it. I'm so mad at you I can hardly see straight. I mean, I've got horrible taste in men. Really bad. My last boyfriend cheated on me with another guy—and that wasn't the first time something like that's happened. And then you come along and I think I've met someone who's different—and dude, you are *different*—but to just announce that whole 'killed a man' thing in the middle of a really good kiss? Do you have any idea how much of an idiot I feel like right now?"

Her voice echoed back to her and she realized that she was yelling. But she did feel better.

"That—" He swallowed as his hands moved from his belt loops to his pockets and back. She almost wanted to give him his hat back so he'd have something to hold. "That wasn't my intention."

"Then what was your intention?" The moment she said it, she realized maybe she'd meant to say something else. Time to clarify. "And I'm not even talking about kissing me. You're looking after that boy and you better have a damn good reason as to why I shouldn't call social services and have him removed from his home." At that, Nobody paled. His gaze dropped and he ran a hand over his ponytail. Yeah, she'd hit a nerve. "So talk. Who did you kill?"

The last word stuck to her tongue like cotton candy on a humid day. Was she seriously having this conversation?

He shrugged. "Didn't know him. Only heard his name at the trial."

"How old were you? What happened?"

She saw his Adam's apple bob, but he didn't look up at her. "Seventeen. I went to bars a lot. Drinking made it... easier to be me, I guess. Didn't have to think as much. Didn't have to remember."

"Sheesh." He flinched at this. "Sorry. It's just seventeen is awfully young to be drinking yourself into oblivion. Please continue."

"This girl... she kissed me." The statement seemed to cause him physical pain. "I didn't kiss her first," he added in a desperate tone. "I fought a lot and sometimes, girls would get drunk and dare each other to kiss me. Because I was big and scary."

"Okay..." she hadn't anticipated a sexual element. "Can't argue with the big part. So she kissed you. How did that lead to you killing a man?"

"Her boyfriend didn't take kindly to it."

Lord, she could see this happening, too. A young, brazen Nobody Bodine getting wrapped up in a woman and then a bigger, older man getting pissed off.

"He threw the first punch, but he was drunk. I ducked. Punched back. He went down. Never got up."

"That's it? You punched a guy so hard you broke his neck?"

"Yes, Ma'am."

"How long ago did this happen?"

"I was in prison until I was 24. Got out six years ago."

She rubbed her eyes, trying to make sense of it all. Brutally attacked when he was thirteen. Living in the woods until he was seventeen. Fighting in bars. An arrest, prison time. Six more years of living in the woods. To think, her life was broken up into chunks by things like high school and college, first job and second—normal stuff. "How'd you meet Rebel? He said he didn't know you before."

There was a pained silence. "I went to see Albert after I got out. He was the only person who ever treated me kindly. Rebel was there. He didn't treat me like a nobody who came from a nobody and would always be a nobody."

The way he said that—like the way that gang guy Dwayne had said it—sounded rote. "Who said that? Who told you you'd always be a nobody?" He didn't answer, but she figured it out anyway. "Your mom, right?"

That got her a sharp nod.

"Jesus, Nobody. What am I supposed to do here? Convicted felons don't get to look after little kids. Hell, they don't get to look after not-so-little kids."

"I know." He sounded defeated about it.

But she didn't feel the same way she had this morning. Damn it all, she didn't know what to do. He'd killed a man with one stupid punch. He was dangerous. And he knew it. But she wasn't sure that made him a bad man. Not like he claimed he was. Just... not a good one all the time. "Why that boy? Why Jamie?"

Nobody shrugged. "He needed someone."

"Like you needed someone?"

"Only I never had anyone."

Dammit. "Why didn't you just tell me this instead of springing it on me and then bolting last night? I swear, I'm not hiding a boyfriend who'd go all ape-shit on you. I need a reason, Nobody. A reason to trust you."

He shrugged, looking more miserable than when he'd been stabbed.

"Did you burn your mom's house down?"

"No."

"Seriously?"

"Some people moved in, started a fire—it was winter. It got out of control."

"Jesus, are they okay?"

"Yeah. They got out."

Okay, so they could eliminate arson. That counted for something. What, she didn't know. But something. "What else? How do you..." Her voice trailed off as she watched him.

Nobody was no longer staring at her or the ground. Instead, he'd gone on high alert. There was no other way to describe it. His shoulders dropped, his head popped up, and his body tensed as he—was he sniffing the air? "What?"

He looked over her shoulder, then up into the air. Without

looking at her, he said, "Get on the horse," in a voice so cold it made her shiver.

"*What?*"

Before she could process what happened next, he had her around the waist and had half-lifted, half-thrown her onto Star's back with so much force that she almost fell over the other side. This was why normal people used saddles—something to hold onto. She grabbed at Star's mane. "What's happening?"

As she spoke, he launched himself up behind her. How did he do that? Then his arm was around her waist, holding her tight. "If you wanted to do this, you could have just asked," she managed to get out as all of his muscles surrounded her. It wasn't like she hadn't touched him before. Hell, they'd already been in this basic position, bodies pressed together.

But there was a world of difference between her holding up a wounded man and a significantly less wounded man holding her. The sheer strength that surrounded her tried to take her breath away. For a man who was physically throwing her around, being in his arms felt *safe*. Not like a murderer kidnapping her. Like a man protecting her.

God, she hoped she wasn't wrong about this.

He didn't reply. Instead, he whipped his hat off her head and slapped it against the horse's flank. "*Hiiii*," he hissed, his voice low in her ear.

Star got the message. She leapt into a gallop like Nobody had jabbed her with a pin. A really big pin.

"Whoa!" Melinda yelled as the whole horse felt like she fell away. For a second, Melinda was flying through the air, anchored only by the arm around her waist.

Then she crashed back onto the horse's back with enough force that she saw stars. *Ow.* "Jesus, Nobody—"

"Shh," was the reply she got as he leaned forward, bending her body with his—asking the horse to go faster. And faster.

There was none of the random, meandering path toward the hills. This time, they rode hell for leather in a straight line to the trees. She held onto Star's mane and tried to grip the animal's side with her legs, but it was Nobody who kept her from sliding off. With each length, her body was pushed back into his and he never moved. Of course, he probably had a lot more practice galloping bareback than she did—which was to say none. Plus, she still had on her backpack. It's not like she could sit back and enjoy the way his muscles pressed against her—not when water bottles were digging into her spine.

She had no idea what was going on. Nothing new there. But something had startled him and she was apparently along for the ride. So she held on tight. It was all she could do.

Star had closed the distance to about three hundred feet when Melinda heard it—a low, droning hum that filled the air around them. *Helicopter*, she realized as Nobody slapped his hat against the horse's flank again. What the hell was a helicopter doing all the way out here?

Looking for something. Or someone.

Oh, hell.

She tried to look around to see if she could spot the helicopter, but when she turned her head, all she could see what Nobody's face. His chin was on her shoulder and she could almost see his eyes. He wasn't looking at anything but the trees.

Star ran faster—much faster than Melinda would have given the old mare credit for. They hit the hill and made it under the trees in what sure as hell felt like record time.

Nobody got the horse to slow down, somehow. A woman had to admire a man who was such an accomplished rider that he could control his animal seemingly by telepathy. Star did a half turn so that both of them could see out through the trees.

A few minutes later, a helicopter went by, far lower than normal. Maybe only a thousand feet off the ground, it flew down the center of the grass valley. As it passed, Melinda saw no police markings or guns. It appeared to be a standard two-seater helicopter. Didn't even look like there was a camera mounted on the outside.

"What the hell?"

"Shh," Nobody whispered in her ear. "Hunters."

"Hunters? Hunting what?" Not him, she hoped.

He leaned forward, following the helicopter as it flew on. When it was out of sight, he said, "Mountain lions, most likely," in a normal tone of voice. "Scouting out where they'll drop a hunting party."

"Did you just say there were *mountain lions* in these hills?" Oh, sweet Jesus. Rebel had informed her that the wolves and coyotes would not come anywhere near the house, but he hadn't said a thing about lions. *Lions*!

He sat up and leaned back. The next thing she knew, he was peeling her pack off her back. "What's in here?"

"Um, water, walkie-talkies, that knife." So, effectively, he was disarming her.

He snorted behind her. She turned as much as she could, expecting to see him drop the pack onto the ground. But he didn't. He slid the straps over his shoulders. Then he ran a hand down her back. "Hope it didn't hurt you too much."

The slow, steady pressure of his hand against her took all the panic she'd felt during the race to the trees and turned it sideways. Her body shuddered as his touch lingered. "Not too much," she admitted, suddenly unable to speak normally. Her voice was low and breathy.

In the distance, she heard the sounds of the chopper growing louder. "They're coming back."

"Yup." He slipped his arm around her waist and pulled her back into his chest. This time, without the pack between them, she could feel his rock-solid chest pressing against hers. "We need to keep moving, in case they've got infrared cameras."

There was no path here and the going was slow for Star. They heard the helicopter pass by again, but they were already deeper into the woods. She leaned back into him, which had more to do with the incline of the hill than the way his body surrounded her. Really. "What happens if a hunting party finds you?"

"Hasn't happened yet."

Yet. Not a terribly comforting word.

CHAPTER TWELVE

They rode on. Nobody kept a firm grip on her. To keep her from sliding off the horse. It had nothing to do with the way she'd been furious with him—but hadn't attacked him or called him names. It had even less to do with the way her back leaned against his chest, warm and soft and inviting. And it had absolutely nothing to do with the way her ass slid back into his dick with each step Star took.

"Are we going back to your camp?" It could have sounded worried. She had every reason to be concerned. After all, he'd heard the helicopter coming and reacted without thinking how she might feel about running for cover. But he didn't hear anything in her tone that told him she was scared.

He hoped. "Not yet." He felt her sigh, her chest rising and falling and pulling his along with her. "Going the opposite way first. Throw them off the trail."

"You're a little paranoid, you know that?"

He chuckled. He couldn't help himself. When he'd heard the copter coming, he'd been terrified that it'd be someone who shot first and asked questions later. That wasn't such a problem for him, but he couldn't handle the thought of anything happening to her. "Just because I'm paranoid doesn't mean they're not out to get me."

She leaned back against him, letting him hold her weight up. Then she rolled her head toward where his was hovering over—not touching—her shoulder. "You know Jack's been watching the clinic and the center, right?"

He swallowed. Jack normally worked for Jacob Plenty Holes, guarding his horses. They had a sort of unspoken gentlemen's

139

agreement not to mess with each other. The fact that the sheriff had seen fit to bring Jack in did not bode well. That, more than anything, was why he'd bolted for the trees. The sheriff wasn't turning any cheek, it seemed. Nobody wouldn't put it past him to have gotten ahold of a chopper. "Jamie told me."

"You know he's not going to arrest you, right? I asked. He said he wasn't. You can come back to work. No more sneaking around in the dark."

He snorted. "Not gonna risk jail on his word. It'd be a big coup for him to catch me." Just thinking about the narrow cell made him break out in a sweat.

Jail. He'd told her everything about prison. Well, not everything. He didn't see fit to tell her about how the good behavior part of his parole actually didn't start until about the second year, when everyone else had learned to leave him alone rather than tangle with him. He would've been out sooner, except for that first year.

"You don't like being inside, do you?"

"No, Ma'am." Being inside was a trap. Didn't matter if it were a closet or a cell.

"What do you do in the winter?"

"Don't mind the cold."

"Really?" She wasn't buying that answer, that much was clear. "What about when it snows? Madeline said you guys get blizzards out here. Real ones."

"That's why I borrowed the trailer."

"*Stole.* You stole it."

"No one was using it. Sat there for years."

She made a clucking sound of disapproval, but instead of scolding him some more she let go of the horse's mane and put her hands on his arms. The ones crisscrossed around her waist. "How do you do that thing where no one sees you?"

"Don't know." That was the truth.

"Have you always been able to do it?"

He shook his head before he realized she couldn't see him. "Couldn't do it before."

"*Before what?* I swear, you are the most infuriating man to have a conversation with." But the way she said it was less disapproving, like her sister, and more something that might have been amused. He hoped.

"Before the closet."

"Oh."

"But when I was in there—I had all these hallucinations. *Dreams.* Visions, Albert said. My vision quest."

"O... kay..." He grinned at her flabbergasted tone. She shouldn't be surprised that things had suddenly gotten all mystical again. Hell, he did have a way of becoming a shadow. That wasn't normal. "What were these dreams?"

He didn't want to tell her. He'd never told anyone but Albert about the dreams—and that was only because he was weak and confused and so scared. He'd never even told Rebel about it, although he'd hazard a guess that the man had figured something close enough to the truth.

Besides, talking wasn't something he was good at. On the other hand, he needed to give her a reason. She'd said so herself, right before they'd been buzzed by that copter. And, given how she was leaning back against him, touching him—he wanted to kiss her again. But he didn't want another kiss with her to blow up in his face, either. Better to get this over with.

He took a deep breath and dug the memory out. The scene was hazy around the edges now, dulled with time. But seventeen years ago, it'd been so real. *So* real. "A coyote came out of the dark. As he got close to me, he changed into a man. Sat with me while I was in there. Talked to me in Lakota. I don't speak it. Don't know what he said. Then he got up and changed back into a coyote and left. That's when Albert came and got me."

She was quiet for a moment, which was something. At least she wasn't calling him nuts or anything. Not yet. "Is that... normal? Or were you hallucinating werewolves? No—wait, you said coyote. Werecoyotes? Is that even a thing?"

"Albert, he said the spirit world had opened up to me. Said my ancestor had come to me and I would be like them—sometimes good, sometimes bad. Sometimes a man and sometimes... not."

A trickster, Albert had said. *Mica,* the coyote, an old figure from an old religion that Nobody didn't believe in, had been a shape-changer who'd played tricks on the old Lakota. Sometimes he'd helped them, sometimes he'd tricked them. Sometimes, those tricks left a man dead.

But he didn't tell her that. He wasn't sure she believed him anyway. Hell, he didn't believe all that crap about *Mica* the trickster who would play games with *Iktomi*, the spider-man, an age-old story of one-upmanship. Those stories were just fairy tales. Not real.

Except...

"You're a what—a shapeshifter? You change into a *coyote?*"

"No, Ma'am. Never had four legs." He sighed. All this talking was wearing him down. "Just two."

"So how do you do it?"

He couldn't tell her. Hell, he didn't even know if he could show her. But he'd try. Only for her.

He let go of her waist and held his arms out straight in front of her. She didn't pull her hands back, but let them rest on his forearms. They were under a canopy of trees that blocked the sunlight from reaching the forest floor. Plenty of shadows. He let himself feel the pull of the darkness. The same darkness that had brought the shapeshifter to his side.

The hairs on his arms stood up and his scalp tingled, but at no point did he become invisible or immaterial. Her hands didn't slide through him. He did not grow hair or paws and claws or anything. Not that he'd expected to, but he knew she was watching for it.

Instead, she jolted forward, pulling her body away from his. "What. The. Hell," she said in an awestruck voice. "Did you just... shock me?"

He shrugged as he let his arms drop back around her waist. He hoped she wouldn't shove him away. Everyone else in this world thought he was a freak, with the possible exception of Rebel. He didn't want her to think that way about him.

It'd been a damn long time since he'd cared what anyone thought of him.

"Okay, so let me get this straight." She leaned back, casually placing her hand back on top of his. She didn't get hysterical and demand to get off this horse or go home right now. "You had a vision of a shapeshifter while you were wounded and starving as a teenager, right?"

Three days without food or water—especially the water—probably counted as starving. "Yeah."

"And since that time, you can... generate a small electrical field? On command?"

"Guess so."

"And everyone has trouble seeing you when you do that."

"Except you." He squeezed her tighter before he wondered if maybe she wouldn't like it.

She hugged his arms tighter around her waist. "Sometimes good and sometimes bad, huh?"

"Yeah. Working on the good part."

She appeared to think this part over. "Do you still go to bars?"

He didn't hesitate. "No." He was too busy these days, what with a regular job at night and Jamie and keeping an eye on things in general. "I don't go looking for trouble."

"But it finds you anyway."

He looked at the woman in his arms. This close up, he could see the faint freckles that dotted her cheeks and nose. Her ears were pierced, but she didn't have any earrings in right now. And her hair—wild red curls tickled against his cheek.

Was she trouble? Maybe. She'd already messed up his careful little world in ways that he hadn't even thought possible. Before Melinda Mitchell, Nobody had trusted Rebel and Jamie and that was it. Now he was riding out to his place with a white woman who talked too much and was absolutely not afraid of him.

"I work at it. Haven't had a drink since that day." Suddenly his mouth was dry. That had been the last time a woman had kissed him—touched him. He didn't count Dr. Mitchell. She touched him, but needles were almost always involved. There was nothing sexual about.

But when Melinda touched him... well, *sexual* wasn't the right word. But there was something sensual about the way her creamy-smooth skin was pressed against his, her heavy breasts resting on top of his arms, her body was reclined against his. The way she'd kissed him last night. "Haven't... haven't done a lot of things since that day."

He felt the tension ripple through her as she looked over her shoulder at him. She stared at him, her mouth wide open. "You... haven't?"

"No." His voice had dropped down to a bare whisper. He wasn't even sure if he'd spoken out loud.

One of her hands reached up and he tensed. But she didn't push him away or smack him. Instead, her fingers skimmed along his hair, wrapping around his head and pulling him down toward her. "Until last night." Her breath mixed with his, sweetening the air around him.

"Until last night," he agreed, letting her pull his mouth to her lips.

The kiss was different this time. Maybe that was because he wasn't at war with himself anymore. He'd told her the worst of it and she hadn't damned him to hell. Instead she was still in his arms, tracing his lips with her tongue. *Yeah,* he thought as he opened his mouth for her and let his tongue meet hers.

Her teeth tugged on his lower lip—not quite the same nip she'd given him last night, but more than enough to take the sensual nature of the kiss to the next level. The half-erection he'd been trying to keep under control went full-on in a heart beat.

"Was that better?" she murmured, her mouth still against his.

Better wasn't the word for it. "Yeah."

"And I can do it again?"

He clutched her tighter, pressing her ass against his throbbing dick. "Yeah."

"Good." She kissed him again, letting her hand slide down to the back of his neck.

He couldn't help himself. Not when it came to her. One of his hands moved up her ribs, over the thin tank top she was wearing, until he was cupping her breast.

God, what a breast. Her flesh filled his hand, firm and heavy and he wanted to get off this damn horse and lay her down and bury himself in her body and hold her for as long as he could.

"Mmmm," she hummed against him. "Gentle." But it wasn't a criticism.

"Okay." He needed to keep his head together and not think with his dick. But he couldn't seem to kiss her and touch her at the same time. Something about being out of practice, maybe.

So he focused on touching her. He kissed her forehead before he settled his chin back on her shoulder so he could watch what he did to her. He let his fingertips trail up the underside of her breast until they reached her nipple—fully pointed through her bra. He gave it a tug. A gentle tug.

"Oh," she moaned, her head still turned to the side. "*Yes.*"

Yes. Best word ever.

He kept stroking her, trying to memorize the map of her skin, but there was clothing in the way. So he shifted to stick his hand up under her shirt.

The bra felt thin—no padding or anything—and lacy. *Lace.* God help him. Going slow was getting harder by the minute. The second.

"I know I ask this a lot," she said in a breathless way, "but how much longer until we get to camp?"

He forced himself to look away from where his skin touched hers—and only because there was the promise of something good in her voice, something that involved little to no clothing in the way. It took a moment for him to recognize where he was, but then he saw the deer path at the top of the hill. "Not far."

"You said that last time, too." Then—Jesus—she wiggled, her bottom grinding against his dick with a pressure that made him lightheaded.

He pressed his feet into Star's side—one forward, one back—and turned her toward the path. Once she was on it, she knew where she was going and he could turn his attention back to the woman who was demanding his attention and so much more.

"I think there's a condom in the backpack," she said as he debated the merits of unhooking her bra or just pushing it down.

"That's... good." That was something he hadn't given much thought to in a really long time. He'd have to get some more of those things if that was how she wanted this to go.

Because any way she wanted it to go was how he wanted it to go.

Finally, he decided to slip his hand underneath her bra. The metal part dug into his hand, but it didn't hurt. Not compared to the heat of his palm cupping her skin, his fingers rolling her nipple back and forth—her moans of pleasure.

"I like that," she got out in tiny gasps.

Yeah, he liked it, too. It was almost too much and not enough at the same time. His other hand started to edge down, over the zipper of her jeans, until he was cupping her.

"Oh, Mr. Bodine," she moaned as he pressed against her until he found the place that made her shiver and grab hold of his arms.

He growled, the name feeling oddly foreign on him—but good, too. Like he was doing this right.

Because he wanted to do this right. Then maybe he'd get to do it again. Back when he'd been a young, stupid punk, he'd taken the comfort a girl would offer him. But that sex had been flavored with whiskey, drunken fumbles in the back of cars or against a wall. Nothing either of them would remember. Just a way to forget.

He wanted to remember this. Every single detail. The pressure of her fingertips digging into the back of his neck as she rode his hand. The little noises she made in the back of her throat as he tugged at her nipple. The sweetness of her breath on his lips. He wanted to keep it all locked in his mind until the day he died.

He was doing this to her. She was letting him. He didn't have to move his hands much. The rocking motion of the horse's pace did a lot of the work for him. He focused on direction. Did she like it better when he went from side to side or in small circles?

She gasped, her back arching against his chest. Circles. Definitely.

"Yeah," she moaned, a breathy sound that brushed over his ears like a kiss. "Oh, Mr. Bodine!"

He liked that name, but when he'd fantasized about a moment like this—and fantasize he had—he'd heard her say something else.

But he didn't want to tell her that right now. He wanted to focus on the feeling of her filling his palm—her breathing and gasping and moaning, all because of him. Because she trusted him.

There were things he wanted to do to her, for her—bite her on the shoulder, grab her—but he didn't want to frighten her. So he focused on the small, gentle things he could safely do. Teasing her nipple, rubbing her clit. Giving without taking. Giving her a reason to trust him.

"Yeah—oh—*yeah*," she groaned, her back going rigid against him, her legs pressing back as she ground her whole weight down onto his hand. "Oh, *yeah.*"

Then she crumpled against him as the tension bled out of her body. "*Oh,*" she said in a satisfied whisper as she sagged back. "Oh, Mr. Bodine."

"Okay?" God, he hoped he hadn't hurt her, done something she didn't like.

"No," she said in a dreamy voice.

Crap. He'd gone too far. Why couldn't he have just kept his hands to himself? Why did she make him want to put himself out there? Why—

"*So* much better than okay," she said in that same voice as she pulled his head down to where her lips were red and warm and waiting for his kiss. "*So* much better."

Yeah, he thought again. He'd done right by her and that was what mattered—more than him being a freak or a felon or a menace to society, he'd taken care of her. It made him feel damn proud of himself, even if he didn't quite understand why that was. Especially given the way his dick was throbbing in frustration.

Then she nipped at his lower lip, dragging her teeth over his skin with just the right amount of pressure. He groaned into her as his dick did a whole hell of a lot more than throb. He would not take a thing she didn't offer—but if she offered—

Yeah, if she offered, it'd be wrong to refuse her, right? Downright rude. And ungentlemanly.

She broke the kiss to say, "I want you. *Now.*"

"Yes, Ma'am." He forced himself to pull his hands away from her welcoming body and grab onto Star's mane. "Hold on."

He hadn't meant for her to hold onto him—he'd thought she'd grab the horse's mane—but she held onto his arms as he urged the horse forward.

They took off at a steady canter, Star easily following the path back to where his camp was hidden in the trees. He needed to cool the animal down after this—a couple of hard runs with twice the weight she normally carried—but he needed to heat Melinda up more.

He was breathing hard, but he couldn't tell if that was from the run or from the woman. Didn't matter.

She mattered.

That was all.

CHAPTER THIRTEEN

One moment, she was flying. The next, the horse was flying. Both made her lightheaded.

Jesus, she couldn't believe how Nobody had reduced her to a quivering mess with just a few light touches. It was like... foreplay. Real foreplay.

Back when she was dating metrosexuals with sexuality issues, foreplay had been very little *fore*, even less *play*. At least, that's how it seemed to her. There'd be some kissing, some oral—almost always her on the giving end—and then sex. Like sex was the only part that mattered and everything else was just delaying the good stuff. Like suffering through crappy previews for movies you didn't want to see before the show you'd paid money to watch.

But in Nobody's hands?

He'd touched her so hesitantly at first, like he was afraid he was going to break her with the pads of his fingertips. Well, he had—but in the very best way possible.

There was something about someone else giving you an orgasm instead of giving it to yourself—she could never replicate Nobody's strong arms surrounding her, holding her up. Or his warm breath cascading over her shoulders. Or the way his erection had pressed into her with such obvious need. No vibrator could ever do that for her.

Her sister Madeline would tell Melinda that she was being stupid—would remind her that little less than a few hours ago, she'd been ready to call the cops on Nobody and have him thrown back into jail and now, here she was, still reeling from the power of the climax he'd unleashed upon her, heading back to his camp with every intention of unleashing a few more climaxes.

But she didn't care. Maybe this wasn't the smartest decision she'd ever made but surely it wasn't the worst, either. How was being with a man who'd fought to defend her, who protected a vulnerable kid, who was working on being good—how was being with him bad?

It wasn't. No worse than being with a man who slept with other men on the down low and lied to her about it. Nobody hadn't lied to her. He'd put her first.

She had things she wanted to do to him, things that did not involve horses but did involve a startling lack of clothing. Even now, her jeans were chafing against the spot where he'd rubbed, an irritating reminder that she was still wearing the damn things.

Then the horse slowed down just as she broke through the trees and into a little clearing decorated with twinkle lights.

"Here," Nobody growled in her ear. The next thing she knew, he'd slid off the horse, his hands trailing down her leg as he went.

She swung her leg over the back of the horse, trying to avoid kicking him in the face. She didn't need to worry—he caught her foot and guided her down.

Then he pressed all those muscles against her back, almost pinning her against the horse. "You... you don't have to do this," he said.

She heard it in his voice then—the same terrified tension she'd heard last night when he'd pinned her arms to her side and then told her about killing a man.

She pushed back against him, feeling the hard bulge in his jeans almost-but-not-quite grinding against her butt. "You don't have to be afraid of me."

"I'm not." It wasn't as defensive as it'd been last night, but his statement did nothing to explain why he was hiding where she couldn't see him.

She turned. He let her. So that was progress. His arms were tight around her waist, his erection pressing hard against her. All good things that could easily lead to great things. But his eyes— his eyes told a different story.

Maybe he wasn't afraid of her. But something about her being here with him had him nervous.

She hoped it was just the long years alone. Thirteen, if she'd understood him correctly. That was a hell of a long time to go without sex. Hell, she could barely make it three months.

She cupped his butt in her hands, feeling the tight muscles shift. Yeah, three months had been a long time for her. Thirteen years was a lifetime.

He growled as she palmed him—but it wasn't a sound of aggression or even anger. She squeezed harder and pushed him against her, feeling the stiff erection that was just waiting for her.

She slid her hands up front and began working at his zipper. Would he tell her "Don't" again, like he had last time? Or would he let her touch him?

The answer to both questions was no. He didn't tell her to stop, but he grabbed her hands just as the button on his jeans gave. "I..." he swallowed hard. "We need to not stand."

She nodded, letting her hand skim over his side. He didn't do anything to betray any weakness—no wincing, no moans of pain—but yeah, he'd been stabbed not terribly long ago. "I'll be on top." That way, he wouldn't have to over-exert himself or pull something.

His face shot bright red, but his only other reaction was a quick nod of his head in the direction of the chaise lounge.

Perfect. Well, not perfect—she hadn't had a lot of sex *al fresco*. That was part of living in a big city—parks were not conducive to a quickie because there were always too many people around. But at least this way they wouldn't have to spend half an hour moving books off a bed. Plus, the chaise lounge was in an upright position. Bonus.

She took his hand and led him toward the chair. He started to sit, but she held him up. For a man who'd picked her up and thrown her onto the back of a horse with no warning—not to mention the orgasm—he seemed more than a little hesitant about this whole thing.

"I won't hurt you," she said as she pushed the straps of the backpack off his shoulders and peeled his t-shirt off. This time, she didn't see the scars so much. Just the muscles. God, the muscles. She let her hands drift over his chest and down his arms before she leaned over and licked his nipple.

He grunted in surprise and tottered back, almost losing his balance.

Right—they were working on that whole not-standing thing. She pushed his jeans down and was surprised to see his enormous erection straining against a pair of black boxer briefs. For some reason, she'd thought a man like him might have gone commando. "Nice," she said, hoping it would put him at ease.

Then she slipped her hands under his waistband and pushed the briefs off. His dick sprang free, at full attention. She wanted to stroke him—to make him moan like he'd done to her on the ride here—but she didn't want to wear him out before they even got to the fun stuff.

Nobody's arms were stiff at his side, like he wanted to touch her but wasn't allowing himself to do that. "Sit," she told him as she put her hands on his shoulders and guided him toward the lounge chair.

He sat, but he didn't look comfortable. Everything about him was stiff, not just the parts that were standing at full attention.

He had no idea what he was doing. The realization hit her like a slap. He hadn't thought about what he was doing on the ride over here—he'd just done it. But now he was thinking and, if last night had been any indication, trying to find a way to talk himself out of this.

"This is the part," she began as she stripped off her shirt, "where you compliment me."

He stared at her breasts with an uncomplicated need. Men weren't really that difficult. A nice bra made everything better. "Compliment?" The word sounded foreign in his mouth, as if the thought had never crossed his mind.

"Here—I'll show you." She undid the button on her jeans and slowly began to wriggle out of them. "Hands down, you have the most amazing muscles I've ever seen. Seriously, you're like a god, only hotter."

His cheeks turned an interesting shade of red, but he didn't look away from her as she stepped out of her jeans and kicked them aside. Then she was in her bra and hipster panties and nothing else. In the full light of day. There was something oddly freeing about being nearly naked outside.

He swallowed. "You're... beautiful."

She struck a pose, her hands on her hips and her breasts thrust out and up. "Good! That was good." Then she turned her backside toward him and bent over, giving him a full view of her butt and the little panties that barely covered it. The groan that came from his direction as she rummaged in the backpack was worth it.

Yup, one lonely little condom down at the bottom. It'd have to do for now. She straightened up and walked over to him. His hands were back into clenched fists held by his side.

But she didn't straddle him, not yet. He was trying to hold onto his control and she was sick of it. So instead of rolling the condom onto him, she lowered her lips to his dick and kissed his tip.

Everything about him tensed, which jerked his dick away her mouth. So she wrapped her hand around his shaft and licked his length.

A low moan—of pain or pleasure, she couldn't tell—pulled free of his chest as she went down on him. God, he was huge. She could barely get her lips wrapped around him. Licking was the better option, so she went with that.

She looked up at him, but instead of him watching her, his head was back and his eyes were closed. And his hands were still clenched at his side. "This is the part," she said as she kissed his tip again, "where you should touch me."

"Don't..." She stroked his length again and he clenched his teeth. And probably a few other muscles, but the teeth were the ones he was having trouble speaking around. "Don't want to hurt you."

For crying out loud. "You won't hurt me. And if you do something that doesn't work, I'll tell you and you'll back off a bit. Simple. Now touch me."

"But—"

"*Touch me*. Pick up that massive hand and stroke my hair while I go down on you." She didn't wait for another reason why he couldn't let himself enjoy this. Instead she took him into her mouth again, swirling her tongue around his tip.

Then she felt it—his hand resting on the top of her head. Not quite stroking, not yet, but it was a start. "Good," she said as she licked him again. Positive reinforcement and all that.

At some point, he began to relax. His hips started to move in time with her hands, his fingers began to tangle with her hair. Then he began to make noise—small noises that sounded as if she were ripping them directly out of his chest.

If she weren't so turned on by this whole thing—having complete control over a man who followed no law but his own—she'd hold him until he'd finished. He'd already given her one orgasm, after all—fair was fair. But she was feeling a little too selfish for that. No way was she going to let this opportunity pass her by. *No way.*

Slowly, she brought the oral to an end. She stroked slower, went from licking and sucking to kissing, then from kissing his dick to kissing his thigh to his stomach, to kissing her way up his chest. She didn't avoid the scars, but she didn't seek them out, either. She didn't want to make him self-conscious—didn't want to do anything to spook him.

Funny how he was the one worried about her—*she* was worried about *him.*

As she made her slow ascent up his body, he untangled his fingers from her hair and let them move over her body. He still wasn't looking at her, but he was breathing hard as he ran his hands up and down her back.

"Look at me," she told him when she was straddling him, the heavy weight of his erection pressing against her. She still had the condom in hand. She needed to remember to use it.

He opened his eyes—the need in them almost took her breath away. *Yes,* she thought with a wicked grin, he was still holding out on her.

She ground her hips against him, feeling his length slide against her. "Do you want me?"

He nodded. Of course he did.

"Tell me you want me."

"I want you." He swallowed as she slid over him again. "You want me?"

She grinned at him as she leaned down to kiss him. He took the kiss, pressing her against his chest. "*So* much," she whispered against the skin of his neck. "I'm going to ride you now."

"Okay."

Yeah, he wasn't one for much pillow talk. She slid back and

half stood, half crouched over him. Quickly, she rolled the condom onto him. He didn't move. She wasn't sure he was even breathing as she scooted back up. And he'd closed his eyes again.

Damn, he was a stubborn man.

She positioned him and let herself fall upon him. Her body, already warmed up from the earlier horse ride and primed from the oral, took him in. "God," she whispered as he filled her. Oh, how he filled her—she shook as he hit parts of her that almost cried out in relief.

He jolted beneath her, his hands on her hips as he kept her from going further. "We can stop."

Stop? Was he insane? That was the very last thing she wanted him to do. "No, the correct choice there was, 'You feel good.'" Somehow, she managed to sound calm about it but calm was something she was rapidly losing control of. She pushed against his hands and let her body settle completely onto his. "Because *you* feel good inside of me. I like it. A lot."

"You do?"

"Oh my God, yes." She raised herself off him so far that she almost pulled free of him, then she took him in again—a little fast this time. A little harder. Then, because it was pretty obvious that he wasn't going to pick up on the finer points of lovemaking on his own, she said, "Kiss me when I do that."

His eyelids fluttered open as half a smile crooked the corner of his mouth. "Yes, Ma'am."

She rose and fell on him again as he kissed her. And he kissed her well. The more she rode him, the better it felt. He was hitting spots that hadn't been properly hit in a long time. She found a rhythm that worked well. "God." Her head rolled back, but he didn't take advantage of his location. "Kiss my breasts."

He pressed his lips against the left one, then said, "Can I do more than kiss?"

"Please." It was supposed to sound all in charge—she was in charge here—but it came out as a whimper because his body was driving up into hers with a little more force now, the friction building as their bodies moved together.

Then he took her breast into his mouth, his teeth scraping along her nipple with the just-right amount of pressure. She moaned, grabbing hold of his head and holding it against her breast.

"Yes," she hissed. "Yes, just like that. Oh, Mr. Bodine."

"Say my name," he said, his voice low and dangerous and the most sexy thing she'd ever heard. Then he nipped at her again.

She was chipping away at his control, bit by bit. She needed him to let go, to give himself up to her entirely. She'd never needed something so very bad in her entire life. "Yes, Nobody." It came out as the barest of whispers, breathy and girly and almost timid.

"Say it..." he shifted his attention to her other breast. "Louder. Say my name louder."

She tilted his head up and looked him in the eye. "Make me."

Maybe it wasn't the smartest thing she'd ever said in bed, but by God, it proved to be one of the most effective. Anything hesitant or restrained about him seemed to shatter under the weight of the challenge.

He grabbed her hips and slammed them down onto his with a guttural growl. "Say. It."

"Yes, Nobody." She purposefully kept it quiet.

He filled his hands with her ass, pulling her apart so he could angle himself in deeper. "Louder," he demanded, slamming up into her again.

This time, she couldn't keep her voice quiet. The force of him driving into her hit her just right. "Oh, Nobody!"

"Louder," he growled again, squeezing her ass so hard she could feel the marks of his fingers on her flesh.

"Yes, like that, Nobody." She didn't say it loud enough, so he bit her on the breast, just above the nipple. "Oh, Nobody!"

He had her now, had complete control over her as he drove up into her body from below. Then he let go of her ass and grabbed her breast, squeezing her nipple while he ran his teeth over the other one.

"Yes—oh, God—yes, Nobody. A little rough, just like that. Oh, God—Nobody."

"You feel so good," he managed to get out as he pinched her nipple between his thumb and forefinger. "Louder."

She was starting to unravel, but the feeling of him giving up his control to her—of him pawing at her—there was something basic and right about it. None of this prissy, fussy sex. Just a man on the edge of reason, pushing her past it.

But she needed something more. She grabbed his face and dragged it up to hers. There was no anger, no pain in his eyes. Just sheer, naked need mixed with old-fashioned lust. "Make me."

"Woman," he growled. A shadow of doubt flitted over his face.

She ground her hips down on his, trying to pull him back from those ridiculous worries about hurting her. "*Make me.*"

He grabbed her by the hips again, but this time, as he drove up into her, one of his hands swung down against the bare flesh of her ass. "Louder," he demanded.

"Nobody!" she cried out—not in pain, no. The quick bite of his hand against her skin didn't hurt—but it did make everything in her body tense up. Including the parts that surrounded his dick. God, it felt good to have everything clench against him like that.

He froze. "Did I—"

"God, do it again. Please do it again!"

He growled—a deep sound filled with longing. "Say it louder," he demanded, then—*smack.*

"Nobody!" she shouted, digging her fingers into his shoulders and holding on for dear life. All she could think about was the way his body had complete control of hers—he could do anything he wanted to her right now and she was powerless to stop him.

He squeezed her ass again—squeezed it hard. "Louder," he ordered again before another smack connected.

"*Ohhhh!*" She couldn't even get the word formed as the climax ripped through her. All she could do was hold onto him as he thrust harder into her. His mouth clamped down on her breast again, the nip of his teeth making sure she was completely undone.

He thrust up once—twice—a third time before he froze. Silently, of course. Then he fell back against the chair, panting.

She collapsed against him, pulling free from him without letting go of him.

They lay there for a few long minutes, chests heaving, skin cooling off. "You are amazing," she whispered against his skin.

"I didn't... I didn't hurt you?" His hand skimmed the surface of her bottom, where he'd smacked her three times.

No one had ever spanked her before. The kind of men she'd always chosen before had been the kind who'd learned everything they knew about sex from watching porn online. Blow jobs. Hard, fast pounding. Anal after the third date.

But not spanking. She would have thought it would have gone against all of her proper feminist views—and maybe it did—but it'd felt different. It'd *been* different. She'd liked it.

"Nope." She let her hand settle over his bandage. "Did I hurt you?"

"Don't care about that," he said, his arms going around her waist as he held her—yes, actually held her.

She let herself sink into his arms. That was another thing her former lovers were not terribly good at—close contact outside of sex. The post-sex cuddle was somehow... pointless to them. The only point of touching was sex. If they'd already had sex, then what was the point of touching some more?

But Nobody? Without her even having to tell him to, he held her even closer. She shifted her legs back so she was able to lean into him even more.

"Well, I care. Does this hurt?"

"No."

"How do I know you're not lying to me?"

"I don't lie to you." He said it simply, as if this were some great obvious truth—and maybe it was—but she felt odd tears prick at the corners of her eyes.

She had such bad taste in men. Always had. The 'bad boy' who had no qualms about sleeping with someone on the side— male or female—who 'broke the rules' not because the rules deserved to be broken but because they got in the way of his selfish needs.

Maybe Nobody Bodine was just a new, improved version of the same old bad boy she'd been chasing for years. But what if he wasn't? He hadn't lied to her—in fact, his honesty had been royally inconvenient. But there was something comforting about a man who was honest even when it wasn't convenient.

"Is that how you thought it'd go?"

"What?"

She pushed herself up to look at him. "I mean, you'd thought about that, hadn't you?"

She liked that faint blush on him. It took all the hard edges of his face and made him look different. Almost as ease. "Yeah."

"Me, too. But with a bed."

His blush got deeper. "I can move some books. If you want to come back out here."

She grinned at him. "After that? You better *believe* that I'm coming back out here. You are an amazing lover, Nobody Bodine."

He hugged her so hard she couldn't breath.

"How did you think it would go?"

"I..." He swallowed again, unable to meet her gaze. Rather than push him, she ducked her head back against his chest and waited. "I thought about you in the shadows of the trees. In the dark."

Her mind filled in the image for her. Nobody pulling her away from the light of the fire and into the dark of the trees. Him, lifting her up and backing her against a tree where no one could see them. Her, wrapping her legs around his back as he held her up and drove into her body hard.

"Oh." She kissed his neck, shivering at the thought of it. "After you heal up?"

"I'd like that."

Behind them, she heard clomping footsteps. Jesus—they were both naked in broad daylight—surely Jamie wasn't about to wander into the clearing, was he?

She lurched up and tried to get free of his arms—to grab her shirt—anything—but he held tight. "Just the horse." Then he sat up. "Damn. The horse. I need to get her rubbed down."

"Oh. Do you have a bathroom or..." she was mildly afraid of the other alternative. She didn't have a lot of experience peeing in the bushes. Especially not bushes that may or may not contain mountain lions.

"Inside the trailer. Plumbing works."

"Okay, great." She climbed off his lap and scooped up her clothes, her legs feeling like jelly.

But it didn't matter. The best sex of her life? Yeah, her legs could just feel like jelly.

She walked into the time-warp trailer again, books stacked everywhere. He was such an odd man, but mostly in a good way. Very different from any other man she'd ever known and, let's be honest, that was a good thing.

But, as she got cleaned up, she remembered that sleeping with Nobody Bodine hadn't been the reason she'd come all this way out to the middle of his nowhere. They had a problem. True, it wasn't as big as it had seemed last night after he'd left her hard up, but they still had a problem.

What were they going to do about Jamie?

CHAPTER FOURTEEN

Nobody got cleaned up and dressed, then he buried the condom and the wrapper in the bottom of his fire pit. The whole time, his head was swimming.

He'd just had sex. With Melinda. What's more than that, he'd hit her. Okay, maybe not *hit* her—but he'd smacked her. A little.

Instead of cowering, she'd... told him to do it again. *Begged* him to. So he had. And she'd liked it, he was pretty sure. He hadn't *not* liked it.

What did that say about him? About her? About them?

He tried not to think about it. Instead, he focused on the horse. Star had already found the small trough he filled up every morning, so he wasn't worried about her getting dehydrated. But he still needed to make sure she wouldn't go into shock.

He got a bucket and scooped out the water from the trough. It was warmish. Good. He grabbed a sponge and began to slop the water onto Star's back, rubbing her muscles to help them loosen up after her hard run. If Jamie were here, Nobody would have the boy do this. He'd gotten good at cooling down horses, which made Nobody feel like maybe he was doing something right for once in his life. Rebel had always talked about how horses were part of the tribe. Nobody wasn't exactly part of the tribe, not really, but he still had the connection of the horses.

His thoughts wandered as he cooled off Star. They didn't go far—just to the woman inside his trailer.

He knew she'd been in there before, but he hadn't been exactly aware of it at the time. Now? Now he knew she was looking at the stacks of books and the odd furniture and the blue bathroom. It made him nervous. He didn't like feeling nervous, and he especially didn't like feeling nervous right after he'd gone and had sex with a woman.

His side began to pull as he rubbed Star down. He forced himself to pause and breathe, to let the pain wash away with the water he was slopping on Star's back.

He didn't know what would happen next—and, worse, he didn't know what she expected him to do next. Was this a one-off, a different version of the same old sex-on-a-drunken-dare he'd had back when he was young and stupid? Or would she think now that they were dating? Hell, he'd never even gone on a date before. He was pretty sure the night where he'd gotten stabbed didn't come close to qualifying.

The fact of the matter was that, aside from remembering the basic mechanics of sex and following his baser instincts to ravish her, as the books said, he had no idea what he was doing. And that sort of cluelessness probably didn't wash with a woman like Melinda Mitchell.

He heard the door to the trailer swing back open, heard her step down the two steps, heard the door close behind her. He tensed, which did nothing for his side. But he couldn't help it. She was going to say something. He just didn't know what.

And there was no point in hiding from her. None. So he had to stand here and take it. Whatever it was.

"Explain to me," she began in a voice that sounded mostly normal, but with a hint of something that reminded him of how her breasts had bounced as she'd ridden him, "why you have *that* many books."

"Like to read." Old habits didn't just die hard. They never died, apparently. He was having trouble finding words.

"Did you graduate from high school?"

"No, Ma'am." She cleared her throat in what sounded a hell of a lot like frustration, so he added, "I didn't finish sixth grade."

His mom had never cared if he went to school or not, but he'd kind of liked it. It wasn't home, anyway, and that made it a good thing.

But he'd never had a head for books or history or math—especially not math—so he'd been held back in fifth and sixth grades until he was too big and they had to pass him up because he was scaring other kids. And then, well, after his mom died, what was the point? He didn't have to escape her anymore.

She was closer to him now—probably close enough to touch, but far enough away that he wouldn't drip water on her. "But you have what appears to be every western ever written."

He shouldn't be nervous about this. She'd seen him at his lowest, barely able to drink from a cup, and she'd heard about his record. Why should his educational failings be as bad?

Because he had so many of them and she was clearly a well-educated woman.

"Got my GED." That was something to be proud of, after all. He wasn't a total loser.

"In prison?"

"Yes." He slopped some more water on Star's back, pretty sure the horse had fallen asleep. That was good. He hated it when a horse was in distress, especially when he was the cause of it.

"Explain that to me." In that moment, she sounded a lot like her sister, but instead of being super-bossy or judgmental about it, Melinda sounded curious.

He took a breath, careful not to pull at his side. "My second year in, they put this white college boy in with me. He'd been caught running drugs over the Canadian border for Mexican cartels."

Ricky Campion. If ever there'd been a guy who wasn't cut out for prison, it'd been Ricky.

"We had this deal. I wouldn't talk about killing and he wouldn't talk about cartels. Nothing about our pasts. I looked out for him—he was easy pickins' for some guys—and he showed me where the prison library was. We spent a lot of time in there. It was safer, you know? Quiet. I didn't read real well, but he helped me study for the GED and he liked to read westerns..."

"You were friends?"

Somehow, it was easier to talk without looking at her. Looking at her made thinking difficult. "Yeah—*just* friends." A lot of people had thought that Ricky was his 'bitch,' but that wasn't how it worked. They'd let people think that, though—made it safer for Ricky if other inmates thought Nobody would kill them for trying anything.

It hadn't been a true friendship but then, Nobody wasn't sure he'd know what a true friendship was if it bit him on the ass. He and Ricky had been more like comrades in arms, fighting prison instead of a war. Outside, they never would have crossed paths. But inside, they had a barter system. Nobody tried to keep him safe and Ricky helped Nobody get an education.

"Understood. What happened to him?"

"Cartels must have decided he was going to talk. Year before I got out, he got shanked."

And the hell of it was, he'd never been able to figure out who'd done it. The wall of silence in that prison was unbreakable. Nobody was probably lucky they hadn't tried to kill him, too—after all, if everyone thought Ricky was his bitch, they might have assumed the skinny white guy would have told him everything.

"Oh, God, Nobody—I'm so sorry."

Nobody shrugged. He knew good and well that if he'd gotten out, he never would have known what had happened to Ricky. Once their paths uncrossed, they never would cross again. In all reality, the most shocking part of it had been that they'd killed him while Nobody was still around. "Prison is a brutal place."

She was silent for a moment longer, probably feeling bad for something that happened a long time ago. She was soft like that in a way that he wasn't. He liked that about her.

Finally, she cleared her throat and said, "Where do you get the books?" in a too-bright tone.

If he hadn't been covered in horse hair and grimy water, he would have turned to her and pulled her into his arms. But soft women probably didn't like smelling like horse and grime. "Thrift stores."

"You don't have a library card?"

He did turn to her then, unable to help the smile on his face. "Don't have an address," he reminded her.

"Sure you do," she said, meeting his grin with one of her own. "Nobody Bodine, Middle of Nowhere, White Sandy Rez, South Dakota. Easy. Anyone could find you."

"No one 'finds' me."

The look she shot him did some funny things to his chest. He didn't like it, but he wanted a lot more of it. "I did."

The sponge splashed into the water as he covered the space between them in two steps. To hell with horse sweat and grim. "I *let* you find me," he reminded her as he pulled her against his chest and buried his face in the crook of her neck.

"Same difference," she replied and even though he couldn't see her face at this angle, he could hear the smile in her voice. Her hands pushed back at his chest and then she was pulling his face up to hers, pressing her lips to his.

She still wanted to kiss him. That made no sense to him. None. He was a felon who hadn't even finished jr. high and had to be taught how to do long division by a drug runner. He was a loser in every single possible sense of the word—and she was still kissing him.

There were some trees right over there. He could pick her up and lean her against one and plunge into her welcoming body again and again. And even then, he wasn't sure he could get enough of her.

She didn't nip at his lip this time, dang it all. Instead, after a really nice kiss that bordered on sweet, she pulled away. It hurt to let her go but he did.

She looked up at him through her thick lashes and licked her lips. Damn, he wanted to kiss her again.

"I'll get some more condoms. I'll make a special trip into town."

"Sounds good," he agreed. She could have told him that she only had sex on the full moon of odd months and he would have agreed that it was a solid plan. Anything, as long as she kept suggesting they were going to have sex again.

He'd never been with the same woman more than twice. That was a record he was looking forward to breaking.

Then Star nudged him in the back, nearly knocking both of them over. "Horse," he said by way of apology to Melinda. "She likes the bath."

"You know, when we used to wash down horses before a show or something, we'd have to tie them up and they'd stamp and kick. How on earth do you train them so well? And how many horses do you have? And *why*?"

He grinned down at her. It was becoming a habit. "I have my own herd."

"Seriously? Just a herd, huh?"

"Come on." He took her by the hand and patted Star on the flank.

With a snort of disappointment—no more bath for her—Star headed down the path that led to the small valley on the other side of the hill. Compared to the sea of grass that separated these hills from the rest of the tribe, Nobody's valley was barely more than a culvert, but the stream ran with fresh water and there was enough grass for his horses.

He didn't let go of Melinda's hand. What was more, she didn't let go of his. There was something so normal about walking through his woods, holding hands with this woman, that felt exceptionally special.

They hiked the four hundred yards down the hill until the path widened. He'd built some lean-to shelters for the horses up under the trees—plenty of cover from the winter winds. They passed those first. Melinda didn't say anything.

Which made him nervous. What if she saw the lean-tos as nothing more than shacks? And she hadn't said anything else about his trailer, just that he had a lot of books.

He couldn't remember the last time he cared this much about what someone thought about him. Never, maybe.

But he cared what she thought. A lot.

Boy, he didn't like that. Not one bit.

He did like the way her hand fit in his and he liked the way she smiled at him and he especially liked the way she'd climbed on top of him without even a glimmer of fear in her eyes.

On the whole, he'd say he was having a good day.

They came into the clearing. Nobody did a quick headcount—he didn't see Red yet. That horse was probably taking the scenic route home. When Nobody had seen Melinda mount up at Rebel's place, he'd gone to find Red, ridden to where he thought she might be headed, and then sent the horse on with a slap on the flank. Red knew where home was. She'd get here sooner or later.

"Holy cow—you have your own *herd*," she said in a breathless voice. "Where did you get all these horses? And don't you dare tell me you borrowed them."

"Didn't." This was what he was most proud of, outside of the boy. "They were wild horses. Found them when I came out here the first time."

The horses had almost saved him the first time. *Almost*. He'd found the group of about fifteen horses hiding in this valley, far away from the Bureau of Land Management and their wild-horse roundups. The second night he'd slept by the cabin, he'd heard the footsteps of horses—at least, he'd hoped they were horses and not another dream animal come to talk to him in a language he didn't understand. So, when he'd been able to explore a little more, he'd eventually found the clearing and the horses.

"Don't know who was more wild—me or them," he told her. "They were matted and dirty and hungry." Like he'd been, except on four legs instead of two.

The horses hadn't been able to find the things they needed. "Let me guess—you stole some horse feed?"

"Borrowed it," he reminded her. "But yeah. Turns out, you feed a starving animal, they follow you forever."

It'd taken time—years—of hauling out sacks of grain he lifted from feed stores to win the trust of the herd. But he was quiet and patient and when the stallion let Nobody pet him for the first time, he knew he'd be able to ride the horse.

He'd done it, too. But then he'd been stupid in a bar and wound up in prison for a while.

The first thing he'd done when he got out was get back here. He hadn't told anyone about the horses—who was he going to tell? Albert? There wasn't anyone else and he wasn't going to be a bigger burden than he'd been on the old man.

That'd been the best day of his life—making his way out to the middle of nowhere, as Melinda had put it, and finding his horses still here. Still dirty and hungry and wild, but still here. Some had obviously died or been caught, some new foals had been born. It wasn't the same herd he'd been forced to leave behind, but the stallion had still been here. Older, lame in his back right leg— but still here. Waiting for Nobody to make things right.

Star caught up to them. He pulled Melinda out of the way as the horse went down to greet her friends. Melinda looked up at him. He knew it wasn't possible that she'd gotten more beautiful in the last fifteen minutes, but she sure as hell looked like an angel.

"How come you never came back for her? I mean, she'd been at Rebel's for days."

This was one of those situations where he didn't think explaining himself would necessarily make things better. But Melinda notched an eyebrow at him in challenge. So he swallowed and said, "She's yours."

"Wait—what?" Her mouth dropped open. "You *gave* me Star? I thought you were just, you know, loaning her to me to get home or something."

He cupped her cheek, wanting to kiss her but not knowing if he should. "Yours now." She blinked at him—too stunned to speak. He couldn't help himself. He lifted her face to his. "She's a good horse. I want you to have her."

I want to have you. The thought popped up unbidden in his thoughts as he kissed her. He wanted her more than he'd ever wanted any one or anything in his entire life. She'd turned everything in his world upside down, inside out and a few other directions he hadn't even figured out yet. He should have hated it. But he didn't. It felt good to be with her. Like being dragged out of a dark closet after days—years—of starving. Starving for the touch of another person.

But he couldn't have her—not more than he had, anyway. Not more than pulling her into the shadows of the night. She was too bright, too soft for a life like his. And him? He couldn't even go inside.

She pulled away from the kiss but didn't go far. She rested her head on his chest as she looked at the horses grazing in the clearing. The simple touch made him feel like he had right before he'd gotten stabbed—he'd die to protect her. He could redeem himself for her, if he had to. If it came to that.

Then she spoke and he knew he'd never be redeemed.

"Nobody, what are we going to do about Jamie?"

CHAPTER FIFTEEN

Ouch. Watching that man shut down on her was not a pleasant thing to endure. His hand dropped away as the light died in his eyes. She didn't see the smile fall away, but that was only because Nobody turned away from her and was walking back up the path to his camp.

A wisp of panic floated through her. God, she hadn't made yet another huge mistake, had she? Sleeping with Nobody Bodine wasn't going to make doing the best thing for Jamie even harder, was it?

Then he paused and looked back at her. He was waiting for her to explain.

"Look, I know you're keeping an eye on him. I understand that. He told me how you saved him. But you can't watch him all the time. The black eye he had when he first came to the center?" Nobody dropped his head in what looked like defeat. She didn't like it on him. "The fact is, as long as he lives with his parents, he's in danger. I don't want something to happen to him. I don't want him to be like you."

The moment the words were out of her mouth she knew she'd said the wrong thing. Nobody's back went stiff and she swore she saw the hairs on his arms stand straight up. She wondered if she touched him, would he shock her? "I mean like when you were locked in the closet," she hurried to explain. "When you were all alone. I didn't mean—" *like you are now*. But she didn't get the chance to say that.

At least he wasn't going into stealth mode on her. He was *just* walking away from her. Damn her mouth. Why was it always doing this to her—forging on where angels feared to tread?

"Wait," she called out as she hurried after him. Her voice seemed extra loud in the still of the woods.

He didn't stop, but he did slow down enough that she could catch up. That was probably as good as it got. "Nobody, wait. Please."

"There is no *we* here, Melinda. I can't do anything more than I'm already doing for the boy," he said, not looking at her. "You know what I am."

She put her hand on his bandage—a gentle touch that wouldn't hurt. She hoped. "I know you're working on being good. That counts for a lot."

"But it's not enough. It won't ever be enough." He shook his head. "It's not enough for you, either."

"You stop that right now, Nobody Bodine," she snapped. "You're just going to have to get used to the fact that I like you." His cheeks shot ruddy red. "And I'm not the only one. Rebel? Madeline? They like you, too."

"Not like you do," he mumbled under his breath.

Now it was her turn to blush. But she wasn't going to let him distract her. "Stick with me here. There is a *we* here because you've given me a reason to trust you and I hope I've done the same."

He didn't reply, but he covered her hand with his and looked at her.

She knew him better now, well enough to see that this conversation was pretty low on his list of things to do—far below getting stabbed and outrunning helicopters. "Trust me, Nobody. I won't take him away from you. But I can't leave him with his parents."

His Adam's apple bobbed as he swallowed, but he didn't say anything.

She sighed. The glow of the good sex was gone and she was back to having important conversations with a brick wall. "Promise me something."

"What?"

This was important. She couldn't do anything for him if he got himself locked up again. "Promise me you won't kill Jamie's father."

Nobody gritted his teeth and she swore she felt a current run over his skin. "You can't hide from me," she reminded him, holding onto him even though it sort of hurt—like a really powerful burst of static electricity. "I just found you. I don't want to lose you again. Promise me."

He moved and she felt herself tense, but then his thumb stroked over her cheek, his callouses rough against her skin. That was Nobody in a nutshell—sometimes gentle, sometimes rough. Always different.

"If he's hurting the boy..."

Melinda closed her eyes. Yeah, that was probably the best answer she was going to get out of him. "Try. For me—and for Jamie."

Then his arms were around her, holding her tight as the shock of his skin seemed to fade away. "I really didn't hurt you earlier?"

He still sounded so nervous about it. About her. "No. I didn't hurt you?"

He shook his head.

"You've been honest with me. I'm being honest with you. It was *just* right." Not too hard, but definitely not too soft. She grinned up at him. "But maybe clear off one of the beds for next time, okay?" Behind her, she heard the clomping footsteps that she now knew were horse steps.

"Red," Nobody said, sounding relieved.

But the horse was a reminder that the outside world could intrude at any moment. "I need to go home. Madeline will be worried sick. I was a tad upset when I left this morning. I don't want her to think..."

He nodded. "I'll have to get a different horse to take you home on. Star needs a rest."

Of course he'd be worried about the horses. Underneath the scars and the scowls, he cared. She stood up on her tiptoes to kiss his cheek. "You can try to tell me you're not a good man, Nobody Bodine, but I know better." She swatted him on the ass—a playful swat, not a violent hit. A sheepish grin pulled up the corners of his mouth. "Now. Please take me home so *we* can discuss *our* plan."

By the time they got back to Madeline and Rebel's house, it was the middle of the afternoon. On the bright side, Nobody no longer looked uncomfortable. She didn't know what was worse for him—talking about what to do with Jamie or talking in the middle of the prairie, with no place to hide or even blend. But she really liked that he was trying.

On the other hand, he was now an unreadable wall. They'd barely crested the hill when Madeline came flying out of the house, a look of pure fury on her face. Yeah, Melinda should have probably used that damn walkie-talkie. Oh well.

Madeline pulled up short when she realized that Nobody was riding next to Melinda. Melinda tried to hide her grin at the wide-eyed shock on her sister's face but, judging from the look Madeline shot her, she didn't do a very good job. "Nobody! In broad daylight!"

"Ma'am," he said with a tip of his hat to Madeline. Melinda could hear how uncomfortable he was. If she touched him, she wondered, would he shock her?

She asked, "Is Rebel home?" If it were up to Nobody, they might stand there all day.

Madeline looked at her like she'd never seen Melinda before. "He had something he had to do. Why?"

"We have a plan."

Madeline was no idiot. She heard the *we*, loud and clear. Her mouth opened but then she got it shut as Melinda watched her get herself under control. "Can you wait?"

They both glanced at Nobody, who looked as if Madeline had made straight for his liver with a spoon. But he nodded.

So they waited.

The wait was excruciating. Nobody tried to keep busy by rubbing down the horses and checking out the land around Rebel's house—anything to stay out of Dr. Mitchell's way—but he wasn't happy about being this visible while the sun was still high in the air. If the sheriff showed up, Nobody would have very few places to hide and he didn't fully trust the doctor not to call the cops on him.

But she didn't. She stayed in the house and no one else arrived. Melinda stayed with Nobody. They talked about which spot on the hill would be good, but that was about it. For once, she was pretty quiet. It was a comfort to him that she was there, but her silence made him nervous all over again.

She had a plan. It was a decent one—far better than anything he could have come up with on his own. He wasn't surprised—she was a smart lady. Smart and beautiful. And, for some reason, with him.

Man. He still didn't get that. She liked him—enough to have sex with him. Enough to trust him.

It didn't feel right. But it didn't *not* feel right, either. To catch Melinda looking at him, that soft, satisfied smile on her pretty red lips—to know he gave her that smile—well, he didn't know what to think. It'd never been his strong suit. So he waited for Rebel.

The medicine man got home just as the sun was setting. If he was surprised to see Nobody sitting at his fire, he didn't show it. And if he was surprised to see Nobody and Melinda holding hands, he didn't show that, either. Instead, he sat next to the fire and said, "What did you decide?"

Nobody's stomach churned. It'd been a rough day—except the sex part—and he was tired. He'd been up for almost twenty-four hours at this point and he needed to go check on Jamie after they got done here. More talking—even if it was with Rebel—wasn't something he was looking forward to. He wanted to go home and lie in his chair and replay the way Melinda had cried out his name over and over again until he drifted off to sleep. Then he wanted to wake up and find her and do it all over again, just to prove it hadn't been a dream.

Melinda waited until Dr. Mitchell had come to sit with Rebel. "I want to get custody of Jamie," Melinda announced.

Nobody winced as her words hung out there. The urge to disappear into the shadows of the trees was almost overwhelming. People didn't talk with him, especially about important stuff like this. Just about him. He wasn't the guy whose advice people sought out. Not like they did for Rebel.

"You want to do *what?*" Dr. Mitchell asked. She sounded stunned.

"Get custody of Jamie," Rebel answered for her. He, at least, didn't sound surprised. But he did sound thoughtful.

"You can't live here with that boy," Dr. Mitchell said real quickly. That woman could be scary when she was in a mood. And with the firelight dancing off her face? Yeah, this was clearly a mood. "I mean, I love you and all," she went on, "but..."

"But children scare you," Melinda said. When Dr. Mitchell glared harder, she said, "Of *course* I wouldn't live here with Jamie. You're doing the most good you can do at the clinic and anything that would disrupt that would be bad for everyone." She turned her attention at Rebel. "And I can't take him off the rez."

Everyone looked at Nobody. This was almost as bad as prison, but he didn't say anything. To do so would invite Dr. Mitchell to tear into him and, given the mood she was in, he'd rather wrestle a mountain lion.

"Where would you live?" Rebel asked. He still sounded thoughtful. Careful, even.

"I thought I could get my own place."

"Where?" Yeah, Nobody was just going to stay out of the sights of Dr. Mitchell right now. "There aren't exactly a lot of available places on this rez that are inhabitable and building permits are impossible to come by since the government holds the land in a trust for the tribes."

But Melinda didn't seem upset by her older sister's sneering tone. "You have a nice house."

"You are *not* moving that boy in with us," Dr. Mitchell said again in an even more severe tone. "I understand you want to save him, but what if his father comes after him? I'm sorry, Mellie, but I'm not going to put myself at risk."

Nobody glanced at Rebel. He didn't appear to be listening to his wife rant. Instead, he was staring at Melinda as if he'd never seen her before.

Nobody didn't like that look. He knew Rebel was an attractive guy. If what was basically his only friend in the world thought of making a move on Melinda...

"We do have a nice home," Rebel said in his thoughtful tone. "I bought it." The fact that he hadn't shut down this whole idea yet was encouraging.

Melinda leaned forward, pulling Nobody with her. "And the water? The electric?"

"I know a guy," Rebel replied. "A guy who can get things done." Then he looked at Nobody.

Jacob Plenty Holes. Nobody nodded in understanding. Jacob sat on the tribal council—if anyone could get through the maze of rules for utilities on the rez, it'd be him. He hired guys to work at a cattle ranch—guys that were loyal to Jacob and didn't ask questions.

Plus, Jacob had bought horses from Nobody. He didn't like Nobody—nothing new there—but when it came to the horses, at least there was respect. Nobody had helped Jacob out last year by catching his boss in some insane scheme to take over the rez and hurt a little albino girl Jacob had adopted. That had to count for a lot, right? If Nobody called in a favor on Melinda's behalf, Jacob couldn't say no, right? Hell, given that the favor wasn't directly for Nobody's benefit probably meant that Jacob would be more likely to agree. Jacob wouldn't like helping Nobody, but he'd respect that Melinda was trying to help the tribe.

With Jacob's political clout and manpower supplies, they could have a trailer set up in a couple of weeks.

"They could run it off your lines." Hell, even he could do that. He'd wired the trailer off that forgotten cabin, after all.

Melinda grinned at him, the firelight catching in her curls as the sky darkened around them. "Perfect! This is a pretty big hill. We walked around earlier and found a nice spot that gets good shade on the north side—no need to crowd together, as long as we could get the utilities."

Nobody's face went hot. Thank God the dusk had settled in enough that no one would be able to see. Shade. She knew he needed the shadows.

He looked up to find Rebel staring at him, a knowing half-smile on his face. Damn it all—Rebel didn't need to see Nobody blush to know what was going on. Nobody tried to take comfort in the fact at least he didn't seem to disapprove, but still.

"Again," Dr. Mitchell said in a cold voice, "not to be the Negative Nancy here, but what's to stop that boy's father from coming up here and exacting revenge for us taking his child?"

Finally, one Nobody had an answer for. "Me."

Dr. Mitchell jumped. "You?"

"Me." But he didn't know what else to say, so he didn't say anything.

Dr. Mitchell was looking back and forth between him and her sister. Nobody would have given anything to be able to slip off unseen into the night, but it was too late for that.

He didn't know if Melinda's plan would work. But he had to try—for the boy, yes. Jamie needed something more than what Nobody could give him. But Nobody had to try for himself, too. One morning in Melinda Mitchell's arms wasn't enough.

"Nobody can't get custody," Melinda said. He had to admire how easily she withstood her sister's frostiness. "But there's nothing to say he can't spend time with the boy. He's already doing that."

"So you're going to, what—move in together?" She gave her sister the look that scared the hell out of people in the Clinic. "You were ready to toss him in prison this morning, remember? And now you're going to move in together? This is too much, even for you."

Rebel put his arm around his wife and said, "Babe, let them explain. Crazier things have happened on this rez, you know."

Dr. Mitchell opened her mouth, but then, unexpectedly, everything about her softened as she leaned into Rebel's arm. It was the sort of contact that had always made Nobody hurt in ways he'd hated before. But that was before Melinda.

Now? He wasn't comfortable mirroring Rebel's actions—not with Dr. Mitchell still trying to kill him with sneers alone—but he had his own contact. Melinda gave his hand a squeeze.

"We're not moving in together." For the first time, Nobody heard something new in Melinda's voice—something harder. Something that sounded more like Dr. Mitchell. "And I didn't have all the facts this morning."

"Oh, so now you do after a fact-finding mission? Is that what they're calling it these days?"

"Madeline." Everything about Melinda changed. Her back went stiff as she launched a pretty damn good sneer across the fire at her sister. "That's *enough*."

The two sisters tried to out-glare each other for a minute. Nobody wanted to do something—anything but sit here. Nothing about this was normal. In his world, when people fought, they fought with their fists. There was no talking—hell, there wasn't even that much shouting. Just fighting until one side didn't get up again.

"So," Rebel said in a calm voice. "Melinda will get a manufactured house, we'll work with Jacob to get the sewer and electric run, Nobody will keep watch and then you'll work through social services to get custody of Jamie?"

Melinda stared down her sister for a moment longer before relaxing. "Basically. I was an advocate for a foster girl back in Columbus—she stayed with me for a month. I understand how the system works—I can go to court. It shouldn't be too hard to prove that Jamie's home is not a safe place."

"Have you discussed this with Jamie?"

"Not yet. But the whole process isn't going to happen overnight. And besides," she added with another icy glare at her sister, "living with you guys is great and all, but I'll be happier in my own place anyway."

"Fine," Dr. Mitchell snapped.

"Good," Melinda fired back.

"Okay, then," Rebel agreed. "This could work. Except for the sheriff..."

"I'll deal with him," Dr. Mitchell said in a huff. "That idiot gangbanger isn't exactly in a position to press charges and the clinic needs to operate at full staff again before we start making people sicker than they already were. Sheriff Means *will* listen to me." The way she said it made it pretty clear that the poor sheriff wouldn't have the option to say no. "But you have to get the child to agree first. I'm not going to be party to pulling a kid out of his home against his will. I won't have it."

Then, unexpectedly, all three of them turned to look at Nobody. "Okay?" Melinda said, stroking her thumb over the back of his hand. "You're still okay with the plan?"

Nobody looked at them all. Melinda's hopeful, encouraging face and the warmth spreading from where she was touching him. Rebel's calm, knowing smile—like he'd *seen* this was how it was going to go down all along. And Dr. Mitchell's arrogant sneer that would have scared the hell out of him if she hadn't just said she'd go to bat with the law on his behalf because she needed him back at the clinic.

This—this must be what having a family was like. People who didn't always agree with what you were doing or why, but who stuck up for you anyway. People who cared what you thought, what you had to say.

He didn't know if he liked it. He didn't know if he *wanted* to like it.

He put his arm around Melinda's shoulder and hugged her to his side. It pushed against his stitches, but he didn't care.

"Okay," he said. "It's a plan."

"Why are we here?" Jamie asked.

Nobody could tell the boy was trying to sound dismissive, but underneath he heard something else.

Jamie was scared.

"Melinda wants to talk to you," he replied.

"About what?"

"About your folks."

"What about them?" This was, hands down, the snottiest Nobody had ever heard the boy talk to him.

"She doesn't want them to hurt you anymore."

"*So?*"

Nobody wanted to wince, but he didn't. This was exactly why he needed Melinda. He was doing a piss-poor job of explaining the plan to the boy. All this talking...

For a moment, he wanted things to go back to the way they used to be—back when no one noticed him, much less asked his opinion or demanded his life's story.

But then, if he went back to that, he wouldn't be looking forward to seeing the woman with the fire-red hair again. And he *needed* to see her again.

"She has a plan," he said. "And you best watch your mouth around her. Drop the attitude."

Jamie made a noise that probably went with eyeball rolling. "Just because *you* like her doesn't mean I have to."

"No, it doesn't," he agreed. Damn it all, this was going to be a disaster.

He glanced back at the boy, ready to tell him to keep his mouth shut and his head down, but he caught Jamie rubbing at his ribs. "What happened?"

"Nothing," the boy lied. "Doesn't hurt."

Damn it all to hell. That kid could sit there and pitch a fit about how he didn't like Melinda and how he didn't want to hear the plan but when it came down to it, he didn't have a choice. Melinda was right about that much. The longer Jamie stayed with his parents, the better the chance he'd be killed in a drunken rage.

Nobody pulled Red to a stop and twisted around to stare at the boy. "You *will* listen to the plan. You *will* be polite. You *will* let her help you because she cares about you." *About both of us,* he added mentally. "Because otherwise, you're going to have to stay with your dad and slowly let him beat you to death."

The blood drained out of Jamie's face. "I just want to stay with you. I like it with you and the horses," he said, his voice barely above a whisper. "Why can't we keep doing that?"

"*Because,*" Nobody replied. It came out more as a growl than regular talking. But then, he wasn't so good at that regular talking thing. That's why he needed Melinda. He took a deep breath and tried again. "Because you're rubbing your ribs. Tomorrow it could be your face again. And after that? Might be something that doesn't heal. We can't keep doing this because it doesn't work and I'm not going to wait while he kills you."

"But I want to be like you—no one messes with you."

He'd failed. That much was obvious. To be like him meant the kid would have to be forgotten and starving, too hurt to save himself. He'd have to do hard time and watch his only friend bleed out on the floor of the prison cafeteria. He'd have to fight and fight and fight without an end in sight. He'd have to be so utterly alone that he couldn't talk to a woman, couldn't even touch her without being afraid he'd hurt her.

"You don't want to be like me, kid. I won't let you."

Then he turned and urged Red forward at a dead run. He made it to Rebel's place in record time. To his credit, Jamie had kept up on Sock. Nobody had been afraid the boy would bolt, but he hadn't.

They dismounted in the shadows of the trees and rubbed the horses down without speaking. Then they walked toward the fire.

Melinda came bounding out of the house, her smile bright. "You're here! I was getting worried. Everything okay?" She pulled Jamie into an awkward side-hug and ruffled her hair. Nobody could see the boy's face crease with pain, but he didn't say anything and he didn't pull away from her. Had Lou Kills Deer broken ribs? Damn it, not killing that man was going to be a hard promise to keep.

Then Melinda let go of Jamie and crossed to him. He didn't know what to do, so he just stood there as she slung her arms around his neck and pulled him down. "Thank you for bringing him," she said in a low voice as her lips brushed his cheek. Just his cheek.

Nobody didn't like this combination of embarrassment and disappointment—embarrassed because she'd kissed him in front of the boy, disappointed because that barely counted as a kiss. He wanted to wrap his arms around her waist and push her up to his mouth and taste her sweetness again and again.

He didn't. He *couldn't*. Not with people watching.

Rebel and Dr. Mitchell came out, holding hands. Why did it look so normal, so *easy* for them but it felt like a mountain he'd never get finished climbing? "Ma'am," he said with a nod of his head to Dr. Mitchell. "Can you check the boy's ribs?"

Jamie glared at him extra hard, but no one seemed to pay any mind. Yeah, this wasn't exactly going well.

"Come on," Dr. Mitchell said to the boy. "Let's get you checked out." She led the way back into the house, Jamie following her with his head down, his feet dragging.

Once they were safely inside, Rebel turned to Nobody and Melinda. "So it's going well," he said with a smile.

"He acts like we're torturing him," Melinda replied. She sounded nervous.

"He's scared." The moment Nobody said it, he wished he could take it back. Jamie would hate him if he knew Nobody was telling people that. "I mean..." But he didn't know what else he could possibly mean. So he let the words trail off.

"Something happened to his ribs?"

"He won't say what, but yeah."

Melinda sighed. "We've got to get him away from those people."

They sat around the fire and talked while they waited for the doctor and the boy to come back out. Rebel filled Nobody in without asking his opinion.

Rebel liked the site Melinda had picked out. He'd already contacted Jacob Plenty Holes about the project. Jacob would be coming out on Wednesday night and he'd appreciate it if Nobody was here to finalize the details.

His wife had already talked with the sheriff once. Rebel reported that Sheriff Means hadn't exactly promised that he wouldn't arrest Nobody if he saw him, but he'd indicated that he wouldn't be specifically looking for him at the clinic. Anywhere else was still fair game. He'd pulled Jack off stakeout duty, at least.

Nobody was—well, yeah, he was impressed. That was a lot of people going to bat for him—and the boy—but for him. But there was something else to it, something that gave him that itchy feeling that always used to send him running for the safety of the shadows.

There was a lot riding on getting Melinda a house, getting Jamie into it. *A lot.* He wasn't used to anyone expecting anything from him beyond predictable violence and a clean clinic. Now he had to meet with Jacob Plenty Holes and persuade Jamie that this was for the best and not let Melinda down. Especially that.

Just as the panic was truly starting to take root in his chest, though, she leaned against him. Her head was light against his shoulder, her body warm against his side. It felt... normal. Easy, even.

He couldn't do this alone, he realized.

But he might be able to do it with her.

It was odd to Melinda, how well she could read this man. Nobody sat next to her, his back straight, his eyes focused on the fire. To anyone else, he probably looked like he'd shut off—not only was the light *not* on, but no one was home.

She knew better. He was all but vibrating with tension as Rebel ran down what had happened over the last few days.

She put her hand around his waist and just held him. Jamie wasn't the only one who was scared about this.

Finally, after what felt like a long time, Madeline and Jamie came back out. His face was pinched and pale and, from the way he moved, it looked like Madeline had wrapped his ribs.

Nobody stood and went to him. He didn't say anything, but Jamie answered the unasked question. "Didn't hurt," he said in a voice that was so much like what she imagined a little-kid Nobody had sounded like that it filled her chest with pain.

They had to get that kid away from his parents. They just *had* to.

Nobody nodded and put his hand on the boy's shoulder. They came back to the fire together and sat a little ways away from Melinda.

She shot a questioning look at Nobody, but she understood. If the boy was nervous, he'd need to feel that he had someone on his side—in this case, literally his side of the fire. So she gave Nobody a reassuring smile and started to talk.

"Jamie, what would you say if I asked you to come live with me?"

He shifted in his seat. Nobody put his big hand on the boy's shoulder again. Not a threatening touch, but a reassuring one. No matter how hard he tried to hide it behind silence and physical intimidation, that man cared deeply.

"Here?" He gave Madeline the side-eye. It was not a warm and fuzzy look.

"I'm going to get a house on the other side of this hill," she explained, trying hard to find the right balance between caring and patronizing. "You'd have your own room and plenty of space for your horses."

"So..." Jamie looked around the fire as if he expected everyone to jump up and shout 'Surprise!' "You want to adopt me?"

"No," Melinda corrected. "Foster you. Give you a safe place to live all the time, where Nobody can still visit you. I've fostered a kid who's dad was in jail before—gave her a place to live until her grandmother could get a better house. This could be a short-term thing, like until your parents stop drinking, or it could be longer."

The boy eyed Melinda suspiciously. "And I'd have to stay with *you*?"

She nodded, trying not to be insulted. "I don't hit. I don't even yell. I like to cook and I don't drink very much, if at all. I like messy art projects and goofy movies. And riding horses," she added, looking at Nobody. "This isn't about taking you away from Nobody. This is about making sure you're safe when he can't watch you. That's all."

Jamie's head bobbed back and forth as he thought about this. "You won't make me change my name, will you? I don't want to have to be a white kid."

Rebel shot her a knowing look. Okay, so he was right about that. "This isn't about being a white kid or being a Lakota," she said gently. "This is about not having to have your ribs wrapped or your eyes blackened—about not having to worry about those things happening. Just because I'll be looking after you won't change who you are. You'll still be Jamie Kills Deer. You can still disappear off to the woods to ride horses and fish and you can still read books."

Jamie looked at Nobody, who nodded. Then he looked at Rebel. "This is the best way," he said in that mystical sounding voice he had—calm, but powerful. "You will only change if you want to. We will always be here to guide you."

Jamie looked at the ground and scuffed a foot against the dirt. "What if I say yes? Then what? 'Cause my dad isn't going to like that. My mom, neither."

"I'll take care of it," Nobody said. Then he looked up a Melinda. "And the sheriff will help. We're not running and hiding. If you come here, the law will protect you. Right?"

"Right," she agreed, but the words felt empty. The law should have been protecting Jamie already, but it wasn't. Instead, the sheriff was more concerned with hunting Nobody down.

Jamie glanced around. Rebel and Madeline were quiet but watchful. "I don't want my dad to hurt anyone," he whispered. He touched his side. "I don't want him to hurt... me anymore."

Melinda's heart broke for Jamie. "We won't let him. But this isn't a free pass. You'll have to go to school every day, do your homework and you'll have chores."

Jamie rubbed his side again. He could protest that it didn't hurt until he was blue in the face but that didn't change the fact that he was, in fact, hurting. Melinda looked to Madeline, who gave her a weak smile. Then she mouthed the words, *Three ribs.*

Melinda turned her attention back to Jamie, who was clearly struggling with the choice. "You've got time to think about it," she offered. "It's going to take a while to get my new house set up and go through social services. Like Nobody said, we're not running and hiding."

"I can't..." He swallowed, his gaze on the ground. "I can't stay now?"

That was a *yes* and everyone knew it. "Not yet, honey. But soon. For now, you keep coming to the center and staying with Nobody as much as you can, okay?"

"And you're always welcome here," Rebel added. "In fact, we'll need your help getting the house set up. Maybe you can come home with Melinda on Wednesday? We're having friends over to plan."

Jamie sniffled, but he nodded.

She exhaled in relief. Thank God.

Now they just had to keep him safe until they could get him away from his parents.

She knew that wasn't going to be easy.

CHAPTER SIXTEEN

Melinda was surprised by how quickly things moved after that. The Jacob that Nobody and Rebel had been talking about turned out to be a mildly terrifying man named Jacob Plenty Holes who wore half a mask on his face. If Melinda hadn't had Nobody standing next to her when she was introduced to Jacob on Wednesday night, she probably would have run and hid from the cowboy in the mask who sat around the fire as the sun set, discussing sewer lines like he did it every day.

But on the bright side, Jacob was married to another white woman named Mary Beth—that made three of them on the rez, as far as Melinda could tell. Mary Beth had a ragged scar on her neck, but compared to the cowboy in the mask or Nobody's scars, it didn't seem like a big deal.

Plus, Mary Beth turned out to be the vet, which meant that at no point did Madeline talk down to her. In fact, the two doctors seemed to be friends. Who knew Madeline actually *had* friends?

If that weren't weird enough, Jacob and Mary Beth had adopted a little girl who was an actual, real albino Lakota Indian named Kip. Kip was about the same age as Jamie. The only reason Kip didn't come to the child care center, Mary Beth explained, was that they lived on the far side of the rez. "She'd love to play with some of the kids," Mary Beth said as the men argued over sewers. "It's so hard for her to make friends. She's a little..."

Melinda looked at the pale girl sitting next to Nobody on the other side of the fire. They weren't talking—just sitting there together, watching the last of the sunset bleed from the sky. Jamie sat on the other side of Nobody, but instead of watching the landscape, he was staring at Jacob. And, more than likely, his mask. "Different?"

Mary Beth looked at her adopted daughter. "Nobody used to keep an eye on her from the shadows," she offered. "He does that."

"I know."

"I always thought they understood each other on another level." Mary Beth grinned as she rubbed the scar on her neck. "Because they're *both* different. Kip can do things..." she shrugged. "Then again—everyone here is a little different, you know?"

The little girl could do things? *What* things? No, maybe it was better not to know. Even if Mary Beth could tell her, the odds were good that Melinda wouldn't be able to make sense of it. Hell, Nobody had shown her how he blended into the shadows and she still didn't understand how he did it. "I'm not *that* different. I don't have any superpowers. Yet."

Maybe she was wrong. She could see Nobody, after all. Maybe that qualified her as different enough to run with this crowd.

Mary Beth grinned at her. "How's the boy doing?"

"Okay, I think. He's still really nervous that his dad's going to show up and do some damage."

Mary Beth clucked. "He'll have to get through Nobody first and that's saying something." She looked Melinda up and down. "It's a good thing you're doing. It's hard to come out here. I used to think I was crazy for leaving behind a normal life to come out to what felt like the Land of the Misfit Toys, you know? Then I met your sister. And you." Mary Beth grinned. "Now I know I'm not the only one nuts enough to do this."

"I don't suppose this is any crazier than anything else I've ever done." She waved a hand over her hair and clothes.

"You don't have to be different to come to the rez." Mary Beth looked at her family. Even in the dark, the love in her eyes was obvious. "You just have to be different to stay."

Then Kip called to her mom and Mary Beth went off, talking a lot and making the cowboy in the mask smile.

Melinda pondered over that. She'd always been the different one—different clothes, different hair, different goals. Nothing like her uptight older sister who followed in the family footsteps.

She'd reveled in being the black sheep of the family but... there'd been times when being different for different's sake was hard. It took energy to be the weird one, to angle for the next big shock.

Here? Here she was normal and different at the same time. She was a white woman—one out of three—on a Lakota Indian reservation. But, as she looked around the campfire at the man who blended into shadows, the albino Lakota girl, the medicine man and the cowboy in a mask, she knew she was one of the more normal people here. Which made her different.

Despite the intimidating mask, Jacob Plenty Holes seemed to be fairly normal. He was on the tribal council and approved of her plan to get custody of Jamie. "Won't happen overnight," he warned her later in the evening, after everyone had agreed on the details for the house. "Things have to be done the right way. The sheriff will have to get involved, but I can make him see our side of things as long as..."

Everyone looked at Nobody. *As long as Nobody stayed out of trouble.* Although his face stayed blank, Nobody's gaze met hers and she saw the panic in his eyes.

So she went to sit next to him, resting her head on his shoulder. She caught Kip giving her a secret smile, almost as if she were thankful Melinda had done that.

She smiled back. She didn't have to be different to come here. She just had to be different to stay.

And she was going to stay.

True to his word, Jacob had men out at the site within the week, clearing the trees, digging the trenches for the pipes and getting the foundation ready. Melinda went in with Rebel and Madeline on Saturday to pick out a manufactured home. She wanted to ask Nobody to come with her, but he was nowhere to be seen and it wasn't like he had a cell phone. Hell, even though she'd been to his place twice, she still had absolutely no idea how to get there.

She wanted to be disappointed—well, she was—but she understood. She imagined that Nobody traveling to the city in the daytime wasn't going to happen in this life or possibly the next. So she bought herself a house with some of her trust-fund money and then they loaded up the car with supplies for the clinic and the center and drove home.

Nobody didn't show up on Sunday, either. Or Monday at the center. She stayed later than normal, hoping that he'd walk out of the dark like he'd never been away, but he didn't. She asked Jamie if he'd seen Nobody, but got a short, "He's doing stuff," as an answer.

"You still okay at home?" she asked him as she ruffled his hair.

Jamie nodded. At least he didn't rub his side and Melinda didn't see any new bruises. "It won't... it won't take much longer, right?"

"Jacob is getting things done as fast as he can," she told him, pulling him into an awkward hug. "And you've got our numbers, right? Call anytime, honey."

Jamie pulled away from her, like he was embarrassed by the hug. But he nodded. "I will."

Then he was gone, wandering off into the dusk toward the last place anyone wanted him to go—his home. She couldn't help but worry. No matter how fast things were happening, it wasn't fast enough. She'd signed up for the required weekly classes for being a foster parent, but the classes were spaced out over ten weeks. She tried to keep up with the reading, since she didn't have Nobody around to distract her. All she could do was hope that, since Nobody wasn't spending his evenings with her, he was keeping an extra close eye on Jamie.

A week passed. Everything else seemed perfectly normal. She got up, went to work, played with kids—Nobody was obviously back on the job. The center was suddenly much cleaner than she'd been able to keep it.

There were just no strange shadows hovering in the distance, no silent man standing in the trees. She would know—she looked.

She resorted to leaving him letters. *Mr. Bodine*, she always started them. She thanked him for a job well done, asked how his stab wound was doing and how things were at Jamie's house after dark. She told him about the progress on the new site.

Every night, she went home, hopeful that he'd either leave

her a reply or show around the campfire. She sat up past her bedtime, watching the trees around her.

Nothing. No shadows, no notes. Nothing but a clean child-care center and a boy without new bruises.

Finally, on Friday night, she left him a final note. *I miss you* was all it said. She taped it to the door so he'd have to read it.

She sat near the campfire that night, waiting. Madeline tried to make small talk, but Melinda wasn't in the mood. Eventually, her sister gave up and went to bed.

Rebel didn't go, damn him. She was in no mood for his particularly irritating brand of wisdom. She worked extra hard to ignore him. Sometimes, a woman just wanted to be alone with her misery. Pity party for one.

"He'll come back when he's ready," Rebel finally said.

She snorted. "Yeah, I guess."

"You understand, don't you?"

"Sure."

This was the problem with talking to Rebel. He never took her at face value. Normal people would have accepted the lie and gone on with their lives, but not him.

"This is... beyond him, you know."

"Is that supposed to make me feel better, Rebel?"

He chuckled. Irritating man. "Nope. But you need to understand. He's existed outside of the tribe for so long, with only a few people to even acknowledge that he's alive."

"And that'd be you?"

Rebel nodded. "Madeline, too. And Jamie. But that's all he's used to. He doesn't think he can handle suddenly having meetings, suddenly having to be somewhere at a certain time—having people expect things of him."

She glared at him. It didn't do much, seeing as Rebel was staring at the fire and not at her. But it made her feel better. "Gosh, that makes it all okay, then! Thanks, Rebel!"

The thing that made it really bad was that she could see how Rebel was right. Nobody had spent more time sitting quietly with Kip the last time she'd seen him than discussing housing plans or working through social services. Even in a crowd of different people, he'd kept himself apart.

He gave her one of his most irritating looks—the calm, peaceful one filled with wisdom. It only made her madder.

"I got it, Rebel, okay? I'm turning his world upside-down, taking him outside his comfort zone—whatever cliché you want to throw at me, I got it. That doesn't mean it doesn't suck to have him suddenly disappear off the face of the earth, okay?"

That man chuckled again, as if Melinda was suddenly the funniest human on the planet. "He'll come when he's ready. He won't be able to stay away for long." On that parting shot, Rebel got up and went to bed.

Melinda glared at the fire for a while longer. She didn't add more wood, though. She just watched it burn down to embers. She hated it when Rebel was right about stuff.

But more than that, she hated how much she missed Nobody. She understood that, yes, she had turned his world upside-down. But didn't he want to see her? Didn't he *trust* her?

Or was it that easy to stay away from her? She'd tried to help him out after he'd gotten stabbed on her behalf. She was doing the best she could to take care of the only other person in the whole world Nobody was comfortable with. Didn't that count for something?

And then there was the sex thing. Even if the process of her getting custody of Jamie was overwhelming—could he really not want to have sex with her again? Had it been bad? Or had she freaked him out too much by enjoying the spanking?

Hell, she didn't know.

The fire died down. She doused the remaining embers and stood, scanning the darkness for any sign of him.

Nothing.

She wasn't going to find out tonight, that was for sure.

Nobody stood in the shadows, staring at Rebel's place. Specifically, he was staring at the window he was pretty sure was Melinda's. It was late—so late, it was early. He'd been stalking Lou and Myra Kills Deer all night, watching them while they got shit-faced at a bar and then following them home. He'd sat underneath their living room window for a few hours until he was sure they'd passed out. He hadn't bothered Jaime—hadn't wanted to do anything that might attract attention.

More than ever, he couldn't risk what would happen if someone saw him take the boy out of his house. Before, it might have sparked a phone call to the sheriff, maybe a search party. But now?

Now it'd put Melinda's plan in danger. He couldn't risk doing anything stupid now. Not when he was so close to making sure the boy was safe.

He'd been following the Kills Deer family for days now, sitting on the ground so he could hear inside their house. To make sure he stayed awake, he'd read the little letters that Melinda had written him over and over. The plan was working. He was tired and sore, but Jamie was okay and that's all that mattered.

At least, that's all that used to matter.

He wanted to see her. It was selfish of him to want that so badly, but he did. He wanted to sit next to her around the fire, just the two of them. No Rebel, no Dr. Mitchell, no Jacob Plenty Holes. Not even Jamie or Kip, although Nobody was pretty sure Kip would have understood anyway. She did, about this sort of thing.

Nobody sighed. For the first time in his life, he was tired of lurking in the shadows—never seen, never heard. Melinda saw him like no one else did.

If it were just that, it wouldn't be so bad.

But she forced everyone else around her to see him, too. She dragged him out of the shadows and carved a place for him around the fire by sheer will.

He didn't know how to be like that—how to act around people. Even if those people were Rebel and Dr. Mitchell and Jacob. Besides, Jamie needed him. That had to come first.

He took out the last note she'd left him. *I miss you.*

No one had ever missed him before. He didn't know what he was supposed to do about it. He was pretty sure the answer wasn't 'tap on her window around three in the morning.' But he didn't have any better ideas and tomorrow, he was going to gather up Jamie and disappear into the back country for a few days.

Courage, he told himself as he pocketed the note and walked up to the window. This was wrong, all wrong—normal people didn't tap on windows. They called or wrote and knocked on the front door during regular hours.

He tapped on the window—once, then twice again ten seconds later. The room stayed dark. He realized too late that Melinda wouldn't know the secret code, but old habits died hard.

He was just about to give up when a light came on. Another momentary flash of panic had him wondering if he'd accidentally knocked on the wrong window and Dr. Mitchell was about to tear him a new one. Then Melinda stood in front of the window, barely dressed in a thin tank top and a pair of panties. Her hair was a fright, but he'd never seen anyone more beautiful.

Her eyes went wide as she yanked the window open. "What's wrong? Is Jamie okay?"

"Fine. His parents were passed out when I left. Should be good until tomorrow."

She relaxed into a huge yawn that she tried to hide behind her hand. "Oh, okay. What's up?"

He couldn't help himself. He reached up and flattened his palm against the screen. "I... I missed you, too." Saying it out loud was harder than he thought it would be.

Melinda stared at him a moment before her mouth cricked up into a small smile. She leaned against the window frame, which did interesting things to her breasts—right at Nobody's eye level. "And you had to tell me that at 3:17 in the morning, huh?"

He swallowed as he dragged his gaze away from the thin panties and top. Face. He needed to focus on her face. "Yeah."

"You could have left me a note, you know."

He nodded. "Didn't know what to say, really."

She leaned forward—God, that body—and slid the screen up. She rested her elbows on the ledge and brought her face down to his level. "You could have told me you missed me, too."

"Could have." He'd thought about it. Felt weird to write something like that down, though. Someone else might have seen it.

"You could have told me when you were going to come by again."

"Didn't know when." She arched an eyebrow at him and he felt his face get hot. "Been keeping an eye on the boy," he offered, hoping that would make her happy. "Don't want anything to happen that would mess up the plan."

"Ah," she said in a breathy kind of voice. "How very responsible of you."

He had no idea if she was complimenting him or not. So he didn't say anything.

She reached out and cupped his face. Her palm was warm and soft against his skin. Something in him relaxed—like he'd let out a breath he hadn't realized he was holding.

"You are an infuriating man, Nobody Bodine." It should have been an insult, but it wasn't, not the way her voice, all warm and soft, wrapped itself around the words.

"My apologies, Ma'am."

Her thumb moved over his skin as she lifted his chin up so he had no choice but to look her in the eyes. "I don't like it when you disappear on me. I know you can't come around the fire every night, but I need you more than this."

He had no idea if he was supposed to feel bad for not showing up or really freaking happy that she needed him. Him! And not because she needed protecting or anything like that—just him.

Then, heaven help him, she leaned forward and pressed her lips against his. Warm. Soft. She needed him.

He needed her. He didn't want to. But he did. Damn it all.

He tangled his fingers in her wild hair, then slid them down over the barely-there top until he hit the edge. But when he started to pull it up, she stopped him.

"Will you come inside?" Her voice was quiet—none of the challenge she'd just laid at his feet.

She leaned back so that he could see the bed—her bed. It was far bigger than the narrow things back in his trailer—bigger than his chair, too. It had pretty white sheets that were all messed up from her sleeping in them and pillows. The whole thing looked soft and warm—just like she was.

But... inside. He shouldn't be afraid of the room. It was just four walls with a door and a window. It shouldn't bother him.

"It's late, Nobody." She could have sounded irritated—she would have been well within her rights to be pissed at him—but instead she sounded tired and maybe a little confused. "Come inside with me. We can leave the window open, if you want. I just..." She sighed. The sound pulled on his chest just as hard as if she'd grabbed him. "I just want to hold you for longer than a horse ride."

He shouldn't, and not just because it was *inside*. Dr. Mitchell might string him up by his toes if she found him in her house in the morning, uninvited and unasked.

But... Melinda. A night in her arms—in a bed—couldn't be a bad thing, right?

"Please." There was something else in her voice—something vulnerable and delicate and so entirely feminine that he almost didn't recognize.

Need. She really needed him. God, what a weird feeling.

He couldn't say no. Not to her. So he nodded. She stepped away and he hefted himself through the window.

Then he was inside. It didn't make him twitch as hard as it normally did. Maybe because she was here, looping her arms around his neck and molding her body against his. "Come to bed," she whispered against his neck. Then she kissed him, right there.

Nobody was not a weak-in-the-knees kind of guy, but in that moment…yeah.

Bed. It wasn't such a bad thing, was it? Just a flat surface. With a woman in it.

He ran his hands down her back until he was cupping her ass. Her body filled his hands. If she hadn't been pulling him toward the bed, he could have just stood there and held her against him.

His dick stirred—and she stirred against him. "Come to bed," she murmured again. This time, her teeth scraped over his skin. "I want you."

"Can we... can we turn the light off?"

"Yes." She didn't hesitate, didn't call him weird or crazy or anything. She just turned off the light and left the window open. For him.

He could love this woman.

The thought terrified him.

He picked her up—not a big gesture, but just enough that she could wrap her legs around his waist. The weight of her body pressed against his dick—no stirring this time. He went hard, straining against his jeans. She made a little noise in her throat, something that was almost a plea.

So he carried her to the bed. He had to. She gave him no choice.

He laid her down on the bed and leaned back just enough that he could strip her panties off. She made a small noise—it felt pretty damn loud in the quiet of the room—but he knew it couldn't be that loud. He paused, listening for any other noises that came from the other side of the trailer. Nothing.

She propped herself up on her elbows. "Don't make me wait." The challenge in her voice was implicit as she traced a single fingertip down his chest. She hit some of the scars, but it wasn't like she was going out of her way to hit them or trying to avoid them. They were just part of his skin. Part of him.

How could something as basic as a finger running over his skin do the things it was doing to him? Because her touch was making him shiver with want. With *need*.

He shucked his shirt and his jeans and leaned down to her. He had a vague feeling that he was doing something wrong. Last time, he'd had the ride to get her all worked up. But this time? He couldn't make her wait.

She pushed him back. "Condom," she said in her quiet voice. Then she rolled over to her bedside table and pulled out a box.

He waited while she got one out and got it open and then rolled it on him. He about lost it, right then and there—just like he had the last time when she'd done it. Feeling her fingers move down his dick, smoothing the condom out—God. This woman. *His* woman.

Then she leaned back and pulled her top off. She was bare before him. In the dark of the room, he couldn't see much—but he could see enough. The palest of lights gleamed off her breasts, so full and soft that he just had to kiss them. The bed made an unholy kind of noise as he kneed his weight onto it. It hurt his ears, but she had her hands on his back and was pulling him down and he let her. He surrendered to her.

If he didn't think about the bed squeaking or the walls around him—if he let himself get lost in her body—it wasn't so bad. In fact, it was pretty damn good.

He joined his body with hers with a hard thrust. Her gasp was small, for his ears only. The sound tickled over his ears, driving him forward again. And again.

She grabbed his butt, squeezing—digging her nails into his skin. Pushing him on harder and harder. "Oh, Nobody," she whispered against his ear—so quiet he almost didn't hear it. "Oh, God, Nobody,"

His name on her lips—not anyone else, just him. In that moment, he wasn't a nobody who came from a nobody and would only be a nobody. He was a somebody in her eyes. He was somebody good.

He leaned up on his hands so he could thrust harder. Her nails bit deep—too deep—so he sat back on his heels just long enough that he could grab her hands and pin them over her head. Then he drove into her body again and again, living for the moment when their bodies were joined, when she moaned, "Oh, God, Nobody."

She pushed against where he held her wrists. Doubt rushed in, just like it had when he'd smacked her bottom the first time. He didn't want to hurt her. Not her. So he stopped and let go.

Her reaction was immediate. Her legs slid around his waist, holding him against her—in her. She cupped his face in her hands and pulled him low. "It's okay," she whispered in his ear. "I want you to hold me like that. I *want* you to."

"Don't want to hurt you," he got out. Suddenly not moving was about to kill him. His dick wanted to keep going, to make her make those small noises again. To say his name.

"You weren't. You won't. I just..." She kissed him then, her teeth scraping over his lower lip before she sucked on his tongue. As she did that, her hips flexed up and she tightened around his dick. "I trust you. Now hold me down, Nobody. Ride me *hard*."

Her body tightened around his again and he couldn't control himself. She made him do these things—pin her wrists over her head, thrust in hard and then harder—she made him skim his teeth over her neck and down her shoulder until he bit down, trying to get a taste of her.

"God, Nobody—yes," she hissed as he bore down on her. "Yes. *Yes!*"

He didn't hold back. How could he? She'd told him not to, right? So he didn't. He gave her everything he had, noise and walls and beds be damned. None of that mattered.

Only Melinda mattered.

"No—Nobody," she got out in a short gasp before she bucked against him. Then her body tightened down on his with more force than he was expecting. He came—there was no controlling this. She made him do it.

He collapsed onto her, both of them panting. "Nobody," she whispered again as her arms wrapped around his neck. And she held him. Just... held him.

He wasn't sure he'd get used to that. But he sure wanted to try.

"Stay with me tonight." Already, she sounded sleepy again. The tension drained out of her body and she was all soft and warm and inviting again.

This was how it was going to be, he realized. She was going to get that little house set up and bring Jamie home to it. He'd planned on keeping an eye on them, of course—but he'd thought he'd be watching from the shadows, hidden away so that if Lou Kills Deer tried anything, Nobody could take him unawares. And if he and Melinda got to have sex, he'd thought he'd pull her into the shadows.

That wasn't going to happen. He wasn't going to pull her into the shadows—she was going to pull him into the light. Even if she turned the light off, she was going to want him to come to her in her bed—and stay there.

She disengaged and started to get up. "Where are you going?"

"I have to use the bathroom." She stood and gathered her top and panties. Then she walked toward the door. Even in the low light—even after just having had her—her body did things to him. She paused at the door. "Will you be here when I get back?"

He didn't answer. He didn't know the answer. She gave him a little nod that seemed... resigned, maybe, and then she had the door open and was walking a short distance down the hall. He heard another door click.

Hurriedly, he took care of the condom. He was tired. Tired of watching Jamie and tired of not solving the problem by dealing with Lou Kills Deer directly. He was tired of assholes like Dwayne thinking they had to take Nobody out to prove how damn tough they were.

But, underneath that, there was another kind of exhaustion. It'd always been there, but he'd never been able to name what it was.

He was tired of being alone, of holding himself apart from everyone, even Rebel. He was damn tired of that chair in front of his fire.

He just hadn't known it until he met Melinda.

But now he did. And knowing that only made things worse because, no matter how nice it might be to wake up with her in his arms, it didn't change things.

Assholes like Dwayne, like Lou, would still be gunning for him. For Jamie, once they realized that the boy was important to him.

For Melinda.

She came back into the room. Her room, not his. "You're still here?" She sounded like her sister, except there was something else to her voice. Something hopeful.

"I..." He hated to destroy that hope, but he couldn't put her at risk. He couldn't. Not her. "I'll stay until you fall asleep." That way, he'd get to hold her a while longer, but he could still go when he needed to. And he needed to, for her sake.

She stood in front of him and cupped his face in her hands. "Will you come back?"

He nodded, slipping his arms around her legs and resting his head against her belly. Soft. Warm. He could stay for just a little bit longer.

"Don't disappear on me, Nobody."

He pulled her down onto the bed and tucked her into his arms. She fit, like she'd always been there. Like she'd always be there. "I won't," he promised.

It'd be a damn hard promise to keep.

But he wouldn't break it.

CHAPTER SEVENTEEN

Melinda woke up when Nobody left. Not because he was loud—he was so silent that she could hardly hear the window shutting. He was doing his best to disappear into the night, a shadow moving with the moon, but he obviously hadn't anticipated one thing.

She knew when his body pulled away from hers. What had been warm and secure and so, *so* right was suddenly cold and empty.

So, through half-lidded eyes, she watched as he slipped out of her room and back into the night. 4:43. He'd stayed for an hour and a half.

Melinda wrapped her arms around herself and drifted back to sleep.

He'd come for her. He'd stayed—not the whole night, but longer than she'd thought he would.

He would come back.

She knew he would.

Three days later, Nobody forced himself out of the shadows. He didn't want to, but he needed to see her and he couldn't have her look at him with that disappointment again.

Rebel and Melinda were sitting around the fire. Neither of them seemed terribly surprised to see him. "Welcome back," Rebel said with a half-smile as he worked in his beads.

Nobody didn't much care for that smile. It was almost as if Rebel knew Nobody had been in his house for a few hours the other morning. Having people know his business was not something Nobody was going to get used to anytime soon.

Then Melinda stood and Nobody forgot all about Rebel and his beads. She was dressed like she normally was—little tank top with the bra straps peeking out, long hippie skirt—but he couldn't remember her looking better. And the smile on her face? Yeah, that's why he was here.

She looped her arms around his neck and pulled him down for a kiss. He let her, even with Rebel watching. When Rebel caught his eye, he shot Nobody a thumbs-up.

This was a form of torture, plain and simple. Plus, if Rebel was sitting at the fire, Nobody really couldn't pull Melinda off into the shadows. Even if he could disappear, she couldn't.

He'd have to come later tomorrow.

Melinda ended the kiss. "You're shocking me," she said in a breathy whisper. But she didn't pull away. If anything, she held on tighter.

"Sorry." He hadn't even realized he was doing it—must have been because he hadn't wanted Rebel to see him kiss her. Too late for that. "I'll stop."

She led him toward the fire. "Everything okay?"

He nodded. "I'll check on him after I leave here."

"I'm glad you came, even if it's just for a little bit."

And the funny thing was, he was pretty glad too.

They fell into a routine of sorts, which Nobody didn't particularly like because routines were, by definition, predictable, and predictable meant it'd be easier to track him.

So it was almost against his will that he and Melinda settled into a routine. Jamie spent the day with her at the center. On the nights he went home to his parents' house, Nobody would be watching, making sure Lou kept his fists to himself until he passed out. Then he'd go back to the clinic and do his job. Finally, in the early hours of the morning, he'd tap on Melinda's window and heft himself into her room—and her bed.

He was pretty sure Rebel knew he was there, but if Dr. Mitchell was aware that he was breaking into her house on a regular basis, she didn't say anything and Nobody wasn't about to tell her.

But sometimes, Melinda took Jamie back to Rebel's house

with her after she closed the center up so he could help work on the house site. Nobody would clean the clinic as fast as he could and then hurry to be with them.

It was still awkward, what with Rebel and Dr. Mitchell watching them, but Nobody found himself hoping more and more that they could get Jamie out here. The boy was still uncertain about the whole thing, but he was getting more comfortable around Melinda and even Rebel. He still didn't care for Dr. Mitchell, but that seemed to suit the good doctor just fine.

And then there were the nights when he got there early enough that Melinda was still outside, but late enough that Rebel had gone in to his own woman in his own bed.

Those were the nights when Nobody would finally, *finally* pull Melinda into the shadows of the tree line, push her up against a tree trunk, and make damn good and sure she cried out his name.

He went to his knees in front of her one night and worked his mouth over her body until she couldn't even say his name.

Another night, he held her up against a tree, her legs anchored around his waist, and rode her until they both collapsed onto the ground, spent and happy.

He was happy.

What a weird thing to be.

Melinda heard the phone from a long way off. She snuggled down into the strong arms around her waist a little more, pushing back against consciousness. Nobody was still here, so it wasn't time to get up yet. He never stayed long, but when he was here...

The phone rang some more. She didn't like it. Who would call at... she pried her eyelid open. Who would call at 2:16 in the morning?

Against her back, Nobody stretched. "Hmm?" he murmured in her ear.

"Phone's ringing. Madeline'll get it." She rolled over in his arms and buried her face the crook of his neck.

He sighed and held her tighter. Yeah, she was going to go back to sleep.

Then she heard it. "Rebel? Tim's on the phone!"

Even through the fog of sleep, Melinda heard the panic in her voice. "Nobody?" she whispered. Tim—the sheriff. Something was wrong.

Nobody got up so fast that he almost threw her out of bed. He already had his pants on when Madeline knocked on the door. "Mellie?"

Oh, yeah—panic. This was bad.

"One sec," she said as she threw on the shirt and yoga pants she should have been sleeping in. She looked back at Nobody, who had his shirt on. Any other time, this would have felt like she was getting busted back in high school with a boy. But Madeline's panic was seeping into the room.

She opened the door to see Madeline standing there in nothing but an oversized t-shirt, her curly hair springing out in every single possible direction. "What's wrong?"

"Normally I wouldn't want to know—but please, *please* tell me you've got a man in there with you." She tried to look around Melinda. "Nobody? Are you here?"

"What's wrong?" Melinda demanded again as Nobody came to stand behind her.

Madeline made an uncharacteristic squeak at his sudden appearance. "Tim—he's got Jamie. It looks like Lou shot his wife and then blew his own head off."

Behind her, she felt a surge of pure electricity pour off Nobody. It made her jump, it was so strong. Madeline made that nervous squeak again. "What the hell was *that*?"

"Just the thing he does." She snapped her fingers, drawing Madeline's attention back to her. "What do you mean Tim's *got* Jamie?"

"Come on." She turned and headed back to where Rebel was pacing a three-step circle as he talked on the phone.

The three of them stood there as Rebel listened. Melinda held Nobody's hand to try and reassure him it'd be okay, but on the inside?

She wasn't cleared by social services to be a foster parent yet. She didn't think the state would release Jamie to her custody. She was a non-family, non-tribal member who wasn't approved.

"Yeah—yeah. Okay. No—no. Tim, listen—" Rebel looked at Nobody. "He's here—has been for three hours. Yeah, I'm willing to swear to that in a court of law. So will my wife and sister-in-law. Yeah, okay." He hung up.

"What?" All three of them—even Nobody—said in unison.

"As best Tim can tell, Lou and Myra had a fight at a bar off the rez, he went out to his truck and got his gun, shot her and then shot himself in the middle of the parking lot. There were witnesses. Tim wanted to be certain that Nobody didn't have anything to do with it."

Melinda clung to Nobody's arm. "He's been here since eleven."

"You know," Madeline said in a put-upon voice, "you guys don't have to sneak around."

Another burst of electricity zapped her. "It's okay," she murmured to Nobody as Madeline gave them both the side eye. "So what about Jamie?"

"Because it happened off the rez, the state's involved already." Rebel sighed. "We can't take the boy."

Nobody's hand crushed down on hers so hard she yelped. He immediately let go of her and stepped away. The energy he was putting off was almost blinding. She knew good and well that if they were outside he'd be gone already, nothing more than a shadow.

"Where?" Nobody growled at Rebel.

"Easy." Rebel held his hands up. "Tim's got the boy down at the police station. They're waiting for social services."

Nobody moved so fast that Melinda barely got her hands on him. "Nobody? Nobody!" She managed to grab his arm and spin him around.

Moving almost as fast, Rebel got between Melinda and Nobody and the door. "Listen to the woman, Nobody." His voice was low and calm, but it carried more authority than Melinda normally heard.

Nobody dropped his hands to his side in loose fists. "I want outside. Now."

Jesus, the last thing any of them needed was for a freaking brawl to break out. "Look at me," she told Nobody, grabbing his face and hauling it down until she could look him in the eye. He let her, so that was something. "We're going to get him back."

A muscle in his jaw twitched. "Now?"

She took a deep breath. "No." He tried to pull away from her, but she refused to let him go. "You listen to me, Nobody Bodine. We have to do this the right way. You go busting up into that police station, the sheriff might not just arrest you—he might shoot you. You might fight back and if you hurt a cop, you'll never see the moon again."

Nobody growled at her.

She wasn't done with him, not yet. "And if you get Jamie? Then what? You disappear into the back country? They will come looking for you—you can't hide from infrared cameras." She thought. Actually, that wasn't proven yet, but she wasn't going to hedge her bets. "They *will* find you and they *will* take that child away. You will never see him again. Is that what you want?"

The muscles in his face didn't move, but his eyes—God, so much pain. She hated having to threaten him like this, but he left her no choice.

"She's right," Rebel helpfully added from his post at the door. "I'll go down to the station and wait with him."

"I'll go too," Melinda added.

"I'm coming." Nobody tried to stand up, but she still wouldn't let him go.

"No, you won't." Rebel at least had the decency to sound regretful about this. "Tim will arrest you. He said he would."

A look of anguish pulled on Nobody's face until he looked like he was going to collapse. "But he'll be scared. What if the sheriff's got him in a cell? What if..."

Melinda honestly didn't know if he was talking about himself or about Jamie. "I know, babe. But he won't be alone. Rebel and I will wait for social services and get the info we need."

"But—"

"No *buts*, Nobody. You are absolutely not to come to the police station. You are not to cause a scene or a fight or anything that will jeopardize our chances of getting him back. You will *not* screw this up. You *will* do what I say. Do I make myself clear?"

Then, before he could come up with a response to that, she kissed him. Hard. Not a kiss of passion or heat, but a kiss of domination. A kiss that left him no choice.

She hoped.

When she broke the kiss, she leaned her forehead against his. His arms went around her waist, which she took to mean that he'd made the correct choice. "Trust me," she said in a quiet voice.

A long moment passed—one in which he looked as if he were really struggling. Good lord—what if he *didn't* trust her? But then he said, "Okay."

She hugged him. That was as good as that was going to get. "We've got to go. You'll stay out of trouble, right?"

Nobody nodded, but he didn't quite meet her eyes. Then he was gone, slipping out the door and into the dark. "Stay away from the police station!" she called after him, but he was gone into the night.

Damn that man.

He wasn't going to make this easy on her.

"He's over there," Sheriff Tim Means said, jerking his thumb over his shoulder. He had some sizable bags under his eyes, making it look like he hadn't slept in a week.

Point of fact, Sheriff Means did *not* have Jamie in a cell. The boy was curled up into a ball on a ratty looking sofa in the police station, which was apparently a fancy way of saying 'an office with two cells in the corner.' A man was in one of the cells, mumbling to himself. Melinda couldn't tell if the man was asleep or just drunk.

Jamie had a stuffed pillowcase at his feet and no socks on. Clearly, he'd been woken up and hustled out of the house. Melinda felt like grabbing the sheriff by his shirt collar and yelling at him. That was no way to wake up a kid, especially not for this.

"Jamie?" She sat down next to the boy and rubbed his shoulder. "Honey, I'm here."

Jamie awoke with a start. "Huh? Oh." He rubbed the sleep from his eyes. "Can we go home now?"

"No, honey, not yet." Jamie's face fell and Melinda felt worse than old gum stuck to the sidewalk. "You're going to have to go to a foster home until I can get approved."

"So... they're really dead?"

Melinda looked at the sheriff, who said, "I didn't show him the pictures. He doesn't need to see that."

Melinda decided to dislike Sheriff Means a tad less. At least he hadn't gone that far.

"Yes. I'm sorry, honey."

Jamie burst into tears and threw his arms around Melinda's neck. She held him and rubbed his back as he cried it out. "I want—I want—I want Nobody!" he wailed at one point.

"I know, honey." She shot a mean look at the sheriff, who promptly busied himself at his desk.

The drunk shouted something that sounded like "Butterflies!"

Melinda tried to block him out. "It won't be long and you can see him again."

Rebel produced a box of tissues from somewhere and set them next to Melinda. He then sat cross-legged on the floor in front of them, just like Melinda had seen him do when Nobody was wounded. *Just waiting*, she thought. *Just in case.*

Finally, after a long time, Jamie calmed down. He wiped his nose on his arm before Melinda could hand him a tissue. "Sorry," he mumbled, not looking at anyone in the room.

Boys. She gave him a tissue anyway. "It's okay."

"I'm just..." Jamie blinked furiously. "They're not coming back, right?"

"Right."

Jamie thought on this for a while, sniffing. "Good." Then he looked at Rebel. "Does that make me bad?"

"No, son. Just human," Rebel replied without hesitation.

They waited, mostly in silence—except for the sniffing, of course. Jamie dozed off with Melinda's arm around his shoulder. If she hadn't been so worried about him—about Nobody—she would have probably fallen asleep, too.

But she was worried. She half expected that man to come busting up in here like some demon from the night. *But he promised me*, she kept telling herself every time she heard a noise. *He promised he wouldn't.*

Dawn had barely cracked when a late-model sedan pulled up in front of the station. A plump woman who looked to be in her late fifties got out. Despite the early hour, her helmet of curled hair was firmly in place and she was wearing a skirt suit with those shoes that older women wore—not quite dress shoes, not quite sneakers, but some unholy combination of the two.

"Jamie, honey—wake up," Melinda said, giving him a squeeze.

Rebel uncurled from his sitting position on the floor and even Sheriff Means straightened the cuffs of his sleeves.

The woman entered the building. "Good morning." Her voice was so perky it hurt Melinda's ears. "I'm Bertha Watterkotte."

Whoa—talk about an unfortunate name, Melinda thought as she barely managed to contain her smile. Morning people should be illegal. She must be getting slap-happy. Not a good sign.

Bertha smiled down at Jamie. "And you must be James Kills Deer."

He flinched. "Jamie," he said in such a quiet whisper that Bertha had to lean forward.

"Of course, dear," Bertha replied in a remarkably good-natured tone. The longer Melinda looked at her, the more the older woman looked like a tough-love granny who'd stopped by the police station on her way to Sunday school.

"I'm Melinda Mitchell, the director of the White Sandy Child Care Center," Melinda said, approaching Bertha with her hand out. Bertha had a firm grip—the kind that said she took no crap from grown women or little boys.

Behind her, the drunk shouted, "Red butterflies! Ohhh..."

Melinda winced. "Can we talk outside?"

Bertha gave a stern look to the drunk. "I suppose that would be best. Jamie, why don't you use the restroom and wash your hands before we leave?"

Jamie looked up at Melinda, who nodded in agreement. He headed toward the back of the station while all four adults headed outside.

"I'm trying to get custody of Jamie," Melinda began with no other introduction. "But my application to be a foster parent is still in process. Obviously, the night's events have both made things simpler and harder. We won't have to work around his parents, but I think you can understand why I was trying to get custody."

Bertha nodded her head, listening intensely. "The trooper I talked to made the situation quite clear. And you have a place for the child?"

Damn it, no. Melinda forced herself to sound upbeat. "Not yet. The house is due to be installed next Thursday."

"Installed?" Bertha's eyebrows quirked up.

"Modular housing," Melinda replied. "The site's almost ready. And, just so you know, I was a foster parent in Columbus, Ohio, a few years ago, so I understand how the process works." And how long it might take. But if she could get someone like Bertha Watterkotte on her side, it might not take as long. "I want to make sure Jamie's in a secure home but not removed from the support system he already has on the rez. This is Jonathan Runs Fast, the medicine man for the tribe." Rebel's other name felt weird on her tongue, but this was all about making a good impression.

Bertha shook Rebel's hand. "A pleasure."

Rebel nodded.

Behind them, a sound like a twig breaking caught all of their attentions. Bertha's head whipped around. "Is someone there?"

"I'm sure it's Nobody," Rebel replied. Sheriff Means glared as he looked off into the distance.

"I understand that the process will take time," Melinda repeated, trying to regain Bertha's attention. "I've enrolled in the required classes and am about halfway done. The home study will need to be completed as soon as the home is ready, which should be in a week or two. But in the meantime, I'd like to be able to come see Jaime. I don't want him to feel alone."

Bertha glanced at the odd circle of people around her. Melinda gave her credit for not looking over her shoulder again. "Yes, well," she began, sounding less warm as she dug a card out of her pocket. "We have rules, as I'm sure you can understand, regarding in-home visits by non-family members. Any visit with the child would have to be supervised at my office. Foster parents do not appreciate unscheduled visits, as I'm sure you can understand," she repeated

"Absolutely," Melinda readily agreed, knowing full well that meant Nobody wouldn't be a part of it. She took the card Bertha offered. "You have a place for him in the meantime?"

"Oh, yes," Bertha said, brightening up. "One of our best homes, I believe. She just had an opening. I'll make it clear to her that this should be a short-term arrangement. We just need to make sure we do what's best for the child, you understand."

"Completely," Melinda said, hoping that Bertha had spoken loud enough that Nobody had heard the 'short-term' part. "I'll email you later today with my information. I'd appreciate being kept in the loop regarding Jamie's care until my application can be approved."

"That's fine," Bertha said as Jamie trudged out of the station, head down and shoulders slumped. "Ah, there you are, dear. Come along." She walked back to the car and opened the backseat door. A child's booster seat was ready at the waiting.

Melinda knelt down besides the boy. "It won't be for long, all right? Take care of yourself, follow the rules and listen to the foster mom, okay? The next thing you know, I'll have the house all ready and you can come back."

Jamie sniffed again. His lower lip quivered, but he was doing a darned good job of not crying, all things considered. "Will you come see me?"

"I'll arrange it with Ms. Watterkotte." She tried to smile for him. "I won't forget about you—none of us will." *Especially Nobody*, she thought. She fought the urge to check out the shadows. At this point, all she could hope was that he wasn't about to materialize out of thin air and grab the boy. *Stay hidden*, she thought. But she didn't look. She couldn't. "It won't be long. You'll be back before school starts." She hoped. She really, really hoped.

"Come along, dear," Bertha Watterkotte repeated.

Melinda crushed Jamie in a hug. "It's going to get better," she whispered. "I promise."

Then Jamie was squirming out of her grasp. Sheriff Means patted him on the head and Rebel shook his hand. Then, just before he climbed into the car, Jamie stared off into a patch of darkness and waved.

Bertha frowned and looked at the same spot, but she must not have seen anything because she shut the door, got into the driver's seat, and drove off.

Melinda, Rebel and Sheriff Means stood there until the taillights disappeared. Then the sheriff spoke. "Dwayne's not really in a position to press charges. The feds picked him up on drug charges and he hasn't posted bail. The feds could care less about how his arm got busted in seven places."

"I see," she said quietly, hoping Nobody could hear.

Sheriff Means scratched his head. He looked more tired than she'd ever seen him. "I think the rest of his gang are scared shitless, so no one else will be stirring anything up. But I'm not going to have a vigilante running around my rez. I see Nobody Bodine, I arrest him. There's plenty of unsolved cases that I can link back up to a man no one saw."

"Understood." Except she didn't, not really. Why was he telling her and Rebel this? "Are you going to look for him?"

Sheriff Means ground his heel into the dirt. "I have better things to do than waste my day looking for a man I'll never find. But if I see him..." He looked at the line of shadows that was fading with the rising sun.

"Got it." She wanted to tell the sheriff that Nobody was working on being good, that he'd kept his promise not to kill Lou Kills Deer—that he'd given her a reason to trust him. But she didn't. She just waited while Rebel and the sheriff shook hands, then got into Rebel's truck and drove back to the house.

It was only then that she allowed herself to feel the tiniest bit optimistic. She wished ill on no man or woman, but it was God's honest truth that, with Lou and Myra Kills Deer out of the picture, Jamie was suddenly much safer than he'd ever been in his life. Plus, she wouldn't have to live in fear of a drunken Lou showing up at her house with a gun and a grudge.

Jamie being in a foster home made things more complicated right now, but in the long run?

Now she just had to make sure that Nobody didn't decide to do things his way. Like the sheriff said, this was not the time for a vigilante to be running around.

This was going to be harder than she thought.

CHAPTER EIGHTEEN

"He's doing fine," Melinda said in that voice that Nobody didn't like because it sounded like she was talking to an idiot who couldn't grasp a basic fact like two plus two was four.

It'd been eleven days since Jamie had been taken—eleven days that felt like a year in prison. "Where is he?"

It was only when she scowled at him, with her hands on her hips just like Dr. Mitchell did, that he realized that he'd maybe said that a little too loud, a little too mean.

Damn it. But he was worried about the boy. That didn't make him the bad guy here. Well, he was already the bad guy here, but it didn't make him even worse.

"You, *sir*, will sit down and chill the hell out," Melinda said in a voice that was downright icy. "I am not going to tell you where he is because I know that you'll slink off into the dark to check on him and that is the absolute last thing that you should be doing right now."

He wanted to argue with her, except she was right about everything except the part where he shouldn't go check on Jamie. "But I—"

"No *buts*. No *ifs* or *ands*, either. Sit." She pointed to the blanket.

So he sat. At least they were outside. And alone. The house was dark, but it wasn't that late, maybe only ten. Either Rebel and his wife weren't there or they were sleeping.

"There," Melinda said, settling in next to him and resting her head on his shoulder. "Now, will you listen?"

He nodded as he slipped his arm around her shoulder. He liked this part—sitting in front of the fire with her, just the two of them. He still found it hard to believe that someone like Melinda wanted to sit with him. Any normal woman would have run screaming from him when he got a little loud and mean.

But not her.

"Jamie's fine. I talked to him today—as much as that boy talks on the phone." She looked up at him. "He gets that from you, you know."

Nobody ducked his head, his cheeks hot. "Sorry."

"I'm going to go see him next week," she went on. "It'll be at the social services office and that woman—remember her?" He nodded. "She'll be supervising."

"I... I shouldn't go, should I?" The woman who had driven Jamie away had looked like the kind of woman who would not take kindly to a man like Nobody.

"I'm really sorry, but no. You just have to trust me, okay?"

He sighed. It wasn't that he didn't trust her—it was that he'd never really trusted anyone before. Most especially when it came to government offices. And government officials.

He knew it wasn't right, but he couldn't help but see Jamie locked in some room, unable to get out. Even just thinking that made Nobody's chest tighten to the point where he had trouble breathing.

"I just want to know he's okay."

"He's okay, babe. I spoke with the foster mother, Ms. Winking. She seemed really nice. Said he's eating well and is amazing at doing chores." She looked up at him again, her eyes bright with affection. "He gets that from you, too."

That made him feel good—he'd done something right by the boy. But he couldn't shake that image..."Winking? Is that her name?" He couldn't tell if that was an Indian name or a white name. He tried to picture the woman that went with it—maybe a little older, a little round. Grandmotherly. Someone who would take care of a boy she didn't know.

If he could just see for himself, he could stop worrying.

But how was he going to do that without breaking his promise to Melinda?

"Nancy." She yawned and nuzzled into his side. "Nancy Winking. He said she doesn't really wink, though. He seemed disappointed."

She seemed unaware that she'd just given him exactly what he needed. "Tired?"

She nodded. "It's been a long couple of days. But I think I'll sleep better tonight, now that I've talked with Jamie." Then she stood, stretching her body right in front of him. Then she held out her hand. "Will you come inside tonight?"

Yeah, that's how it was. She asked him almost every night now, and he'd started using the door—walking into the house as if he owned the place. Him. Inside. Every night.

Her house was here now, but still empty, still not hooked up to those things a woman like Melinda needed—lights and water. But by the end of the week, she'd be set up in her new place. And he'd be able to walk in like he owned the place any time he wanted. She'd said he could. No slinking around in the shadows anymore.

"Yeah." He'd stay until she fell asleep.

And then?

He had to find out where Nancy Winking lived.

It took a little work—Nobody had never turned on the computer at the Clinic before, but it was the only place he knew he could use the internet without anyone noticing.

It took him over an hour to figure out how to use the Google, but by 3:15 in the morning, he had an address for Nancy Winking.

He borrowed a car—not Melinda's—and was gone. He'd be back before anyone noticed the car was missing.

He had to go see about a boy.

Nobody tapped on the window—once, then paused for ten seconds, then quickly two more times. If Jamie were in there, he'd recognize the signal.

He crouched low under the window and waited. He was pretty sure this was the right address—the number matched—but he had no idea if this was Jamie's room or not. The house was a small ranch home, probably from the sixties, so he had that going for him, but it had draperies, so he couldn't see inside. He'd chosen this window because the other one had what might be lace on the edges of the draperies. An older lady might have lace in her room.

Nothing happened. He'd give it one more try and then he'd have to bail. Anything more and he'd attract the wrong sort of attention. Damn it, he just wanted to make sure the boy was okay.

While he waited, he looked around. It was about 4:45 in the morning—still early enough that the neighborhood was quiet. He didn't have much time, but then he didn't need much—just to check on the boy.

Nice place—all the windows had glass in them and the yard was mowed. So this Nancy Winking person took care of her house. That was a good sign, right?

Doubt crept in. Melinda would kill him if she knew he was here. She'd asked him to trust her and he wanted to. He really did. But the boy...

Above his head, the window opened. "Hello?" a small voice—Jamie's—whispered into the dark. "Nobody?"

The tightness in his chest unclenched so fast that it made him dizzy. He looked around one final time—no curtains fluttered, no lights popped on in any of the houses he could see—so he stood up.

"Nobody!" Jamie said in an excited whisper as he threw his arms around Nobody's neck.

"Hey, boy," Nobody replied, patting him awkwardly on the back. "Came to check on you."

"I knew you would—I knew it!" But then his excitement drained. "I don't want anyone to see you—you better get inside."

Nobody hesitated. Knocking on a window was one thing. Actually going inside?

"Please? I can show you my room."

Nobody nodded. He wouldn't stay long, he reasoned. He'd just make sure that the boy's room was okay—that he wasn't locked in or had any new bruises or anything. Then he'd go.

He hefted his weight up and climbed into the room. Jamie turned on the small lamp next to his bed. Nobody flinched at the light, but he looked around.

The room was plain—a blue rag rug was on the floor, a twin bed with a blue blanket was next to a small white table with the lamp and a white dresser stood off on one side. There was a small bookshelf with books and a few worn looking toys on it next to a rocking chair. He could see someone sitting in the chair to read stories to a child in bed.

It wasn't a dark, dank cell. It was actually pretty nice.

Jamie sat down on the bed. "It's not bad here," he said in a quiet voice. "She thinks I should eat a salad every night. I don't like salad, but she won't let me have carrots for lunch and dinner."

Nobody half grinned at this as he tested the doorknob. It opened.

"The bathroom's down the hall," Jamie went on. "I have my own towels and everything, but I hafta hang them back up."

"Melinda said you were doing your chores real well," Nobody replied as quietly as he could. He looked around the room again. He wouldn't fit in the chair and besides, that felt... well, for some strange reason, that felt like he'd be trespassing too much. The chair belonged to the woman.

The bed was out, too. It was just a twin—and besides, it probably squeaked. So he folded himself up on the floor. Which squeaked. Damn it. "I'm real proud of you for that."

"Yeah..." Jamie shrugged. He mimicked Nobody's cross-legged posture. "It's okay. Better than home used to be, but not as good as camp with you. I really miss the horses. Miz Nancy doesn't even have a dog."

Nobody nodded. Anything would be better than home—even living in a strange house with a strange woman. He'd have to see if Melinda would let Jamie have a dog. She'd probably know how to get one without borrowing it.

The silence grew between them. "You doing okay?" He swallowed. Talking about feelings wasn't really his strong suit. But he was going to make himself try, for the boy's sake. "About your parents?"

Jamie looked away. "I... I wake up, you know? I wake up thinking that this has all been a really weird dream and I'm back in my old room with the dresser against the door and Dad's going to come in and hit me with his belt because I hoped they were dead." He curled up onto himself, head against his knees. "I don't want it to be a dream. I don't want them to come back."

His body began to shake, even though he didn't cry. Damn it. This was the sort of thing Nobody needed Melinda for, or even

Rebel. Emotions were messy and painful—they could be used against a man. Against a boy. That's why he tried not to have them

But beyond that, he understood exactly how Jamie felt.

He'd been there, after Albert had opened the closet door and carried Nobody home and laid him on the couch. After Albert had rubbed bear fat on Nobody's festering burn wounds and dripped water into his mouth from a rag so that Nobody wouldn't die of thirst but wouldn't guzzle the cup full so fast it would make him retch.

Of how seeing the man who wasn't a man but a coyote stand in the doorway and smile down at Nobody and say something that he didn't understand right before Albert came in and told Nobody that his mother was dead and her boyfriend was dead, too. And not believing the old man because to believe it was to hope and Nobody didn't know how to do that.

It'd taken him weeks to fully accept that his mom was gone and not coming back. And even when he'd recovered enough to believe that, he'd still been afraid that her ghost wouldn't let him be, that her *sica* spirit would haunt him until she drove him mad.

That fear, more than anything else, had pushed him into bars and brawls and women's arms as he tried to get away from the fact that, even though he never saw her, his mom was still torturing him.

Nobody got up. So he wasn't so good with words. The boy didn't need words. He wouldn't believe them anyway, not yet. Maybe after they got him back home, safe in Melinda's new house—the one that Nobody could walk into any time he wanted—maybe *then* Jamie would start to believe that they were dead and gone. It'd be different for the boy than it'd been for Nobody. Jamie wouldn't be alone.

Just like he wasn't alone now. Nobody went to the boy's side and sat on the edge of the bed. It squeaked, but he tried not to care. He put his arm around the boy's shoulders like he'd seen Melinda do and sort of hugged him.

It took a long time, but eventually the boy stopped shaking. By then, the sky outside his window was starting to show hints of color. Nobody found a clock hanging on the wall. It was almost six—hell. He hadn't planned on staying this long, but the boy had needed him.

"I have to go," he said, rubbing Jamie's back before he stood. "Will you come back?"

Nobody didn't know the answer to that. "Melinda's going to see you next week. And you won't be here too much longer. You'll be home soon."

The boy nodded. "Okay. I'm glad you came."

Nobody actually smiled. "Me, too." And he was. The boy was okay. This was a nice place to stay for a little while and soon enough, he'd be back where he belonged, where Nobody wouldn't have to hide in the shadows to see him.

Filled with these good thoughts, Nobody turned and climbed out of the window. His feet hit the ground in the same moment he realized that something was wrong. He dropped into a fighting crouch but he was too late—a bright light hit him square in the face. He couldn't see a damn thing.

"All the way down—now!" a voice shouted.

Nobody tensed. He didn't need to see with his eyes to know where the man was standing. He could hit him hard and—

"Nobody!" came Jamie's cry from inside.

Then there were more voices—a scared sounding woman and another man's voice. "You heard him, buddy," the second man said. "All the way down."

Something hard jammed into the top of Nobody's head from above. A gun.

Shit.

He fell to his knees and put his hands behind his head. He didn't want to go all the way down—too easy to be kicked. But he also didn't want to be shot. Bullet wounds hurt like a son-of-a-bitch.

"You're under arrest for breaking and entering," the first man said. Nobody heard a noise that sounded like a gun being holstered, then the metallic clink of handcuffs. "Don't make my partner shoot you."

"Don't hurt him!" Jamie cried from inside. "Nobody!"

"Come away from the window, Jamie," the woman's voice said. She still sounded terrified but there was steel in her voice. "*Now.*"

"*Don't hurt him!*" Jamie wailed. His voice grew distant, as if he'd been pulled out into the hall.

The gun jammed into his scalp pushed. "Are we going to do this the easy way or the hard way, buddy?"

If it were just him, they'd do this the hard way. He was pretty sure the cops knew it, too. He couldn't go back to jail, couldn't be found guilty and be sent back to prison. He'd be a repeat offender—his record would be Exhibit A that he was a bad, bad man who shouldn't see the light of the moon for years to come. He could bulldoze his way through these two cops with hopefully only a few collateral flesh wounds. No one would believe Jamie that it'd only been 'nobody' in his room.

Nobody could disappear again. He might have to move his camp, but he could do it. He could survive. He had before, he could do it again.

But if he did that—if he fought his way out of this like he always used to...

"*Nobody!*" Jamie cried from somewhere in the house.

He'd never get to see the boy again. Worse, he'd never get to see Melinda again. He'd be completely, utterly alone.

Melinda.

Jesus, she was going to kill him.

He lay down on the ground and didn't make a sound as the first cop's knee drove into his back. His arms were wrenched behind his back and his wrists were cuffed.

A thud came from behind him—the second cop jumping out of the window. Together, the two cops picked him up. Nobody's shoulder popped out of joint, but it didn't hurt. He wasn't about to make a sound that the cops would take as a sign of aggression—or a sound of pain that Jamie might hear.

"You picked the wrong house to bust into," the second cop said as they walked him back to a black and white. Nobody was slammed against the side of the car before the cop opened the door and shoved him into the backseat. "I installed that security system myself. *Nobody* messes with my aunt."

Yeah, that sounded about right. Nobody had messed with the guy's aunt.

Now there'd be hell to pay.

CHAPTER NINETEEN

Melinda tried not to worry. She hadn't seen Nobody in two days. There'd been a time when two days without Nobody was just the tip of the iceberg.

But something about his absence this time felt... off. Like the fact that the clinic and the center didn't get cleaned. The only time Nobody had failed to do his job was when Jack had been staking out the place and even then, Melinda was pretty sure Nobody hadn't made it in only because of that whole stab wound thing.

So for him to just disappear without a trace was problematic.

Then there was the call she got from Bertha Watterkotte at eight a.m. on the nose Wednesday morning. There'd been a disturbance at the foster mother's house, she told Melinda in an all-business voice. A man had been arrested leaving Jamie Kills Deer's room at 5:52 in the morning two nights before.

Ms. Watterkotte hadn't provided any other details—indeed, she'd stressed that she was only informing Melinda of this because Jamie was refusing to talk to anyone about what had happened that morning and perhaps Melinda could come in this afternoon to speak with the boy?

Melinda hung up the phone in a daze. Jesus, what a mess. And it'd happened two days ago! Somehow, she knew exactly what had happened.

That man had tracked down the foster home and gone slinking off into the shadows and gotten caught.

By God, she was going to wring his neck.

Anger got her moving. Someone had to be the responsible adult here and that someone was her, apparently. She didn't have time to waste. Rebel was already gone, doing whatever it was a medicine man did, so Melinda was on her own here. She called Tammy and informed her that she wouldn't be in to the center today, so Tammy should just do the best she could. Then she dressed in her best suit—okay, it was the only suit she'd moved out here, the one she wore when she had to go to the board meetings for the Mitchell Trust Fund—and headed to the police station.

When she walked in, Sheriff Means did a double take. "Ms. Mitchell?"

"Sheriff Means, we have a problem."

He regarded her for a second. "What'd he do?"

Yeah, the sheriff wasn't a stupid man. "He tracked down Jamie in his foster home and got arrested." Then she remembered—she'd told him Nancy's last name. And when a person's last name was Winking, there probably weren't that many listed in the phone book. Damn it all to hell—this was her fault.

Well, her fault up to a point. That man had promised her that he wouldn't make trouble and look what had happened. Trouble with a capital Nobody. "I don't know where he is. I only just found out he'd been arrested."

Sheriff Means gave her a startled look, but then he sat down and fired up his outdated computer. "He *got* arrested? What'd they do—taze him a dozen times? I didn't think Nobody would ever go quietly."

That was a good point—one she'd hazard a guess as to why. "If they cornered him around Jamie, he might not have wanted to risk getting the boy caught in the crossfire."

Sheriff Means snorted, like he didn't believe this was possible. Melinda let it slide. "I can track him down, but it might take a little while." Then he looked up at her again. "You going to go visit him?"

"No," she replied, not even knowing if what she wanted was possible. "I want you to get him in your custody and bring him back here."

Sheriff Means let forth a low whistle as he leaned back in his chair. "You want me to do *what*, now?"

She straightened her shoulders and gave the sheriff her best Mitchell sneer. It was never as good as her sister's, but it was good enough. "I believe the charges against him will be dropped and he'll be released. I don't want that to happen—not right away. I want him transferred to your custody and I want you to keep him locked up until I have custody of that boy. Do I make myself clear?"

Sheriff Means' mouth dropped open. "You *want* me to lock him up?"

"For a while," she clarified. "I'm sure you have some outstanding warrants you can use to get custody transferred to you—tribal jurisdiction or something. He won't be able to post bail. Anything to hold him long enough that he can't do something stupid to jeopardize me getting custody of that boy." She gave the sheriff a hard grin. "I can't have a vigilante running around here."

"Oh, sure—you say that now, when it's convenient for *you.*"

She ignored him. "Now that Jamie's an orphan," she went on. The word sounded rough in her mouth. Now that he was alone in this world, just like Nobody had been. "It'll be harder to track him through the system. If I lose him..."

She shook her head. If she didn't get custody, Jamie was the kind of kid who could fall through the cracks—alone, mostly quiet like Nobody had taught him to be. The chances were decent that he'd be shuffled around, a sitting duck for bullies and predators.

It might not happen. There were a lot of good foster families in the world, people who cared about kids and did their level best to make sure those kids had a good start in the world. But she knew enough of the world to know that not everyone had a kid's best interest at heart.

"I can't let that happen," she finished. "Can you?"

Sheriff Means tilted his head as if he were debating this. "I might be able to help you out—provided the current charges are dropped against Nobody. You have the power to make that happen, do you?"

She didn't. Not yet. But Nobody wasn't the only one who could figure out where Nancy Winking lived. "Do I have your word that you won't lock him up and throw away the key? You'll release him when the time is right and that you'll treat him fairly while he's here?"

Sheriff Means scratched at his neck in a way that was probably supposed to look lazy but instead came off as almost predatory. How long had he waited to get Nobody in his custody? A *long* time.

In that moment, she almost backed out of it. Putting Nobody in a cell—even one in this small office—was tantamount to breaking him one day at a time. She didn't want to do that but he'd gone back on his word to her and mucked up the whole process of getting Jamie in her custody. She was as mad as hell that he hadn't trusted her, hadn't trusted that she would be able to navigate the system and get Jamie home in a matter of months, if not weeks.

He could just sit in a cell for a few days and think about what he'd done while she cleaned up his mess.

"Tell you what," Sheriff Means said in a too-casual voice. "I'll do my best to get him here and hold him and we'll go from there. Deal?"

It was a crappy deal and they both knew it. But she needed Nobody someplace safe, where he wouldn't get himself killed and he wouldn't put Jamie at risk by being a stubborn idiot.

"Deal."

Sheriff Means chuckled. "Lady," he said as she headed out to her car, "you are a piece of work."

She didn't bother to reply.

Melinda knocked on the pristine white door of a pristine ranch house. The moment the sound faded, she reconsidered. If her sister Madeline knew what she was doing—barging in on Nancy Winking three hours before they were to meet at the social services office, Madeline would say that Melinda was no better than Nobody Bodine was—headstrong, stupid and above the rules.

She'd be right. But it was too late now.

The curtain moved, but the door did not open. "Yes?" said a worried voice inside. Melinda could just barely see an older woman through the glass.

"Ms. Winking? Hello." Melinda pulled one of her hot-off-the-presses business cards out of her handbag. She held it up so Ms. Winking could see the card through the window. "My name is Melinda Mitchell and I'm the director of the White Sandy Child Care Center. We've spoken on the phone about Jamie Kills Deer. May I come in?"

Ms. Winking made no attempt to open the door.

"This is about the other morning," Melinda added. "I understand that Jamie's not talking. I think I can explain what happened."

After a moment longer, the door opened. "My nephew's a police officer," Ms. Winking said. "He keeps an eye on me."

Melinda nodded in understanding. Ms. Winking wasn't the kind of woman who could threaten anyone outright, but the implication was clear. "Of course. Did your nephew arrest the man?"

Ms. Winking nodded. She still hadn't invited Melinda in.

"As well he should have. What happened was unacceptable and I'm glad that your nephew is able to help you out. I imagine that, when you're a foster parent, you can't be too careful." She smiled her most comforting smile. "You're doing the best you can for Jamie and I appreciate it."

Ms. Winking opened the door a bit more and looked Melinda up and down. Melinda had her hair pinned back. Her make-up was understated and, of course, the suit was perfect for trust-fund board meetings—or court hearings for custody cases. "You're hoping to get custody of Jamie, is that right?"

Melinda nodded. She pulled out her phone and called up the photo of her new house. "While my application is being processed, I bought a house that would be perfect for Jamie to grow up in. As I'm sure you know, he had a rough home life."

"Yes," Ms. Winking said, stepping forward to look at the photo. "I read his file, of course. And since the other morning... well, he stopped talking once they took that man away. I can hardly get him to come out of his room." She shook her head in what looked like desperation. "I've seen a lot of tough cases in my time—I was never able to have children and after my husband passed, may he rest in peace, I started taking in children."

Melinda nodded again. Her comforting smile was beginning to hurt her cheeks, but this was progress.

"But Jamie is—well," Ms. Winking went on. She shuddered. "There've been confrontations before, you know. Angry parents, the like. That's why Mark—he's my nephew—installed that security system. But this is the first time I've ever had someone actually break into my home."

"I'm sure it was unnerving," Melinda agreed. "I'd like to fill in a few of the blanks for you. I think that, if you understand the whole picture, you'll realize you were never in danger."

Ms. Winking nodded again and stepped back to hold the door open for Melinda. "Come in. Shall I get Jamie?"

"Not just yet. I'd like to have this conversation without him around. I don't want to upset him even more." Because when she told Ms. Winking that she'd arranged for Nobody to remain in police custody until Jamie was no longer in her care, Jamie was *going* to be upset.

Ms. Winking led her to a cozy kitchen that looked to be original to the house. *Harvest gold appliances*, Melinda thought with an inward smile. *Nice*. A worn high chair was tucked into one corner and the refrigerator handle had been dulled by countless little hands opening it, but everything was clean and neat, much like Ms. Winking.

She was probably in her mid-sixties, a heavy-set woman with a grandmotherly air about her. Her long, gray hair was rolled back into a loose bun and the wrinkles around her mouth and eyes indicated that she laughed easily and often.

"Have a seat. Coffee?" she asked as she bustled around the kitchen, assembling the cups before Melinda could say 'Yes, Please.'

"So you don't know anything about the man who was arrested in your home?"

"Jamie called him Nobody," Ms. Winking said, sliding into her seat. "Mark—my nephew—said his name was Nobody Bodine and that he had a record. He served time for killing a man?" She shuddered so hard she had to put her coffee cup down. "I'm sorry."

"Don't be. I understand completely." Melinda took a sip to give Ms. Winking the chance to compose herself. "Mr. Bodine—Nobody—is an unusual man. He was involved in a brawl at a bar where he punched a man and that did lead to the man's death. He was quite young at the time—seventeen—and had been living on his own for about four years when the fight happened."

Ms. Winking blinked. "My, that is young—he'd been alone since he was thirteen?"

Melinda nodded. She felt badly about this—it was not her story to tell—but Nobody would never get the chance to set the record straight. "He'd survived incredible abuse at the hands of his mother. She tortured him."

"Oh, my," Ms. Winking said, not looking at Melinda.

"I only tell you that to help you see why he was here," Melinda hurried to add. "Mr. Bodine never had anyone to look out for him. When he found Jamie—a young child being beaten by his parents with no one else to rely on, he decided to be a... guardian angel, you could say. The kind of guardian angel he'd needed but never had." The sheriff would say *vigilante*, but Melinda was going for an image make-over here. "He watched over the boy, gave him a safe place to go and defended him when necessary. I think it's fair to say that he's the only reason Jamie's still alive."

"I see," Ms. Winking said in the kind of voice that suggested she didn't, not entirely.

Melinda sighed. This wasn't going poorly, but it wasn't going well. Not yet. "As I'm sure you can gather, Mr. Bodine hasn't always operated within the bounds of the law—or reason. He promised he would trust me—that Jamie was safe here with you and that no one was hurting him. But, as you know, he didn't keep that promise to me. It was important for him to see with his own eyes that Jamie was well."

It shouldn't sting—but it did. He'd broken his promise to let her handle this. He hadn't trusted her.

She wanted to wring his neck all over again. But she didn't. She just smiled at Ms. Winking.

"He looked so dangerous," the older woman said in a quiet tone.

"I know that his looks can be intimidating, but please believe me—he was no threat to you. He was so worried about the boy that he just didn't think through the consequences of his actions." Like the possibility of a security system or a cop for a nephew.

"He's been the one constant in Jamie's life," Melinda went on. "The one person he's always been able to trust. I understand if you want to press charges against Mr. Bodine, but I'd like to ask you not to. I believe that locking Nobody Bodine up will only harm Jamie. I'm working to build a bond with him, but without Mr. Bodine..."

"He has been so upset," Ms. Winking murmured. "He was never a talkative child, but now he won't even look at me. I've been so worried that man did something to him but..." she sighed heavily. "You should have seen him when Mark arrested that man—screaming and crying out for him."

Melinda's heart broke. Yeah, that was why Nobody hadn't fought back. He'd realized that would have only made things worse for Jamie.

"I just want what's best for Jamie. We all do."

They sat there for a moment, sipping the coffee. It was growing cold.

"I understand what you're saying," Ms. Winking finally said into the silence. "But I can't have that man breaking into my house again. What if there'd been shots fired?"

"I've made plans for that. If you decide not to file charges against Mr. Bodine, I've arranged for him to be turned over to the tribal sheriff. Sheriff Means has promised me that he'll hold Mr. Bodine until Jamie is no longer in your care. Mr. Bodine will be unable to make bail."

Ms. Winking looked up at her in surprise. "You want me to have him released so you can lock him up?"

"Basically," Melinda readily agreed. "I don't want to discount the trauma he put you through, but I don't think he needs to spend three to five years in prison for it, either." Another three years in prison would break that man. Who could guess what Nobody would be when he got out again?

She remembered him telling the story about how he got his GED by guarding the college frat-boy drug runner, how the frat-boy got shanked. How many people had Nobody beat up—people like Dwayne, who were also in prison?

Who could guess what Nobody would be *if* he got out again?

Ms. Winking swirled what was left of her coffee in her cup. "And you're confident that'll be best for Jamie? To allow him to continue to be with a convicted felon?"

"I believe Nobody Bodine would die to protect Jamie, if that was what was best for the boy."

That was the truth. Nobody would die for Jamie—or go to prison again, which was basically the same thing.

"You can think about it. Mr. Bodine isn't going anywhere," Melinda said as she stood. "I won't take up any more of your time. I think it'd be best to stick to our scheduled meeting with Jamie at Ms. Watterkotte's office this afternoon, don't you?" Maybe by that time, Ms. Winking would have decided to drop the charges against Nobody.

"Yes, I suppose," Ms. Winking said. Melinda might have been wrong, but she thought the older woman looked relieved that Melinda wasn't going to press the issue by calling Jamie in and telling him what might happen. "Thank you for stopping by. I do feel better about the situation now."

"I'm glad." And she was. "I'll see you in a few hours."

She left the house. Nobody was still in jail and he might be there for a long time, but at least Melinda had done what she could.

Now she just had to wait.

CHAPTER TWENTY

"Let's go," the cop said. It was a different cop, but Nobody wasn't exactly keeping track at this point. He didn't know how long he'd been here—maybe eight days, maybe ten. He couldn't think about it. "Arms in back."

He could still fight. But he was inside, with walls and bars and razor wire between him and the night sky. He could only fight if he wanted to die.

So he turned around and held his arms in back. Cuffs were slapped on his wrists again. He wanted to think they were letting him go, but even he knew you didn't cuff a man to turn him loose.

There were two options. Either they were moving him. Maybe he'd get a window this time. If he could just see the sky...

The other choice was that someone was here to see him. He wanted to hope it was Melinda, but at the same time he didn't want her to see him like this, locked up like an animal. She'd be plenty mad at him, that was for damn sure.

Maybe it was Melinda. Maybe she'd have the boy with her. Maybe she'd bailed him out. He knew he didn't deserve it, but for a brief moment, he allowed himself to hope. The thought of her—sitting next to him in front of the fire, curled up in his arms while she slept, riding him with her wildfire hair all crazy around her beautiful face—well, that'd kept him going. But he didn't know how much longer he could hold onto those images. Hope was a damn dangerous thing when a man was in jail. Better to keep his head down and get through each day as it came.

The cop led him down the long hallway to the booking area. He kept his head down—no sense looking around. He didn't want to start anything with other prisoners. "Here he is," the cop said, giving him a little shove forward. "Don't talk much, though."

"Yeah," said a voice that sounded like home—but with an attitude. "We're used to it."

He knew that voice. Jack.

What the hell was Jack doing here? Nobody took a cautious look up. Jack was leaning up against a desk, a smirk on his face. Nobody wasn't exactly happy to see him, but there were worse people in the world.

Like Sheriff Means—who stood up from the chair behind Jack. He did his best to stare down at Nobody. Nobody didn't even flinch. He wouldn't give Means the satisfaction. "He didn't give you any trouble, did he?"

"Nah," the cop said. "Never said a damn word."

Nobody wanted to ask what was going on—why were the sheriff and Jack here? But he didn't want to admit that Means knew anything he didn't, so he kept his mouth shut.

"You got all the paperwork?" Means said.

"Yup," the cop replied. "He's all yours."

What? Means had come for him? Nobody didn't like this. Not a bit. He'd rather be moved to a new cell. But he didn't have a say in the matter. So he kept his mouth shut.

Jack walked back behind Nobody and changed out the cuffs. He locked Nobody's hands in front of him this time. "I can't believe you *let* yourself get arrested, if you don't mind me saying. Never thought I'd see the day."

He'd only gotten arrested for one reason. He didn't want to give Means anything to go on, but Nobody couldn't help it. "The boy?"

Jack laughed. "Man, you are a piece of work."

"The boy's fine," Means said. "It's the woman you should be worried about. That Melinda Mitchell?" Means whistled. The noise made Nobody flinch, but he managed to keep his face blank. "I'm going to be holding onto you for a while longer." He smiled when he said it. "Understood?"

Nobody gave him a curt nod, just enough to let the sheriff know he got it.

Means gave him a mean grin. "Officer, if you'd follow us out, I'd appreciate it."

The cop snorted. "You think he'll run? *Shit*. He hasn't done anything but sit in his cell the whole time we've been here." The cop made a move to prod Nobody in the side.

Hell, no. Nobody gave him a look and the cop backed up a step. "Yeah, okay," he said, a new respect in his voice. "Once he's in the car, he's all yours."

"Don't try anything funny," Jack said in a kind of quiet voice. "You know he's got it in for you."

Nobody gave another small nod. He wouldn't try anything, not yet. Means was taking every precaution—even bringing in Jack as back-up. There would be no opportunity to run, not yet. He was just exchanging one cell for another, one jailer for another. He deserved nothing less.

Would he ever see Melinda or the boy again?

Nobody had been in the sheriff's cell for three days. He knew that because watching the sun move across the floor was the only thing to do in a place like this.

He'd mostly been alone. There'd been some guy Nobody didn't recognize in the other cell—the one with the window—when they'd brought Nobody inside. But that guy had made bail, apparently. So now Nobody was alone.

Well, not entirely alone. Sheriff Means appeared to expect Nobody to go up in a puff of smoke or bend the bars with his bare hands or something, because he and Jack were doing twelve-hour shifts of staring at him. Nobody was never left to his own devices.

Means didn't talk to him. Of course, he didn't taunt him or throw crap at him. Nobody would have guessed that the sheriff would have jumped on this chance to exact a little revenge on him—but he didn't. He brought Nobody his meals—decent food, better than what he'd been getting in the other jail—and even offered Nobody a cup of coffee every time he made a new pot. But mostly he shuffled paper and took calls.

Maybe Nobody had figured the sheriff wrong. After all this time, he'd figured the lawman would have had it in for him, just like Jack had said. But he didn't.

It was different with Jack. Jack would turn on the little black-and-white TV set the sheriff had and watch cartoons. He played solitaire and drank a lot of coffee, but that was about it. Nobody wanted to ask Jack what was going on or if he knew how long he'd be in here, but he couldn't figure out a way to ask the question without betraying weakness and he couldn't do that. Weakness got a man killed in prison.

Nobody was alone and ignored. It shouldn't have hurt—it was a far sight better than the sheriff getting it into his head that maybe Nobody needed to be put in his place—but it hurt anyway.

This was his fault. All of it. Even the loneliness was his fault. He'd let himself get comfortable with Melinda—with being around other people. With stepping out of the shadows and into the light. He'd thought he'd hate it, but now that it'd been taken away from him, he missed it all the more.

He should have stuck to the shadows.

And now he couldn't even do that.

He tried. He'd always been solid, always had just the two legs. He didn't shift his shape and he was no *sica*. But, a few times when the midnight hour had long passed and dawn was still a ways off—the hours he should have been sliding into Melinda's bed and taking comfort in her arms—he tried. He sat as far into the corner of his cell as possible and tried to let the darkness—what little of it there was in a room with the lights always on—pull him into the shadows.

It didn't work. No weird tingling on his skin. His hair didn't even stand on end. Nothing.

The morning of the fourth day, the door of the station opened. Nobody didn't look up. He just wanted to be invisible again, where no one could see him and he could come and go as he pleased. He missed Melinda. He missed the boy. He missed the horses. And the night sky. He missed all the things that had made him who he was. Gone. They were all gone.

He sat on the floor, back against the wall of his cell, and tried to remember the last book he'd read, the one about the Sackett brother that had to kill a man. Nobody couldn't remember all the words, but if he concentrated, it was almost like he was watching the movie of the book in his mind. It was enough to keep him from going truly insane.

"Sheriff," a tight female voice said as heels clicked over the floor.

"Ms. Mitchell," Means said. "This way."

That got Nobody's attention. He looked up to see Melinda—

his Melinda—standing there. His chest unclenched and he felt himself breathe. She hadn't forgotten him. She'd come for him, his Melinda. He hadn't been wrong to hope that she would.

Except she wasn't his Melinda. The woman who was stalking her way back to where he was locked up like a stray dog had her hair smoothed back into a severe bun. She wore a gray suit and tall black heels that made her look like a lawyer. There was nothing wild or free about her—especially not about her face. The change was so different that, if it hadn't been for the red hair, he would have thought Dr. Mitchell had come to scowl at him.

Melinda and the sheriff stopped in front of his cell. She didn't say hello or ask him how he'd been. She just looked down at him with nothing but contempt. "When did you get him?" she asked the sheriff. Her eyes—cold and unfeeling—stayed on him.

"A few days ago."

Nobody ignored the sheriff. Melinda had come to see him. Maybe she'd come to get him out?

Melinda turned enough to fix that scowl on Means. "You were supposed to call me when you got him."

Ah, so that'd been Means' punishment. "Been busy," Means replied. But he did wipe that grin off his face. Even a lawman was afraid of Melinda when she was mad.

And she was *mad.* Means' words came back to her—"It's the woman you should be worried about." He hadn't just been blowing smoke up Nobody's backside, that much was obvious.

"I can see that." Melinda's voice would have turned the White Sandy river to ice in the middle of July.

Then she swung that scowl back to him. "Why isn't he in the cell with the window?"

"It was occupied by another 'guest' when we got him here."

"It's empty now. Move him." It was not a request.

That was when he realized she hadn't come to get him out. She was going to leave him here. With a window, but still. More than anyone else in the world—even more than Jamie—she knew what being behind bars did to him. And she was going to leave him in here.

He knew he deserved it but it still went down bitter.

"I'll have to call Jack in. In case he tries anything funny," Means said. "That's extra overtime."

"So call him in." Means opened his mouth to argue, but Melinda cut him off. "I'll wait."

Nobody wanted to smile at her for putting the sheriff in his place, but he didn't. He couldn't—not when she turned those pale blue eyes in his direction. They were all the more cold now.

She waited until the sheriff headed back to his desk and picked up the phone. Then she crossed her arms and glared at Nobody as if she were going to reduce him to dust with looks alone. "You should have trusted me."

Nobody swallowed. He didn't know what to say to that but he got the feeling if he didn't say something, she might tell the sheriff she'd changed her mind and Nobody could stay in the cell without the window. He wanted to tell her that he'd tried, he really had—but he'd needed to see with his own eyes that the boy was okay. Which would have just proved her right—he hadn't trusted her.

So he just said, "Yeah," and hoped that was the right thing.

It wasn't. He wouldn't have thought it possible, but she got even meaner looking. "I needed you to trust me. I needed a *reason*, Nobody."

For the first time, her voice softened. Hell, her whole face softened and she looked sad. Worn down and worried and tired, but above all that, sad. She knew exactly what being locked up would do to him. And she was going to leave him in here anyway. "I needed a reason to trust you. And you..." Her voice caught. She looked like she might cry because of him and it tore him up. Just tore him up. "You didn't give me one."

He stood and tried to go to her. He wasn't so good with words, but there were other ways to say he was sorry. Except there were some damn thick bars in between them. They clanked when he put his hands on them. He didn't know what he was going to say until the words were already out and he couldn't stop them. "I tried. But I didn't... I didn't know *how*."

Which was true. He'd never trusted anyone. Albert had saved him, Rebel had welcomed him to the fire—but he'd never trusted either of them enough to even know where he lived. *How* he lived. He'd let Jamie into his world because the boy... the boy had needed him.

Melinda had needed him. And he'd let her down.

"Everything okay over there?" the sheriff said in a loud voice.

Nobody's sudden movements must have caught his eye.

"Fine." Anything soft or sad about Melinda vanished and suddenly Nobody was eye to eye with a woman who would leave him to rot. "So," she went on, all that ice back in her voice, "Ms. Winking decided not to press charges against you, but because you *didn't* do what I asked you to—because you *didn't* trust me, you will stay here until I get custody."

He nodded. "I'm sorry," he whispered, as if he were apologizing for having to stay. He couldn't argue with her—and even if he tried, it wouldn't make any difference. She could walk right out of here and he couldn't. "But the boy?"

She sighed so heavily that he thought she might deflate. "The boy is fine, Nobody. He was fine before. He didn't need to see you getting hauled off at gunpoint, but he'll be fine again."

"Can I see him?" He knew the answer before the words got out of his mouth.

"No," she said, her voice somewhere in between disgust and menace and sadness and pity. It looked like it hurt her to say it. It sure as hell hurt to hear. "You're *going* to have to trust me. You have no choice."

"Will you come back? I need you." The words were out before he knew it—an admission of his weakness. He swallowed. He was all in. Might as well be *all* in. "I need you more than this." He'd always thought that other people would use his attachment for Melinda and Jamie against him, but now?

Now he saw he was wrong.

She would. Because she knew what she meant to him.

She touched him then. Her hand slid between the bars and her fingertips stroked over his cheek like the answer was going to be *yes*. But it wasn't and they both knew it. "I need you, too. I just wish you'd realized it sooner."

He tried to lean into her touch—to hold the contact for as long as he could—but then her hand was gone and her back was turned to him. "Rebel will be by," she said. Then she stalked toward where the sheriff was sitting, watching them. "Move him to the cell with the window," she said as she stalked past him. "But don't let him out until I say so."

"Will do, Ms. Mitchell." But the sheriff's words fell on deaf ears.

Melinda was already gone.

Nobody sat down to wait for Jack to come so he could get a window to look out of.

He had no choice in the matter.

Melinda sat in her car and cried. *Ugly* cried. She was trashing her conservative, understated makeup all to hell but she couldn't stop.

God, what was she doing? She couldn't just leave him in there.

Could she?

She'd seen Nobody when he was wounded and bleeding, when he was in so much pain he couldn't even sit up in his chair. She'd seen him anxious and nervous and worried and mean. She'd seen him take out six men.

She'd never seen him like that. It'd been like... like he wasn't even in there. His eyes had been as close to dead as she'd ever seen them—and, considering how close he'd gotten to actual death, that was saying something.

She'd wanted him to sit and think about what he'd done wrong. Like a time-out for a grown-up.

But that wasn't what was happening. She couldn't help but feel that she was killing him, one day at a time in that cage. Because that's what it was. A cage. Like he was nothing more than an animal that had gone feral.

But she had to, she told herself. She hadn't told him any lies—she couldn't trust him not to muck things up worse than he already had. She had to leave him in there, for his own good.

For so long—most of her life—she'd been the flighty one, the weirdo, the black sheep in the family. The one who made a scene at fundraisers and a mess of her personal life. She was not the responsible one who got good grades and made wise decisions. She was the flake, the screw-up with horrible taste in men.

That part, at least, hadn't changed. She was in love with a man who she'd not only *not* bailed out, but who deserved to be behind bars in the first place.

For maybe only the second time in her life, Melinda had a greater responsibility than herself that she had to consider—Jaime.

The boy had no one else in this world now, except for her and Nobody. And if she didn't do the right thing here, that child wouldn't have either of them. Melinda would lose custody and Nobody? Well, she didn't even want to think what would happen to that man if Jamie were taken away.

She couldn't leave him in there. But she *had* to.

She couldn't stand to see him locked up like that—caged and desperate. She just couldn't stand there and try to be the grown up when he said he needed her. In that moment, she'd wavered. But if she'd made the sheriff unlock the door, what promise did she have that he wouldn't slip off into the night to check on Jamie again? What guarantee did she have that he wouldn't wind up behind bars again?

She couldn't trust him. And she couldn't bear to see him suffer. She'd never felt so miserable in her entire life.

Being the grown-up sucked.

Slowly, Melinda managed to get herself back under control. She had some powder and lipstick in her purse, so she tried to fix her face as best she could. There was no solving the red eyes, but it'd have to do.

Then she made the long drive into Rapid City to meet with Bertha Watterkotte for her official foster-parent interview.

One step closer to having custody of Jamie. The modular house was hooked up now and she'd started moving her things in, getting things for Jamie set up in anticipation of the home study. If everything went according to plan, she might get custody of him in two weeks.

Two weeks. It was a long time to keep Nobody behind bars. It'd already been close to three weeks since he'd been arrested. She'd missed him more than she could even put into words. No little taps on the window at night. No man walking out of the shadows to sit at the fire.

No Nobody. And after seeing him like that today?

But what choice had he given her?

This was the only way.

She had no idea how to make it better.

CHAPTER TWENTY ONE

The days were long. The nights were long. Basically, being in jail was one of the better ways to stretch time.

Rebel did come and sit with him. He brought in his beading and sat on the floor, telling Nobody what was happening in the world without him. If Nobody closed his eyes to block out the bars that separated him and Rebel, he could almost pretend they were back around the fire.

Melinda had gotten herself approved to be a foster parent. Jamie was due to be handed over any day now, Rebel said. He'd helped get some of the furniture in Melinda's new house put together, too. Said it shouldn't be too much longer, but what did that mean when Nobody was locked up in a place where time had very little meaning?

Rebel told him what else was going on, too. Said Clarence was getting mighty tired of doing Nobody's job for him. Said Dr. Mitchell was tired of listening to Clarence complain about doing Nobody's job, but she hadn't hired anyone to replace him. Nobody couldn't figure if that meant that he was going to get out soon or not.

Melinda had said he had to stay in here until she got custody, hadn't she? And if Rebel said she was going to get custody soon... she'd come for him, wouldn't she?

Maybe she wouldn't. He hadn't given her a reason to trust him. How could he, when he was behind bars? For all he knew, he might be in here a while longer.

On the whole, it could be worse. He knew that first-hand. He didn't have to share his cell with anyone, no one picked a fight with him and he got to keep his window. He spent a lot of time staring out of it—so close to being outside, but so far away. Fall was coming in fast. His horses would start to grow out their winter coats. They were probably doing okay now, but if Nobody didn't make it back to take care of them before the winter snows buried the grasses, they could starve. He didn't want that. If he didn't get out of here soon, he'd have to tell Rebel how to get to his camp. Maybe, if Melinda got Jamie, Jamie could take Rebel out there. Just so long as someone took care of the horses.

Sometimes, he retreated into his imagination and played out one of his stories—a man alone, making hard choices in a hard land. That'd always been how Nobody had felt before. Now? Now the stories he'd spent years reading seemed to ring hollow for him.

But most of the time, when he looked out his window, he thought about Melinda. She'd be settling into her own place now. Would she have a fire pit outside, like Rebel did? Would she build her own fire and spread a blanket out next to it?

Or maybe she was doing crazy things to her house—cutting metal to fit over the door in wild patterns, painting rooms in bright colors that wouldn't suit anyone but her. He wanted to see what she did with her own place.

He didn't know if he'd get to.

Even if he got out of here, he had no idea if she'd let him back into her bed. She'd let him see the boy, he was pretty sure. Kind of sure.

He had to trust her. He was beginning to realize he didn't have the first idea how to actually do that. And that wasn't even including the fact that she'd left him in here.

He'd thought... he'd thought he might get to be happy. With her, he'd been closer to happy than he'd ever thought he'd get to be, right up until he'd gone off and done things the way he'd always done them before. He'd brought her into his world and she'd made a place for him by the fire. A place for him in her bed.

Why hadn't he let that be enough?

He couldn't go back to the way things had been before. He knew that now. That was the truth of coming into the light. For a short while, he'd been a part of something that had always been beyond him—the love of a good woman at the end of a day, the boy looking up to him. Things had been better than he'd ever thought he deserved them to be.

And he'd thrown that all away. Because he hadn't trusted her.

So he sat and he waited. He hoped he'd get out soon.

He hoped he could give Melinda a reason to trust him again.

He just wasn't sure how he was going to do that.

Sheriff Means answered the phone. "Yeah. Yeah? Hey— that's great. Now? Yeah." He hung up the phone and announced, "Today's the day!"

Nobody looked at him out of the corner of his eye. What did that mean? And why did he sound so damn happy about it? Besides, the sun was on the verge of setting. The day was mostly over. "The day for what?" His voice felt creaky from lack of use.

Means waltzed up to the cell door, handcuffs in his hands. "Four whole words that time," he whistled. "A new record." He bounced the cuffs in his hands. "You know the drill."

Nobody did. He turned around and stuck his arms out behind him. Means slapped on the cuffs. Then he stepped forward so Means could get the door to the cell open.

It didn't happen. Instead, Means looked at him for a moment. "Don't get any funny ideas," he said. His hand was resting on the butt of his pistol.

Damn it, he was getting really tired of people saying that to him. He turned around to give Means a proper glare. Behind bars *and* cuffed? What funny ideas was he going to get? A career in comedy?

Outside, a horn honked.

"Let's go," Means said. Finally, he opened the damned door. He grabbed Nobody by the arm and started walking him up front.

Nobody didn't like the man touching him like this. Suddenly, after weeks of not being able to do anything, he tensed. His hair stood on end and he felt *it*—whatever the hell *it* was—move over his skin.

The shadows were growing long. He was so close to being free. So damn close.

"Hey, what the hell?" Means yelped in what sounded like actual pain. But he let go of Nobody. "What the hell was *that*?"

Nobody didn't reply. He didn't know what was waiting for him on the other side of the door. Another cop car, another move to another jail—another cage? Or something else?

If it were just him, he'd head-butt Means until the man was down and then he'd kick him just for good measure. Then Nobody would be gone. He'd get the cuffs off somehow and...

Never see the boy again. Never have the chance to prove to Melinda that she could trust him.

He stopped. Just stood there while Means got his act together again. "Don't you *ever* do that again," Means said. He didn't put his hands back on Nobody but he didn't shoot him, so that was something. "Walk, damn you."

So Nobody walked. He walked right out the front door and into the dim light of early evening.

He blinked, his eyes adjusting to the dusk after weeks of non-stop fluorescent lighting. The back of his neck prickled as he breathed in air that didn't smell of the sheriff and stale piss.

He was still alive, by God. He'd survived this far. He could make it.

"Why is he handcuffed?" Melinda's voice cut through the air like a knife.

Melinda. She'd come back.

"Ma'am," Means said in a voice that wasn't quite respectful enough for Nobody's tastes, "Mr. Bodine is still a guest of the tribe."

"You've got to cuff him to let him go?"

Nobody smiled—actually smiled for what felt like the first time in months. *Let him go.* He was almost free.

But he also smiled at the way she said it—she wasn't buying Means' line of bull. He focused on the direction her voice had come from. His eyes adjusted to the low light and she came into focus.

Melinda was leaning against her car. Gone was the harsh suit and slicked-back hair. She looked just like he remembered her—wildfire hair all around, one of those skirts she liked so much and a tank top that gave just a hint of what was underneath.

And she had a grin on her face that made him think that maybe it was going to be okay. She was glad to see him—not like the last time, when she'd left him behind bars.

Jamie stood next to her, vibrating with so much energy that Melinda had to keep an arm around his shoulders. He waved, the biggest smile Nobody had ever seen on his face. The boy looked happy. Actually happy—the kind of joy that wasn't crowded out by worry or pain. He looked like a kid should look.

They were okay. They were fine, just like she'd said.

"Hey," Means shot back at her in a voice that Nobody didn't particularly care for, "I'm not taking any chances with him. Hell, he just—I don't know what he *did*. He shocked me or something."

"Yeah," Melinda said dryly, "I'm used to it."

Means stood behind Nobody and undid the cuffs. "All charges against you have been dropped," he said in an official tone. "You are no longer in custody of the White Sandy Reservation. But stay out of trouble and stay the hell out of my way."

Nobody flexed his wrists. He didn't bother to look back at the sheriff. He just walked down the steps.

His head was a mess of emotions, ones he wasn't used to. He wanted to run to her and the boy, swoop them up in his arms and break down in tears. Tears. What the hell? He didn't cry, for God's sake. He *didn't* cry.

But his deep breaths of clean air were suddenly gasps that didn't give him enough to actually survive on. As much as he wanted to run to them, the night was pulling at him. There was safety in the darkness, where no one could see him. No one would know he was there.

She'd left him in there. Because she'd had to, but she'd been able to leave him there.

She'd walked away from him without a look back.

Maybe she didn't want him to wrap her up in a big hug.

The boy broke away from her, charging up at him. Nobody flinched when the boy tackle-hugged him. "I missed you so much," he said in a quiet voice. Even as he said it, he kept a cautious eye on the sheriff.

Nobody didn't know what he was supposed to do. Everyone was watching him, expecting him to do something. But he didn't know what. The last time he'd been released from prison, no one had been waiting for him. No one had expected anything from him.

The shadows reached up and pulled at him. *Free.* He was free. He just... he just needed to think, to figure out what he was supposed to do now.

"You're all right," he said almost as much to himself as to Jamie. That's what he'd wanted, right? To see with his own eyes the boy was all right.

Well, now he'd seen it. The boy was fine. Just like Melinda had promised he would be. She'd take good care of him. Better than Nobody could, that much was clear.

He patted the boy on the head. "I've... I've got to go."

"What? Go where?" Jamie took a step back. "Don't you want to come see the house? I got my own room and everything! I was waiting for you!"

Nobody looked over to where Melinda was still leaning against the car. She wasn't scowling at him, not like she'd been last time, but she wasn't throwing her arms around his neck, either.

"I'll come see you," he said to the boy. Then he took a step— not toward the boy, not toward the woman. And definitely not toward the sheriff. "Stay with her, you hear?"

Toward the shadows. Toward the safety of the night.

"Nobody?" Melinda called out.

But he didn't turn back. He ran into the shadows and was gone.

It was better this way.

Oh, God. He'd just... disappeared.

"Nobody?" Jamie yelled. "*Nobody*!"

"How the hell does he *do* that?" Sheriff Means said, rubbing at the back of his neck.

"He just does," Melinda replied, trying so very hard to keep her cool. "Jamie, honey—let's go. He won't come back here."

"Better not," Sheriff Means replied. The phone rang inside. "Ms. Mitchell, always a pleasure." Then he went inside.

"Where'd he go?" Jamie all but wailed. "I want Nobody!"

Melinda looked into the lengthening shadows, trying to find the darker one. She didn't. "He'll come back," she said, although she didn't know if she was trying to reassure herself or the boy.

"But why didn't he come home with us now?" Jamie asked, his voice growing tight. "You said he could—you said he *would*!"

She crouched down in front of Jamie and held him by his shoulders. "First off, you need to calm down. Second off, he's been in jail for a long time." Almost five weeks. That was her doing. Oh, God—what had she done?

But she had to keep it together for Jamie. "He just needs to... I don't know. Get things sorted out again, you know?"

Jamie nodded and sniffled. She pointed him back to the car, proud that she'd managed to be normal and not go running off into the dark after that man.

He'd just gone, so fast that she'd hardly been able to see him.

She drove Jamie home, trying to figure out what had happened. She hadn't lied to the boy, she was pretty sure. Five weeks was a long time for Nobody to be locked away. He probably did need to get things straightened out in his head.

Or maybe... maybe he didn't want to see her. Maybe he was mad at her. Could she blame him?

"Let's build a fire," she told Jamie. She didn't say it, but she thought, *for Nobody.* They roasted marshmallows—something Jamie had never done before—and talked about how they were going to paint his room that weekend. He wanted spaceships and planets, so Melinda told him they could paint the solar system on the ceiling, if he wanted.

As she and Jamie talked, she kept her eye on the trees around them. Nobody would come, she decided. He had to. He'd have to come and see that Jamie was okay, right?

He'd have to come see her, wouldn't he?

But he didn't. She tucked Jamie into bed and sat by the fire a while longer before deciding that maybe, if she went to bed, there'd come a tap on the window in the middle of the night and Nobody would climb into her room and into her arms.

She lay awake for a long time, listening with all her might for any possible sound that could come from a man outdoors. As she lay there, she was forced to confront the fact that he might *not* come.

She'd left him in there, locked away from everything he loved. She hadn't told him she was waiting for him because... because she'd been so mad at the time. Because she'd been worried and overwhelmed with everything she was suddenly responsible for, she hadn't been able to think about what would happen next.

Had she really believed that Nobody would walk out of that jail and into her arms like nothing had happened? And they'd waltz off into the sunset, an almost normal family of sorts—a child, a foster mother and a father-figure?

That's what she'd wanted to happen.

That's not what happened.

As she drifted off to a restless sleep filled with coyotes slinking through the tall prairie grass, she decided they'd make another fire tomorrow night.

Nobody stood by the creek, rubbing his horses' noses, one after the other. They hadn't forgotten him, he was happy to see. It didn't matter where he'd been or why he'd been there—he was back now and that was all that mattered. They hadn't been brushed in a long time and they all looked a little ragged, but otherwise, they were the same as they'd ever been. Red was so glad to see Nobody that the horse almost knocked him off his feet when she nudged him. Star was still here—he wondered when the old girl had gotten back. Had Melinda let her go or had she taken off by herself?

If Melinda had let Star go that meant that she didn't want him back.

Even though it was probably the truth, he pushed the thought away. He couldn't think of that right now.

After he'd touched each one of his herd, he walked the dark path up to camp. It was probably close to three in the morning—he'd taken a long, winding path back here, just in case the sheriff got it into his head that he should maybe track Nobody back to his home. It was too late to start a fire, so Nobody flipped on his Christmas lights and sat in his chair.

He was free again. He could come and go as he pleased. He could stay out here as long as he wanted. Things could go back to the way they used to be.

Back to being alone.

Worse than that. Back to being lonely.

It wouldn't be so bad, would it? He'd been alone out here before and he'd survived all right. He had his horses and his books. That had been enough before.

But as he sat in his chair and watched the night sky, breathing in free air and letting the shadows hold him close, another thought filled his head.

He could slink into Melinda's place, tap on her window. He could slip inside and tell her how much he'd missed her—then *show* her how damn much he'd missed her.

He could stay the whole night, not just until she fell asleep. In the morning, he could see the boy, maybe go for a ride with him.

He was half out of his chair before the image of her, all mean and scowling, came back to him. What if...

What if she said no? What if she closed the window in his face?

He wanted to think she wouldn't do that, not to him, but then—she *had* left him in that jail.

Nobody sat there for a long time, arguing with himself before he realized the truth of the matter.

She had said she needed him, too—it wasn't like she'd told him to go to hell. She'd asked him to trust her, asked him to give her a reason to trust him.

Well.

He sure as hell couldn't do that from out here.

CHAPTER TWENTY TWO

"What's a some-more again?" Jamie asked as he roasted a marshmallow over the fire.

Frankly, the marshmallows were the only things still keeping him here. Another day or two and Melinda knew that he'd slip off into the woods to go look for Nobody himself.

So she'd upped her game—marshmallows plus chocolate. "S'mores. Because they're so good you want some more. S'more. Say it fast."

Jamie looked at her like she was nuts. "Yeah, okay. Got it. What are they, again?"

Melinda arranged the square of chocolate on the graham cracker. "Here—put your marshmallow here." When he did, she squished the two halves together. "Count to ten so you don't burn yourself, then *voilà*! Eat!"

The boy rolled his eyes at her. "I'm not a baby." But even as he said it, he took the s'more from her. "Mmmm," he said around a mouthful. "Good."

Melinda grinned at him, but then she turned her gaze to the trees that surrounded her house. Her house. The one with the boy she was now legally responsible for.

It was a lot of responsibility.

The shadows looked normal. No extra-dark spots that were roughly the size and shape of a man. A specific man.

If he didn't come soon, she'd let Jamie track him down. She'd have no choice. She had to tell Nobody she wanted him to come back—that she *did* trust him. Jamie could find him. And if Nobody wouldn't come, well, she'd have Jamie take him to her.

This couldn't be the end of it. It just couldn't.

She and Jamie made a few more s'mores. The night fell faster now that autumn was upon them.

The thought of long, cold winter nights without Nobody's warm arms to snuggle into made her feel sad in new and painful ways. And what about him? Sleeping out in lawn furniture, for God's sake, until he was finally driven into his trailer of books by a blizzard? The image was so depressing that not even Jamie pulling off the perfect s'more could make her smile.

Then ... it started out as a small prick on the back of her neck. Just a tickle. The sensation cascaded down her back, making her muscles twitch. The air around her took on a heavy feel to it, like lightning was on the verge of striking.

Like someone was about to shock her.

She grinned as she poked the fire. He'd come. She hadn't even had to track him down.

Still, she wanted a moment with him before Jamie tackled him again. "Time for bed," she said to the boy. "You know the drill—wash, brush, jammies."

Jamie gave her a funny look as he wiped chocolate off his face with his forearm. "What—now?"

"Now," she replied with more force. "Go. When you're done, you can come back out for a little bit." With any luck, Nobody would still be here.

Jamie mumbled under his breath, but he got to his feet and went inside. Melinda waited a moment, but the static electricity didn't fade away. He was still here, watching her.

She should have known—he'd always come back to watch her. To make sure she and Jamie were safe. It was his way. "Good evening, Mr. Bodine." She stuck another marshmallow on her stick and sat. It was his move to make.

He didn't make her wait long. Out of the corner of her eye, the darkness seemed to bend and then break away and a man stepped into the firelight.

"How'd you know I was here?" he asked. But he didn't come any closer.

"You're stealthy but not invisible." She looked up at him. He seemed thinner now, still worn down by his time behind bars. But he'd come. That was the important part. "I could feel you."

The corner of his mouth moved, as if he wanted to smile at her but was afraid to. He didn't say anything else.

"Did everything check out?"

"Yeah," he said. Then he took a small step forward. The air seemed to almost shimmer around him. Melinda swore she could feel the charge from this far away.

Nervous, she realized. *Scared.*

Scared of her.

"I was worried about you," she went on, knowing full well he wasn't going to say anything else. "I was going to give you another day or so and then I was going to send Jamie after you."

"You were?" Another step into the light.

"I was. Don't sound so surprised by that. I've been worried about you for weeks."

He stopped. "But I thought—I thought you'd washed your hands of me. I screwed up and you were done with me."

She stood and walked to him. "I never said that, did I?" He flinched when she touched him, even though it was just her palm to his cheek. "It hurt, to see you like that. It hurt me to know that leaving you in there was for the best. To know that I was doing that to you. I couldn't... I couldn't see you like that."

He stared down at her. For a second, she thought he was going to bolt on her—hit her with a burst of electricity and be off again. But then he leaned into her touch, his hands resting on her waist. "I didn't want you to see me like that, either."

"So I stayed away. I focused on getting Jamie. I got the house ready and passed the classes and got custody. But I *never* forgot you, Nobody." She looped her hands around his neck, pulling him down to her. "I couldn't. Not you."

He sighed, like he'd been hoping she'd say that but was afraid she wouldn't. But instead of kissing her, he stopped just short. "I was a damn fool. I should have trusted you. I should have waited."

"It's okay. I understand." She stood on her tiptoes, her lips almost brushing his.

He jerked his head back. "But I don't—see, I don't know *how* to give you a reason to trust me. I don't know what I can do to show you that I trust you." The words ripped out of him with so much anguish—five weeks' worth of it.

"Come sit with me by the fire. Come inside with me. Stay with me until I wake up." He gave her something that might have been a grin if it hadn't been so worried. "Help out with Jamie," she went on. "Go riding with him, show him how to work with horses. Make him do his chores. You can't ever do just *one* thing to make me love you, Nobody."

"I can't?"

"You can't. And I can't either. I have to show you every day that I trust you, that I love you. So come and sit with me. When Jamie comes out, ask him how his day was. Ask him what a s'more is." She swallowed, suddenly nervous. His hands were still on her hips, but there was no give to him. He was still holding himself apart from her.

Maybe she deserved that. She'd left him in jail, after all. She'd gotten him moved to a nicer jail, gotten him a window—but it was still a cage with a lock. He might hate her for that. And she wouldn't be able to blame him.

"You... you love me?" His voice was so quiet it barely even qualified as a whisper.

"I do. Even when you go behind my back." She traced her fingers over the round of his cheek, down his jaw and over the scars. "I want you to stay with me. And—" Her voice caught. There was no give in his body, none. He wasn't going to come sit with her. "And if you can't stay, I want you to come back. There will always be a place for you at my fire. There will always be a place for you in my heart, Nobody Bodine."

"I've never loved anyone. I don't know how to love you."

He said it gently, but it broke her heart anyway. Tears pooled in her eyes and she started to nod.

But then he cupped her face in his hands, tilting her lips up to his. "Will you show me how?"

"Yes." The word came out harder than she meant it to, but that's what happened when someone tried to talk and not cry at the same time. She searched his eyes and saw the fear.

No one had ever loved him before. No one had ever seen him before, so how could they love him? She was the only one crazy enough to look at what was right in front of her—a man. An imperfect man who was going to make mistakes, yes, but a man who would always, *always* do the right thing, who would protect her and Jamie, who would love them in the only way he could.

"I want to love you," he whispered as his lips touched hers. "I want you *so* much. But I'm scared I'll screw it up just like I screwed this up. I'm working on being good, but..."

"I'll help you," she managed to choke out. "We'll work on it together."

He leaned back and looked at her. "You're crying," he said, terror in his voice. "Did I hurt you?"

"No—God, no. I'm just so glad you're going to try. I'm not going to give up on you, Nobody. All I can ask is that you don't give up on *us*."

He rubbed a tear from her cheek. "*Us*. Never had an *us* before."

She opened her mouth to tell him that now he did—him and her and Jamie all together. But the door to the house slammed open. "Nobody!" Jamie launched himself out of the house. "You're here! Did you come to see me? Did you come to stay?"

Nobody looked down at her and smiled. A real smile, honest and true. A small flash of electricity made her skin tingle, but he didn't melt into the shadows and he didn't bolt. He just held her all the more tighter.

"Yeah," he said as he held her tight. "I did."

MYSTIC COWBOY
(Men of the White Sandy #1)

The White Sandy Reservation needs a doctor, and Madeline Mitchell needs to do a little good in the world. It seems like a perfect fit, until she meets the medicine man, Rebel Runs Fast. As far as Madeline can tell, Rebel's sole mission is to convince her patients that modern medicine can't help them. And the fact that he makes her heart race every time he looks at her only irritates her more.

Rebel swore off the white man's world—and women—years ago. But he's never met a woman like Dr. Mitchell. She doesn't speak the language, understand the customs, or believe he's anything more than a charlatan—but she stays, determined to help his people. He tries to convince himself that his tribe doesn't need her, but when patients start getting sick with strange symptoms, he realizes that he needs her more than ever.

Excerpt from *Mystic Cowboy*

And suddenly, it got a whole lot less boring. Tara gasped in shock as the fan was kicked out of the door. *Now what?* Madeline spun around in her pitiful supply closet.

Two men stood in front of Tara. Well, one man stood. He was tall and straight, all the more so compared to the broken people she'd looked at all day. His jet-black hair hung long and loose under a straw cowboy hat, all the way down to his denim-clad butt. Even though he was supporting the other man, he was moving from one black cowboy boot to the other, his hips shifting in a subtle-but-sexy motion. He was wearing a T-shirt with the sleeves torn off, revealing a set of honest biceps that looked like carved caramel—the best kind of delicious.

"Find a nice cowboy." Mellie's voice floated back up her from their last conversation. *"Ride him a little. Have fun!"*

Now, Madeline wasn't exactly a thrill-seeking adrenaline junkie. On more than one occasion, she'd been accused of being the party pooper, the stick in the mud, a real-bring-me-downer in the room. Several times, it had been pointed out that she wouldn't know fun if it walked up and bit her in the ass. And that was just what Mellie said to her face. God only knew what everyone else said behind her back.

But there he was, standing in her waiting room. Fun in cowboy boots. No biting in the ass required, because she knew him immediately, and all she wanted to do was find a horse and ride. With him. The heat started at her neck and flashed southward. She could feel her curls trying to break free into a full-fledged frizz with the sudden temperature change, which only made things that much worse.

"Jesse!" Tara said in a voice that was just one small step below shouting. "What did you do now?"

"Give me a hand, will you?" Fun in Cowboy Boots called back to Clarence. He pivoted just a little, revealing the other man who was leaning all of his weight on Fun's right side.

Not good. The second guy's leg was being held together with what looked like broomsticks and duct tape. His right arm hung limp, and his scratched face was contorted in pain.

"Damn, Rebel, what happened?" Clarence was already hefting the broken man—Jesse?—onto the nearest free table, leading to a volley of clenched grunts from the injured man. "I thought we might get through this month without you trying to kill yourself, you know."

Did Clarence really just call this guy *Rebel?* Well, it was official. She'd heard it all today.

Rebel—if that was his real name—was shaking his head

when he caught her staring. He had beautiful black eyes, the kind of black that didn't so much show you the window to his soul, but reflected yours back on you. Those eyes widened in surprise. "You know how it goes, Clarence," he said, his gaze bearing down on her with enough heat that the rest of the clinic felt suddenly cool by comparison. "Life with Jesse is always an adventure."

Tara was next to the exam table now, holding Jesse's hand as she felt his head. "Do I even want to know?"

"Not really," Rebel replied, taking his time as he looked her over. His thumbs were hanging from his belt loops, which only made the shifting thing he was doing look more intentional. Aside from the long hair, he looked like every cowboy fantasy she'd ever had. Did he have a horse, or was her imagination way out of control? "You must be the new doctor, ma'am." He took off his hat and nodded. All that black hair, so straight it made her jealous, flowed around him like a cape.

Oooh, her first *ma'am*. From an honest-to-God cowboy, no less. She felt the sudden urge to curtsey, but then realized what he'd said right before the ma'am. She was the doctor, and she had a job to do. Wrenching her eyes from the caramel-colored cowboy to the patient, Madeline tried to regain her professional composure. "Dr. Mitchell, please. And this is Jesse?"

"Yes, ma'am."

That wasn't helpful. "I need to know how this happened, Mister…"

"Rebel," he said, those hips still moving.

She was *not* staring like a schoolgirl at this man. "Excuse me?"

"Just Rebel, ma'am."

A shiver ran down her spine. One more ma'am and she might swoon. "Dr. Mitchell," she said with more force as she turned to her patient.

Buy the Book / Leave a Review / Sign up for the Newsletter

MASKED COWBOY
(Men of the White Sandy #2)

Mary Beth is the kind of woman who wishes she had a five-second delay on her mouth. The swath of verbal destruction she leaves is why she goes west to start over. But any resolve to hold her tongue is lost immediately when she meets Jacob, a Lakota cowboy who says next to nothing – especially about the black leather mask that covers half his face.

Jacob's silence is his armor in a white man's world, but even that isn't enough to protect him—or the mute girl he guards—from forces he can't control. Fascinated by the masked cowboy and drawn to defend the girl, Mary Beth finds herself in the middle of a decades-old power struggle that only she could talk her way out of.

Excerpt from *Masked Cowboy*

Mary Beth followed Robin's gaze, blinking through the streaking evening sun.

Down the center of the street, a cowboy was riding a horse, leading another behind him. As he got closer, Mary Beth could see the cowboy was shirtless. The golden light settled over his dark hat and shimmered off his bare shoulders. His front was still in light shadows, but if the rest of him was as carved as those dark brown shoulders, things were about to get interesting.

"Mmm," Robin hummed and Mary Beth swore the whole restaurant was humming in pleasure with her.

As the lone rider got closer, the shadows eased back a bit, and

Mary Beth realized that there was something different about this cowboy.

He had an eye patch.

Whoa, hunk on the hoof, just like in a romance novel. But as she blinked through the angular sunlight, Mary Beth realized that the patch was far larger than the kind a pirate would wear. The swath of dark leather started at his left temple, covered his left eye and continued down over the center of his face, coming to a sharp point over his nose.

Mary Beth shook her head, but the patch remained the same. "He wears a mask?" she whispered to Robin, afraid to break the spell that gripped the café.

"Shhh," Robin hissed.

The masked cowboy rode right up to the café and stopped mere feet from Mary Beth's table before he slid out of the saddle, his leg muscles twitching through his tight jeans the whole way down. He paused for split second, clearly enjoying every female eye trained on his bare torso before he walked up to Mary Beth's table.

"Robin," he said, gently tipping his black felt hat, its brim creased from countless such tips. His one eye, nestled between a strong eyebrow and a stronger cheekbone, swept over the scene before it settled on Mary Beth.

"Jacob," Robin practically sang. She held out the tray with the towel and the water.

Jacob, the masked, shirtless cowboy, gracefully lifted the glass of water from the tray before he set his hat in its place. He took a huge drink, then grabbed the towel, leaned forward and poured the rest of the water over his head.

The water rushed through his slightly overgrown jet-black hair as he stood up, his mask covered with the towel. Rivulets raced down his browned, chiseled chest before he slowly mopped them up, his gaze grabbing Mary Beth's face and refusing to let it go again.

She was sure her mouth was on the table, but she couldn't help it. Every fiber in her body was vibrating as she watched the towel trace passed his pecs, down his lean abs—the muscles moving just beneath the smooth surface of his skin—and follow a faint trail of hair that ended in his jeans. The mask notwithstanding, this man was quite possibly the most ideal specimen of masculinity she'd ever laid eyes on. Nothing like pasty Greg Meyers.

A hint of a smile on his face, Jacob handed the towel back to Robin, took the to-go bag, pivoted and walked to the saddlebag of his paint. Mary Beth admiringly noted the huge tear in the seat of his pants, just under his left butt cheek. It was hard to tell what was more promising—his rock-solid chest or that flash of ass. Pausing again for just a second, he tucked the meal in the bag after he whipped out an Anthrax T-shirt that might have been black back in the 80s.

As he began to unbuckle his jeans, Mary Beth heard the entire café suck in a hot breath.

He won't. Mary Beth's brain stuttered in shock. *He wouldn't!*

The top button gave under his nimble fingers, and then the second. Mary Beth couldn't help but stare at the treasure trail of dark fur that crested at an even darker line peaking just over the undone buttons.

Jesus Christ, is he even wearing underwear? She gasped, unable to look away as she squirmed in her chair.

Jacob slipped the tee over his head, tucked it in and buttoned back up. As he took his hat off Robin's tray, the whole café—the sum total of women in Faith Ridge—sighed and leaned back in their chairs. Mary Beth wondered if there were enough cigarettes in town for the collective orgasm that had just happened in broad daylight.

Buy the Book / Leave a Review / Sign up for the Newsletter

ALSO AVAILABLE FROM SARAH M. ANDERSON

Men of the White Sandy
Mystic Cowboy
Masked Cowboy

Lawyers in Love
A Man of His Word
A Man of Privilege
A Man of Distinction

The Boltons
Straddling the Line
Bringing Home the Bachelor
Expecting a Bolton Baby

Rich, Rugged Ranchers
A Real Cowboy

The Texas Cattleman's Club
What a Rancher Wants

Rodeo Dreamers
Rodeo Dreams

The Beaumont Heirs
Not the Boss's Baby
Seduced by the Cowboy
A Beaumont Christmas Wedding

ABOUT THE AUTHOR

Award-winning author Sarah M. Anderson may live east of the Mississippi River, but her heart lies out west on the Great Plains. With a lifelong love of horses and two history teachers for parents, she had plenty of encouragement to learn everything she could about the tribes of the Great Plains. When she started writing, it wasn't long before her characters found themselves out in South Dakota among the Lakota Sioux. She loves to put people from two different worlds into new situations and see how their backgrounds and cultures take them someplace they never thought they'd go.

She's sold over eighteen books to Harlequin Desire and Superromance, as well as Samhain. She won RT Reviewer's Choice 2012 Desire of the Year for *A Man of Privilege*.

When she's not helping out at her son's school or walking her rescue dogs, Sarah spends her days having conversations with imaginary cowboys and American Indians, all of which is surprisingly well-tolerated by her wonderful husband.

Readers can find out more about Sarah's love of cowboys and Indians at:

Her Newsletter: http://eepurl.com/nv39b

Her website: www.sarahmanderson.com

On Facebook: www.facebook.com/pages/Sarah-M-Anderson-Author

On Twitter: @SarahMAnderson1

On Goodreads: www.goodreads.com/author/show/4982413.Sarah_M _Anderson

By snail mail at: Sarah M. Anderson, 200 N 8th ST #193, Quincy IL 62301-9996

Made in the USA
Charleston, SC
03 May 2014